MURDER

at

WRIGLEY FIELD

MURDER
at
WRIGLEY FIELD

TROY SOOS

KENSINGTON BOOKS
www.kensingtonbooks.com

KENSINGTON BOOKS are published by

Kensington Publishing Corp.
119 West 40th Street
New York, NY 10018

All Kensington titles, imprints and distributed lines are available at special quantity discounts for bulk purchases for sales promotion, premiums, fund-raising, educational or institutional use.

Special book excerpts or customized printings can also be created to fit specific needs. For details, write or phone the office of the Kensington Special Sales Manager: Kensington Publishing Corp., 119 West 40th Street, New York, NY, 10018. Attn. Special Sales Department. Phone: 1-800-221-2647.

Kensington and the K logo Reg. U.S. Pat. & TM Off.

First Kensington Hardcover Printing: April 1996

ISBN-13: 978-0-7582-8741-0
ISBN-10: 0-7582-8741-0
First Kensington Trade Paperback Printing: May 2013

eISBN-13: 978-0-7582-8780-9
eISBN-10: 0-7582-8780-1
First Kensington Electronic Edition: May 2013

10 9 8 7 6 5 4 3 2 1

Printed in the United States of America

Acknowledgments

Throughout this series I have been fortunate to have Pat LoBrutto as my editor, and it is a pleasure to finally express my appreciation. His guidance, encouragement, and humor have improved my work while making it seem like fun.

I am also grateful to my agents Meredith Bernstein and Elizabeth Cavanaugh for all their efforts in making sure that the Mickey Rawlings manuscripts become published books.

A number of institutions graciously provided assistance during the research of this book: the National Baseball Library & Archive in Cooperstown, New York; the Chicago Public Library; the Chicago Historical Society; the Government Documents Room of Harvard University's Lamont Library; the Dewey Library at the Massachusetts Institute of Technology; the Boston Public Library; and the North Cambridge Public Library. I am indebted to all of these for so generously making their resources available to me.

Chapter One

Thirty-six ounces of tight-grained American white ash, painstakingly carved and sanded into a sleek, tapered cylinder thirty-three inches long. The supreme achievement of the woodworker's craft: a Mickey Rawlings model Louisville Slugger.

"Atten . . . *tion!*"

A baseball bat. An object simple in design, yet with a quiet elegance to its form and a latent power in its core. In the hands of a major-leaguer, it's a versatile instrument with a dozen uses.

"Present . . . *arms!*"

And I knew most of them. I could slip one hand up the barrel to drop a bunt down either foul line or choke up with both fists to poke the ball to right on a hit and run. If a sacrifice fly was needed, I could slide my grip down to the knob and swing from the heels to lift a drive deep enough for a runner to score from third. Deep enough for a fast runner to score, anyway.

"Shoulder . . . *arms!*"

I raised my right forearm, lifting the bat to my shoulder. The thick end was cradled in my upturned palm; I could feel nicks where I'd struck it against my spikes to dislodge clods of earth. The handle, stained with sweat and grime from having been squeezed between my fists a thousand times, rested next to my collar bone. And every muscle and bone in my body screamed at me that this was no way to hold a baseball bat.

I never imagined any bat—much less one with my name stamped below the Hillerich & Bradsby imprint—could feel so unnatural to me. But then, the one thing I never expected to do with a baseball bat was use it for a make-believe rifle while I played soldier.

The entire Chicago Cubs team stood in formation, four rows of four players each, in foul territory behind first base. We faced the infield, our backs to the first base dugout. The team was arranged in order of height, with the tallest players in the back. I was in the front row, my toes touching the edge of the chalk foul line.

"Forward . . . *march!*"

I promptly stepped forward with my left foot. Willie, next to me on my right, started with his right foot, as did several others. Some didn't move at all until bumped from behind; then they shuffled clumsily forward to catch up.

As we marched in the direction of second base, the teen-aged Army lieutenant in charge of our training chanted in his high-pitched voice, "Left . . . left . . . left, right, left . . ." It took quite a few paces before the footsteps of the Cubs players matched the instructions he squeaked out. We were not a spit and polish kind of squad—despite the fact that we did do an inordinate amount of spitting.

And we would be of little use if Kaiser Wilhelm's army

decided to invade the North Side of Chicago. Hell, we were going to have enough trouble defending Cubs Park from the visiting St. Louis Cardinals.

We were simply putting on a show orchestrated by the baseball owners. It was an attempt to impress Secretary of War Baker, who was threatening to shut down major league baseball. Baker believed that healthy young men belonged on battlefields, not baseball fields. The team owners thought that by marching us around with bats on our shoulders they could convince Uncle Sam we were training for war, not merely playing a game. I thought not even the U. S. government could be that gullible.

There was still some reason to hold out hope for a reprieve though: Baker had already given deferments to actors and opera singers for providing "essential entertainment." I figured if *opera* could be considered essential, surely the national pastime was.

As we reached second base, the lieutenant yelped, "Right turn . . . *March!*"

I spun to my right and collided with Willie turning left. "Your other right, Willie," I said. I grabbed his shoulder with my free hand and turned him around.

He had a bewildered look on his young face and his cap was askew. It was also too large for his head, making him look like a kid whose mother had bought it for him with the hope that he'd grow into it. "This just ain't natural," he protested. "You're supposed to turn left at second and go to third. Who the hell runs out to centerfield?"

"We're not practicing triples," I said. Although he was right: nothing about this felt natural.

We said nothing more, which I'm sure the lieutenant appreciated since we weren't permitted to speak at all during drills, and scampered to catch up to our teammates marching toward right field.

Any other park would have had an outfield fence to mark the perimeter of the playing field. Except for a high wall that ran from the left field foul pole to left center, that useful feature was omitted in the design of Cubs Park. In right field, bleachers sprouted directly from the grass; only a low railing separated the seats from the field of play. With few fans occupying them, the bleachers looked like a wide squat staircase. It appeared we could march up those steps and walk right into the second-floor windows of the Sheffield Avenue row houses that overlooked the park.

"Company . . . *halt!*"

I halted. Fred Merkle ran into my back.

As the Cubs players stumbled into each other trying to maintain some semblance of formation, I decided it was a wise move on the part of the Army not to equip us with real rifles. One of us would have probably ended up getting his nose shot off.

•   •   •

This little patch of Chicago, four acres of ballfield nestled in the juncture of Addison and North Clark streets, was a baseball oasis—a green cathedral in a blue-collar neighborhood.

The field itself was splendid. The turf, a lush mixture of bluegrass and clover, shimmered with life, and the dark earth of the base paths looked fertile enough to grow crops.

After a week of sporadic thunderstorms, the weather was finally cooperating as if nature herself wanted to see a ballgame. Gentle, cooling breezes blew off Lake Michigan. They sent wispy white clouds drifting across a high sun to provide soft shade for the park below.

Taking in the view, one could almost forget that across the Atlantic young men were dying by the thousands in trench warfare. Almost, but not quite.

The war in Europe had taken a toll on baseball that was most evident in the dugouts. The players seated with me on the Cubs bench were far from prime physical specimens, and the Cardinals across the field in the first base dugout weren't any better. Not since the 1899 Cleveland Spiders had there been a major league baseball team comprised of such wretched-looking ballplayers. This year, with rosters decimated by players leaving for military service, it was the norm. Teams had to fill holes in their lineups with sandlot players too young to fight and old-timers too aged. It was often a challenge for a team simply to field nine players by game time.

It was also a challenge to fill a ballpark with paying customers. Factories were running round-the-clock to produce materials for the war effort, and even on Saturday few people could take an afternoon off to watch a baseball game. Of the eighteen thousand seats in the park, only about two thousand were occupied. There wasn't enough of a crowd for the fans to feel part of, so they sat in self-conscious silence. The sounds that filled the park came from the streets outside: automobiles with bleating horns on Addison and trains rumbling past the entrance behind home plate.

With the game about to begin, the Cubs' public address announcer walked to a point between home plate and the pitcher's mound. Through a megaphone that wasn't necessary, he gave the St. Louis starting lineup, then began to read off Chicago's. The crowd listened with indifference until he announced, "Batting third and playing shortstop: Willie *Kay*-ser."

Jeers and boos immediately came from the stands, first scattered and then in unison as individual hecklers pooled their meager courage into one voice. The announcer had intentionally mispronounced Willie's name, but they knew what it really was.

I looked down the bench at Willie. Willie Kaiser, that is. His head was down and he gave it a slight, sad shake. In the summer of 1918, "Kaiser" was not a popular name. All season long, in a dozen malicious ways, spectators and opponents continually reminded Willie of this fact.

So did the newspapers. A year ago, Willie was working in a meatpacking house and playing amateur ball for the Union Stockyards. Now in his first full season with the Cubs, he had a .322 batting average and the best glove since Honus Wagner. He should have been the sports pages' biggest story. But the papers chose to avoid putting his hated name in print and rarely mentioned Willie in their coverage of the games. The box scores, which couldn't omit him entirely, abbreviated him as "WKsr."

After their outburst of patriotic disapproval at Willie's surname, the crowd quieted down and remained in a dormant state through five scoreless innings.

Not until the top of the sixth did they come to life, when the Cardinals' Cliff Heathcote led off the inning with a line drive single over first base that almost took Fred Merkle's head off. The crowd gasped with one breath at Merkle's near decapitation.

With Heathcote on first, heavy-hitting Rogers Hornsby stepped up next to face our Hippo Vaughn. Murmurs of anticipation came from the stands. The crowd was thinking base hit.

I was thinking double play. From my second base position I gave a glance at Willie. I could see his thoughts were the same as mine. We'd turned enough twin killings this season that Kaiser-to-Rawlings-to-Merkle was on a pace to beat the record of an earlier Cubs' double play combination, Tinker-to-Evers-to-Chance.

After Hornsby took a fastball for ball one, Willie picked up the catcher's sign for the next pitch. He passed it on to me, flashing two fingers from behind the protective shield of his mitt. Curve ball. With Vaughn a lefty and Hornsby right-handed, a curve will break in on him. He should be pulling it. I started to cheat toward second as Vaughn released the ball.

Hornsby ripped it, a hard grounder up the middle. I was off, sprinting back and to my right. The ball skimmed the pitcher's mound and veered to my side of the bag.

At the last possible instant, I threw my glove out, letting it pull my body along in a low dive. The ball snagged in the palm of my glove at the same time that my belly hit the ground. Skidding face-down on the outfield grass, I couldn't see second base, but I knew Willie would be there. I flipped the ball over my left shoulder, then twisted around to watch the end of the play.

In one fluid move, Willie caught the ball cleanly, dragged his foot across second base, and transferred the ball to his throwing hand. Then the amazing part: with Hornsby two steps from the base, Willie snapped off a sidearm throw to first that nailed him with time to spare.

There wasn't another shortstop in baseball who could put that much smoke on the ball. Not many pitchers, either.

Although Willie was no more muscular than me, there was explosive strength in his wiry build. As cheers came from the crowd, I thought to myself that I'd give anything to have an arm like that. For just one throw I'd like to know what it felt like to unleash that kind of lightning.

Willie showed no joy in the play though. He trudged back to his position at short, looking as if he'd done nothing more thrilling than change a flat tire.

Jeez, Willie, let yourself have some fun. There's only one thing that feels better than turning a play like that, and you can't do it on a baseball field. Not during a game, anyway.

The yells from the stands continued, and people rose from their seats. I thought they wanted Willie to tip his cap in acknowledgment, and I was happy that he was being cheered for a change.

Then I saw that the fans were scrambling for the exits, and the one word they were all shouting became clear: "Fire!"

• • •

It took almost an hour to get the game going again. There had been no fire, only lots of acrid black smoke from a couple of smoke bombs in the grandstand seats near first base.

The final four innings were played before an empty stadium, so there was no one to boo our 3–1 loss to St. Louis.

I was the last one into the showers after the game. By the time I finished washing, most of my teammates were getting into their street clothes.

Wearing a towel tied at my waist, I sat down on a wooden stool in front of my locker. Willie Kaiser dressed slowly at the locker next to me, pulling on an ill-fitting suit of faded blue seersucker. His face sagged with worry.

"Hey, *Wilhelm,*" a voice called out. "I guess that was some of your German buddies that tried to burn down the park!" It was the nasal bray of Wicket Greene, a washed up infielder. Greene had earned his nickname earlier in the season by consistently giving ground balls free passage through his legs. For the same reason, Willie unseated him as the Cubs' starting shortstop. Greene retaliated by launching a persecution campaign against the rookie.

Willie ignored Wicket Greene and continued glumly buttoning his shirt.

C'mon, show some gumption, I silently prodded him. Don't take any guff from Wicket.

Greene continued his goading. "Oughta send ya back to the *fatherland* is what they oughta do!"

Willie remained silent.

I didn't. "Shut your mouth, Wicket," I warned. Greene knew, but didn't care, that Willie was under my protection. When Willie had come up to the Cubs I was assigned as his roommate. For the first time in my career, I'd been considered a veteran. As such, it was my job to introduce the rookie to life in the big leagues and keep him from getting into trouble. I took my job seriously. Besides, you don't ride a teammate about his nationality or his religion or what part of the country he's from. No matter his background, once a fellow joins your team, he's family.

Greene lumbered over to us. When the Cubs drilled, he marched in the back row with the other six-footers. He stopped on the other side of Willie, folded his arms across his chest, and tried to look menacing. He succeeded only in looking ugly. Greene had thinning black hair combed straight back from a prominent forehead and a receding chin dotted with stubble. Through a tangle of brown teeth he said, "I wasn't talking to you, Rawlings."

But I knew he was. We'd gone through this before, and Greene could always get a rise out of me before he'd get one out of Willie. By now, Willie had almost become an excuse for Greene and me to go at each other.

"What's your problem, Wicket?" I taunted him, rising from my seat. "Riding the bench giving you a headache?"

"Son of a bitch! You think you're a big deal playing second? I'd rather be a batboy than a second baseman."

"Too bad you don't got enough talent to be a batboy."

Greene's dark eyes narrowed and he snarled, "I could get *your* job in a minute if I wanted it."

"*Sure* you could, Wicket. Don't know how you'd run the bases though. All them splinters you been picking up, you got more wood in your ass than in your bat."

"Well it ain't second I want. I'm gonna be playing short-stop! Soon as they deport this little krauthead." He feigned a slap at Willie's head. Willie didn't flinch.

"Watch yourself, Wicket," I warned again. I suddenly realized I was still dripping wet and wearing nothing but a towel. It's hard to look menacing in a towel. Between that and the fact that he outweighed me by thirty pounds, Greene wasn't likely to be worried.

Other locker room conversations trailed off into silence. The staccato drip of a leaky shower echoed through the quiet clubhouse. Greene and I each took a half step toward each other while Willie sat silently between us.

Greene leaned forward, trying to intimidate me. It didn't work. I knew that he moved slow and thought slower. He growled, "What are you, his protector?"

I held back, waiting for Willie to act. C'mon Willie, stand up for yourself. If that right arm of yours can throw an uppercut the way it can throw a baseball, Greene's gonna be real quiet real fast.

Willie did nothing.

Greene stepped around Willie and poked me in the shoulder. "He need you to protect him? Is that it?"

"No, he don't need me, but he got me." I followed that with a hard shove to Greene's chest, and we started grappling together. Neither of us threw an actual punch—baseball players hardly ever throw good punches.

Fred Merkle yelled, "Break it up!"

Teammates soon pulled Greene and me apart.

Merkle stepped between us. He was a strong, smart fellow with a mournful face. Greene wouldn't argue with his muscle, and I wouldn't argue with his wisdom. "Come on now," Merkle said, looking first at Greene and then at me. "Don't take the loss so hard. No reason to go squabbling with each other." He knew the loss had nothing to do with the argument, but he didn't understand what was really behind it.

Neither did I. All I knew for sure was that I was mad. Irrationally, seething mad. I was angry at Greene, of course. More so at Willie for not standing up for himself. And I was mad at something I couldn't quite identify: a cruel intolerance, a perverse brand of nationalism that had taken over the country and intruded itself into baseball—*my* game.

I glanced at Wicket Greene. There was more than anger on his face. There was hatred, pure hatred burning in eyes aimed straight at me.

I knew we'd be going at each other again soon.

When we did, I didn't want anyone around who could separate us.

Chapter Two

Rube's pink tongue lapped my wrist as I scratched him under his chin. He sat on his haunches, his tail happily thumping the hardwood floor.

"I think his leg's getting better," I said. "He seemed to be putting more weight on it when I walked him." Although it was hard to tell with Rube, the dachshund's legs being so stubby.

"Mmm," said Edna in a pleased tone. For her, that nearly amounted to a speech. She wasn't one to use words when a nod, a smile, or a shrug would do. She didn't need to. Edna could convey exactly what she meant through the smallest gestures. Her concise means of communication never seemed brusque though; she always nodded, smiled, or shrugged in the nicest ways.

If I could choose only one word to describe Edna Chapman, it would be "nice." If allowed all the words I wanted, I would be hard pressed to elaborate on that description.

Edna wasn't beautiful, though she wasn't bad-looking, either. She had a round, fair face that always looked freshly washed. Her dull blonde hair was pulled back and pinned in a simple bun. High Slavic cheekbones pulled up the corners of her blue eyes, giving them a slightly exotic touch, almost oriental.

Nor was she particularly intriguing. Edna rarely expressed an opinion on anything, and there were few indications that she had any she was keeping to herself.

Edna Chapman was simply a quiet girl who was comfortable to be with.

It was probably just as well that I didn't find her any more tantalizing than that, for she was Willie Kaiser's little sister and there were tacit rules about proper conduct with a teammate's sister. She was his half-sister really, but Willie had made it clear to me that he considered her to be his sister, period.

Edna was bent over, feeding the other dogs. They were all dachshunds, all victims of the hysterical campaign to erase everything Teutonic from American life. People with dachshunds were accused of being German sympathizers. Those with German shepherds were reported as spies. As a consequence, dogs of both breeds were often cast out by fearful owners.

A couple of months ago, Edna had taken in several abandoned dachshunds, giving up her small bedroom to house them. Willie and I had moved her bed and belongings to a sitting room outside their mother's bedroom upstairs. Edna now had less space and almost no privacy, but she never showed signs of regretting her sacrifice and treated the residents of her former bedroom as welcome guests. Like I said: nice.

A contented rumble came from deep in Rube's throat.

Edna straightened up. Her figure was more sturdy than

shapely and stretched a couple of inches taller than mine. "He likes you," she said. When Edna did put a few words together, I was always surprised at how childlike her voice sounded. She was a full eighteen years old. Or as Willie kept reminding me, "going on nineteen and not getting any younger."

"He's a good dog," I said, stroking his smooth brown coat.

Rube was my addition to the kennel. I'd found him on Belmont Avenue, cringing against the wall of an apartment building. A big drunk had been kicking the little dog while yelling about "goddamn wiener dogs" and "goddamn Huns." I'd objected to the drunk's behavior, and he'd objected to my interference. By the time we'd finished scuffling and punching, I found myself guardian of a dachshund with a busted hind leg. I named him "Rube" after the old Athletics pitcher Rube Waddell. The dog didn't look anything like Waddell, but he was the first creature I ever got to christen, so I named him after my boyhood hero. Rube took to his name, and to me, as if he fully appreciated the honor.

I couldn't keep Rube myself since I spent half the season on the road, so Edna gave him a home and I helped her care for the dogs. It was one of two activities we did together. The other was going to the movies every Saturday the Cubs were in town.

"What would you like to see tonight?" I asked, though I could guess what her answer would be.

Sure enough. *"Tarzan of the Apes,"* was her quick response.

Every Saturday this month we'd gone to the Crystal Theatre on North Avenue to see Elmo Lincoln as Tarzan. There wasn't much else to choose from. Most movies currently playing were propaganda films, like *To Hell With the Kaiser* and *The Beast of Berlin*.

"How about Charlie Chaplin?" I suggested as a change. *"Shoulder Arms* is a comedy—it's not really a war movie."

Edna shook her head with distaste. No. Comedy or not, no war pictures.

There was a western playing at Covent Garden, a theater that was only a short trolley ride down Clark Street, but the movie starred Norman Kerry and I was boycotting his pictures. He used to be Norman Kaiser until he'd decided his career would benefit from a name change. I figured it was cowards like Kerry who made things tougher on people like Willie.

I gave in. "Okay. *Tarzan* it is."

She flashed a smile at her victory.

I patted Rube on the head and stood up. "I'm going to talk to Willie for a bit before dinner."

Edna's gaze dropped. I think she sometimes wondered whether I preferred to spend time with her or her brother, but she never asked.

• • •

Willie's room was the same size as the one Edna had relinquished to the dogs—about eight foot square with one tiny window, sparsely furnished and tidy. A high maple bureau and a narrow iron rail bed with a navy wool blanket pulled taut over the mattress were the only pieces of furniture.

On top of the bureau was a mail-order set of *The Complete Works of Mark Twain,* with the green cloth-bound volumes lined up alphabetically by title. Willie had probably agonized over whether to arrange them alphabetically or by year of publication. I knew from rooming with him on the road that he liked things neat and orderly. Even in hotels that provided chambermaids, he made his own bed and cleaned the wash basin after shaving. He still had some things to learn about living like a ballplayer.

Willie stood before a small framed display on the wall. Inside the dark wood frame were two brass disks hanging from bright-colored ribbons.

"I know," I said from the doorway. "You want some of your own."

He ran his forefinger over one of the medals, a bust of Admiral Dewey attached to a striped ribbon of blue and gold—the Manila Bay Medal. Then he dropped his hand. "I don't care about medals," he said. "It's what you do to get them that's important." Before Willie was two years old, his father died in America's "splendid little war" with Spain to earn those medals. "And I'm gonna go fight," he added.

I immediately resorted to the same argument I'd given him many times before. "What about Edna and your mother? How are they going to get along without you?" The U. S. government sided with me on this: it had given Willie a deferment. Other than the pension his mother received as a military widow—a two-time military widow—he was the sole support of his family.

Willie shrugged off the question. "I'm an American. America's at war. I should be fighting in the war."

I thought for a moment and tried to remember if the world had seemed that simple to me when I was twenty-one. If it did, it had sure gotten more complicated in the five years since I was Willie's age.

"You don't have to prove anything to anybody," I said.

"Stay here, play out the season. Your mother and sister need you."

Willie was unfazed by my words. His eyes were fixed and his face hardened with determination.

Rookies. Sometimes there's no talking sense to them. I gave it another try anyway. "If it's about Wicket Greene," I said. "Don't let him get to you. He's not half the ballplayer you are."

"It ain't about Greene," Willie snapped. Then he asked, "I ever show you my father's picture?"

He had, at least half a dozen times. I sighed and surrendered. "No, I don't think so. Can I see?"

I sat down on the bed and Willie went to the bureau. He pulled an iron strongbox from the bottom drawer and a rusty key from the top drawer, then sat down next to me. With the box on his lap, Willie unlocked the padlock and pried open the lid. He pulled a creased photograph from the box. Holding it carefully by the edges, he looked at it for a few seconds, then handed it to me.

The tinted photo was of a young man in the smart uniform of the United States Marines. Corporal Otto Kaiser looked a lot like his son and not at all like a soldier. His build was spare and his features delicate. The dark cap he wore was similar to a trolley conductor's and much too big on him. Just like Willie in his Cubs cap. His eyes were like Willie's, too: bright and determined.

"Looks like quite a man," I said. "But, you know, you don't have to go to war just because he did."

"That ain't it either," Willie said. He put the strongbox on the floor at our feet. "I just know I got to go fight."

I looked down at the contents of the box. The most prominent item was a revolver: Colt .38, Model 1892, double-action. Willie had recited its specifications to me numerous times. There were a few more photos in the box and some papers.

"My mother wanted to throw all this out," Willie said. "The medals, too. But she kept it. Said otherwise I wouldn't have nothing to remember him by." He reached down and took the revolver from the box. It was not an attractive object: the blue steel of the barrel was scratched and nicked, the trigger guard was bent, and the plain walnut grip was chipped.

"Careful with that," I said.

"Don't worry. No bullets." Willie swung open the cylinder to show me it was empty, then clicked it shut. Touching his forefinger to the trigger, he aimed the weapon in the direction of the window. "You think they'll let me use his gun over there?"

I sighed. "Your mother's going to wish she did throw it out."

"I'm going to tell her at supper. I'm enlisting."

From the kitchen, Mrs. Chapman called, "Dinner!"

I had the feeling indigestion was going to be the main course.

• • •

"It's terrible, this war," said Mrs. Chapman. "Keeping people from their beer."

I shared her unhappiness with the wartime prohibition. "And it looks like it's going to be permanent," I said mournfully. One state after another was ratifying the Eighteenth Amendment; there was little doubt that the ban on alcohol would soon be written into the Constitution.

Willie sat at one end of the small dinner table, Mrs. Chapman at the other. She looked like an older version of her daughter, with hair that had lightened halfway to silver, skin creased with character lines, and a settled figure—not quite shapeless, but the shapes were less defined and at lower altitudes than they were on Edna.

Unlike her daughter, Mrs. Chapman had no end of opinions and no reluctance about expressing them. "A good pilsner," she said, "could make even this food taste good."

I doubted that. Not with the wartime restrictions on food in effect. Herbert Hoover had decreed this to be a "Meatless Saturday," so instead of beefsteak we were dining on the recommended alternative: whale meat. There wasn't a beer in the world strong enough to make whale meat palatable. Nor was there one that could improve the "liberty bread," which was made with little wheat and a great deal of an unidentified substitute—sand, I suspected. The best part of the meal was the pungent sauerkraut, on which there was no prohibition, though it was supposed to be called "liberty cabbage." We called it "sauerkraut."

"It's a delicious dinner, Mrs. Chapman," I lied.

Willie had hardly touched his plate, but he murmured in unconvincing agreement. Edna, seated at my right, nodded.

Hans Fohl, the only other dinner guest, snorted. He was a cousin of Willie's. Presumably a distant cousin, for there was no physical resemblance. He was a burly fellow of about thirty, with dark bristly hair that needed trimming.

Fohl sat across the table from Edna and me. "Told you before," he said to Mrs. Chapman. *"I* can get you beer. Just got to know the right people." He had a gravelly voice and loose jowls that quivered when he spoke.

"And I've told *you,*" she responded firmly. "We're good citizens. We obey the law. No beer."

"We have to eat this pig slop because the good food's being shipped to England and France. And we can't even have a beer to wash it down with?" Fohl shook his head. "That's too much."

With irritation in her voice, Mrs. Chapman said, "If you don't like it, why come to dinner? Go out with your friends."

"I will. Later." Fohl turned to Willie. "How about you coming along? We're having a meeting at the church. Nine o'clock."

"Why would I want to go to that?" Willie asked with a pronounced lack of interest.

"Because it's about them smoke bombs at the ballpark. They say we did it, you know."

I assumed the "we" referred to German-Americans, and I thought of Wicket Greene. "There's always people saying stuff," I said. "What difference does it make?"

Fohl didn't like my interruption. "None to you, maybe. You're not one of us. You don't know what it's like."

"I'm not going to any meeting," Willie said. He took a deep breath and announced to his mother, "I'm going to the recruiting office. I'm enlisting."

"You're doing no such thing!" Mrs. Chapman cried.

"What are you, a traitor?" cried Fohl.

Mrs. Chapman turned on Fohl. "Don't you ever call my boy a traitor!"

The two of them fell to quarreling about Willie, fighting over him the way Greene and I had, as if he wasn't there. Mrs. Chapman and Fohl were arguing the same side of the question though, in agreement that he shouldn't enlist.

I suddenly realized how very alone Willie must feel and

thought I was starting to understand his desire to join the Army. He was looking for an answer. Not an easy answer, but one that was at least clear: go fight for your country and you're doing the right thing. Almost everyone agreed on that. Not even those opposed to the war blamed it on the soldiers who did the fighting.

During a moment when both Fohl and Mrs. Chapman took a breath, Edna softly said, "I wouldn't like for you to go to war."

Everyone looked at her, but no one spoke. I think we were partly surprised that she'd said something and partly embarrassed that we'd forgotten she was in the room.

The silence lingered a while, then I thought of a possible compromise. "Look," I said to Willie. "Why not wait until the end of the season? It might be just a few more days."

"Or three more months," he countered.

"Could be," I said. "But the betting is that the War Department is going to shut the game down sooner than that."

After a minute's thought, and under the persuasive stares of everyone at the table, Willie gave in. "All right. I'll wait."

Mrs. Chapman let out a breath. "Good. That's settled, then."

"And if I wait till the season's over, you won't try to talk me out of it?" Willie asked.

"Of course I will," she admitted with disarming honesty.

"So will I," said Fohl.

Mrs. Chapman waved a finger at him. "You be quiet." Then she said to Willie, "I gave two husbands to this country's wars. I don't intend to give my only boy."

Willie shrugged. There wasn't much he could say to that.

Mrs. Chapman settled back in her chair, comfortable that at least Willie wouldn't be going off to war tomorrow. "All I want to do is raise my children," she said. She glanced at Edna and me with an encouraging smile. "And someday grandchildren."

Edna blushed.

I asked Willie to pass the bread.

• • •

The Saturday post-dinner ritual was carried out in a routine that was now familiar to me. Edna took the leftovers to the icebox. Willie and I cleared the dishes, pushed the dinner table back against a wall, and—under Mrs. Chapman's strict supervision—arranged the furniture to make the front room a parlor again.

It was a cozy parlor, clean and neat, with braided oval rugs and floral wallpaper of muted reds and greens. The wood of the heavy, old-fashioned furniture glistened from polishing.

Then, as always, Mrs. Chapman declined our offer to help wash the dishes with her customary behest, "No, no. Young people should be out now. Go have fun." To Edna, she added meaningfully, "It's going to be cool tonight. Better get your coat."

I almost protested that it was balmy outside but held my tongue. Mrs. Chapman wasn't one to argue with unless you liked losing, which I didn't. Edna smiled and went upstairs.

Hans Fohl, who didn't visit often enough to have a role in the ritual, sat quietly sipping his ginger ale until we'd finished tidying up. Then he asked Willie again to go to the meeting. At Willie's curt "No," he thanked Mrs. Chapman for "the grub" and sulked out the front door.

Mrs. Chapman said jokingly to Willie, "He's from your father's side of the family, you know."

Willie wasn't listening. His thoughts were off someplace else, the location of which he wasn't revealing to anyone.

Edna rejoined us. She handed me her coat and turned around. I held it open for her as she slid her arms into the sleeves.

On an impulse, I said, "Say Willie, why don't you come with us?"

Edna spun around to face me. I'd never seen her eyes so wide. She looked as hurt and angry as if I'd kicked one of the dogs.

Then I noticed the garment: a belted velour jacket of golden brown with white piping. It had large turned-back cuffs and triangular patch pockets. The coat was more fashionable than anything I'd ever seen her wear, obviously brand new and probably an extravagance.

Willie rescued me. He said, "No, not tonight, thanks."

Edna quickly tied the belt of her jacket and pinned a small woven straw bonnet to her hair. She tucked her hands into a fox muff.

I jumped right back into the fire. I knew there was something important troubling Willie—something more than whether or not to enlist—and I didn't think he should be left alone. Despite Edna's pleading eyes, I said, "We're going to see *Tarzan*. It's a good picture. C'mon. We'll have a good time."

"Can't. I got plans."

He didn't elaborate. Meanwhile, Edna was nudging me toward the door.

It was strange. Usually I could understand ballplayers but not women. Tonight, I had no idea what was going on in Willie's head, but I knew exactly what Edna was thinking.

Chapter Three

Baseball stars like Ty Cobb and Walter Johnson collect batting titles and strikeout crowns. The game's top managers—John McGraw, Frank Chance, Connie Mack—collect championship pennants. Me, I collect scars.

During eight years of professional baseball, my legs had been slashed, gouged, and impaled by the spikes of the game's best ballplayers. And I was proud of every calling card they'd left on me. I didn't think of my legs as marred but as properly broken in, like a fielder's mitt softened and creased from use.

I'd picked up two more bruises in this afternoon's game. One was from a foul tip that I'd hit off my left instep, the other from a bad hop that I'd stopped with my right kneecap instead of my mitt. Neither would leave a scar, but they were both begging to be soaked in a hot bath.

Deciding to let them beg a while longer, I settled into the comfortable green Morris chair in the corner of my parlor and picked up one of the newspapers stacked next to it on the floor.

The papers were a week's worth of the *New York Press*. I subscribed to the New York paper not because it was any more informative than Chicago newspapers—it wasn't—but to keep tabs on a friend of mine, a reporter who'd gone to Europe at the end of 1914. His reports on the war had appeared regularly in the *Press* until last summer, when they'd abruptly stopped. I didn't know if he was alive or . . . otherwise.

I flipped through the first paper, looking for his name. I read none of the articles and noticed only a few of the headlines:

Spanish Influenza Epidemic in German Army
President Urges Suffrage on Senators
Czar and Family Executed
Commission Reports War Profiteering on Enormous Scale
Republicans Seek to End Party War

As I mechanically went through page after page, I thought about the night before. Mrs. Chapman was getting more brazen in her hints, and I had no doubt she assumed Edna and I would get married someday. I didn't know for sure what Edna thought, but I was starting to get the impression that her mother wasn't the only one with that notion. To me, our dates were as innocent as if she was my own sister, and I assumed nothing more than that we'd be going to the pictures again next Saturday night. Although it might be wiser not to. Perhaps it would be better to end things now. I wondered how Willie would take it if I stopped seeing his sister.

I started on the second issue of the *Press* and couldn't help noticing the theme that ran through many of the stories: if you weren't supporting the war effort, you were a slacker;

if you were a slacker, you were a traitor; if you were a traitor, you should be hung. My thoughts turned to my own feelings on the war, feelings that changed from day to day. I didn't know what the war was about exactly, nor why it was something I should be eager to kill or die for. Since my number hadn't come up in the draft lottery, I figured I'd just keep playing ball. Even though playing baseball for a living sometimes seemed a meaningless chore this year.

Except during the game itself. From the umpire's cry of "Play ball!" to the final out, I felt fully alive and the world made sense. Perhaps that's why, with all the craziness that had taken over the world, I clung so desperately to baseball. It was one thing—sometimes the only thing—that I understood.

I threw down the last of the papers without having seen a "Karl Landfors" byline. I knew I could have simply called the *Press* office and asked about him, but definitive news could also be bad news. I preferred to believe that if I just kept checking the papers, someday his name would reappear.

After skimming the newsprint and all the thinking, my head needed a douse of cold water as much as my legs needed to soak in hot. Prodded by a pang in my knee, I went to prepare the bath.

I cracked open the hot water tap above the tub. Nothing came out. I spun the faucet all the way open. Not a drip, not a belch. I tried the cold tap and a torrent gushed forth. Okay, there's water. So why not hot water?

Before renting this cottage, I'd always lived in apartments or boarding houses, so home maintenance wasn't my strong suit. I did remember, though, that in the cellar were some pipes and plumbing fixtures.

I went through the kitchen, out the back door, and stepped into the narrow alley that ran behind my house.

The cellar entrance was next to the back steps. I lifted the flimsy sheet of wood that covered it, climbed down three rickety steps, and pulled the string of an electric light. The bulb struggled to produce a dim glow.

My eyes took a few seconds to adjust to the darkness. After they dilated, I saw that the cellar was almost bare, pretty much the way I remembered it. A few empty wood packing crates, a small pile of bricks, and a coal shovel were its only contents.

I started to explore, walking hunched over to avoid bumping my head. The light wasn't bright enough for me to see the cobwebs that tickled my ears as I made my way to a location under the bathroom.

By following the pipes running under the floor joists, it took only a minute to discover the problem: the hot water tank was gone. Where it had been was a small puddle of water on the concrete floor. I ran my thumb over the end of one of the pipes that dangled above the puddle. It had been sawed through.

Relying on my apartment dweller instincts, it took only another minute to figure out what to do: call my landlord.

Back upstairs, I did just that, and asked him if he'd had the tank removed for some reason. He insisted he hadn't, which I believed since he wouldn't have cut the pipes to disconnect it. He also insisted that I now owed him fifteen dollars for a new one, which I argued about until he hung up on me.

I went out back again and looked around. There wasn't much to see. The dirt alley, with the back doors of Wolfram Street homes on one side and those of the larger George

Street homes on the other, wasn't wide enough to allow automobile traffic; it served primarily as a community back porch, a storage place for brooms and carpet beaters and a place for neighbors to gossip. No such neighbors were out now, no one to ask if they'd seen anything.

Lake View—which really didn't provide a view of Lake Michigan—was a good neighborhood. It was a peaceful area, mostly residential with single and two-story homes, not a part of the city where crime was a problem. But then, what kind of neighborhood does have a problem with stolen hot water tanks?

From the street in front of my house, I heard a familiar blustery voice call, "You kids beat it now! Scram!"

Leaving the alley, I squeezed my way between the side of my house and that of my next-door neighbor and emerged on Wolfram Street. The red brick homes on the block were essentially all the same. They were a step up from row houses in that there was a good foot and a half of space between each one.

This was "Gasless Sunday," so the street was as devoid of traffic as the alley. A herd of children had taken advantage of the empty street to play crack-the-whip. They were hand-in-hand, strung out across the width of the road. Yelling at them from the sidewalk was Mike the Cop, a large pudgy man with damp crescents under the arms of his blue uniform. It was Mike's personal mission to keep the neighborhood free of noisy children; and since there's no other kind, he routinely chased away anyone under the age of sixteen.

"Go on! Get! Ya snot-nosed little . . ." As he yelled, he flourished his billy club like Tom Mix twirling a six-shooter. I knew the kids were in no real danger from the stick. Mike was actually pretty harmless for a cop.

The kids finally ran away laughing, and I approached him. "Hey, Mike. I've been robbed."

He ignored me, his eyes remaining fixed on the kids as they scampered toward Southport Avenue. Mike had his priorities. "And don't come back neither!"

Mike was red-faced and breathless, either from the exertion of yelling or from the tight fit of his uniform. After he was satisfied that they were far enough away, he took a few puffs of air and turned his attention to me. "Robbed, you say?"

Good thing I wasn't reporting a shooting, I thought. "Yeah. Somebody stole my hot water tank."

His face fell. "Stole your *what?*"

"My water tank. You know, for hot water. It was in my cellar and now it's gone. Somebody took it."

Mike pushed up the visor of his cap with the end of his stick. "Uh-huh," he said flatly.

"Cut it right off the pipes and—"

Mike's attention had turned back to the street. "Well, would ya look at that," he said, pointing the stick at a passing Model T. A creative motorist had hitched a team of horses to the front of the car so his family could enjoy a Sunday drive without using gasoline.

I didn't appreciate Mike being so easily distracted. "About my water tank," I reminded him. "What are you going to do?"

"Me?" He was clearly astonished that I expected him to do anything.

"Yeah."

"Well. . . . I'm not gonna do nothing," he decided after a moment's thought. "I think that's crazy is what I think." He then nodded amiably and walked off, twirling his nightstick and trying to whistle.

After a couple of minutes, I went back into my house, slamming the screen door behind me. He's right, I thought, it's crazy.

•   •   •

I struck a match and put its flame to a piece of kindling in my kitchen stove. As the fire spread to the rest of the wood, I filled all the pots I had—three, including a coffee pot—with cold water and put them on top of the stove. One way or another I was going to have a hot bath, dammit.

"Hello! Rawlings, you in there?"

Mike the Cop must have decided to investigate after all. Leaving the water to boil, I went to the front door. The man who took form through the wire screen wasn't a cop. It was my boss. *The* boss: Charles A. Weeghman, President, Chicago Cubs.

"Mr. Weeghman," I said with surprise, pulling open the door. I'd never had a manager in my home before, never mind a team owner. "Uh, would you like to come in?"

He said nothing, but his scowl answered, "Obviously. What a stupid question." Weeghman, an ungainly fellow of about forty, had sunken eyes with dark bags under them and could produce a spectacularly frightening scowl.

He stepped in without removing his derby. Over his shoulder I saw a glossy black Packard at the curb, with a driver behind the wheel and the engine running. Gasless Sunday didn't apply to people who could afford Packards.

Weeghman's clothes were at the same end of the price scale as his car. The tailored dark suit couldn't disguise his awkward build though. And the droopy green bow tie wasn't exactly flattering.

Once inside, Weeghman gave the room a cursory glance and said, "Nice little place." He stressed the "little."

"Can I take your hat?"

"No," he grunted.

Despite his lousy manners, I was determined to be a good host and offered him my chair. He shook his head no and proceeded to half-sit on a sideboard that I didn't think could hold him.

I settled into the chair he'd declined and waited for him to tell me what he was doing in my nice little place.

I didn't have to wait long. "I want to know who's trying to put me out of business," Weeghman demanded.

I was tempted to suggest that he'd come to the wrong place, for I had no idea what he was talking about. "What do you mean?" I asked.

"Just what I said. Those smoke bombs yesterday. And the bleachers that collapsed." Last month, several of the right field bleacher seats had broken through, upending some fans.

"They just broke, didn't they?"

"They were sawed."

Like the pipes to my water tank.

He leaned forward. "And the pretzels a couple weeks ago."

Somebody had put pretzels in all the concession stands at Cubs Park, and Weeghman was pilloried in the papers for serving German food.

Did he think I was involved in any of this? "I don't know anything about it," I said.

"Don't expect you to . . . yet. But I expect you to find out. I want you to do some digging around for me."

"Oh." This sounded like an opportunity I'd rather pass up.

Weeghman noticed my lack of enthusiasm and his lips pursed. He looked down and began tugging at his shirt cuffs, carefully adjusting and readjusting them until they both stuck out exactly the same length from his jacket sleeve. As he fiddled, he softly said, "You know, the Work or Fight order takes effect tomorrow."

Know? It was almost all I'd thought of since the government had issued it in May. According to the order, every man of draft age had until July first to find essential war work or be drafted. Tomorrow was July first.

"Yeah, but if the Secretary of War decides baseball's essential, it doesn't matter," I said, with more hope than conviction. It sounded ridiculous to say those words. The Secretary of War ruling that baseball was essential. Not likely.

"True . . ." Weeghman nodded solemnly. Then, with a hint of a smile, he added, "Of course, if you're not playing baseball, it doesn't matter what Baker decides. You'll be off to the trenches."

Weeghman had all the subtlety of a bean ball. So that was it: do what he wanted or I was off the team. He could have asked nicely, explained why he needed my help. Instead, he starts off with a threat. A damned effective threat.

"You really think somebody's trying to put you out of business?"

"I *know* it," Weeghman snapped. "And I got an idea who, but I want to know for sure."

"Who do you think it is?" I half expected him to answer "Germans."

Weeghman hesitated. "Rather not say."

"How can I help if you don't tell me?" Not that I was

going to anyway, if I could avoid it, but I was getting curious.

Weeghman removed his derby and spun it idly in his hand for a minute. "It's Wrigley," he said abruptly.

"William Wrigley?"

His scowl told me it was another stupid question.

A splash and a sizzle came from the kitchen. The water! I bolted from my chair and ran to the stove. Removing the pots from the stove top, I wondered what Wrigley could have against Weeghman.

I knew Charles Weeghman wasn't the sole owner of the Cubs. He'd put together a syndicate of Chicago businessmen to buy the team two years ago. William Wrigley was one of a number of partners.

Back in the parlor, I pressed Weeghman. "Why would Mr. Wrigley want to put you out of business?"

"Bastard wants to take over my team."

That cheered me somewhat. I generally like it when owners fight among themselves—it's the only time they leave the players alone.

"When did Mr. Wrigley start this?" I asked, playing along.

"Right from the start of the season." Weeghman leaned forward and said confidentially, "I don't have proof of this, but I would bet you it was Wrigley who talked Alexander into enlisting." Weeghman had bought Grover Cleveland Alexander, the National League's premier pitcher, from the Phillies last winter. After three games with the Cubs in April, Alexander had enlisted and gone to France with General Pershing and the American Expeditionary Force.

"Maybe he enlisted out of patriotism," I suggested in Alexander's defense. I owed a lot to the players who had given up baseball to go to war, such as my promotion from utility player to starting second baseman.

Weeghman shook his head. "Nah, it was Wrigley. I'd bet money on it." When an owner's willing to risk money on something, he must feel it's a sure thing. He went on, "William Wrigley's got the biggest goddamn ego I ever seen. Did you know he used to own a semi-pro team that played out in Ogden Grove?"

"I heard that, yeah."

"Know what the name of the team was?"

"No—"

"The *Wrigleys*. How's that for ego?"

An owner with an ego. There's something new.

"If he takes over the Cubs," Weeghman said, "you might be wearing the name of a chewing gum on your uniform."

I didn't like that idea at all. It sounded like something slimy and writhing.

He added, "At the least, he'll change the name of the field to Wrigley Park or something."

I chose not to point out that Weeghman had christened it Weeghman Park when he'd opened it for his Federal League team four years ago.

And I really didn't care enough about the name of the park or the team to want to get involved in investigating anything. I'd done it before and had picked up a bunch of scars and broken bones in the process; I had no desire to add to that collection. If my career was going to end with a fatal injury, I wanted it to be from a fastball to the head, not a bullet in the back.

I finally asked, "But why me? What makes you think *I* could help you. I've never even met William Wrigley."

"I don't want you to check out Wrigley. He didn't plant them smoke bombs himself. Not the pretzels neither. And he sure didn't saw them bleacher seats. He's got somebody working for him. I want to know who it is."

"I wouldn't know where to begin."

"Start by finding out what your buddy Kaiser is up to."

"Willie?"

The scowl again, more severe, telling me that my questions were getting dumber. Hey, if you think I'm so stupid, I thought, get somebody smarter to help you.

"No, the other one," Weeghman said sarcastically. "Yeah, your roomie. Willie Kaiser. He went to some German meeting last night."

"He did?" But he'd told Fohl he wouldn't go. "How do you know that?"

Weeghman gave me a look that showed he didn't feel obligated to explain anything to me. But he grudgingly said, "These are unusual times. I need to know what my players are up to. So I keep tabs on—them." He'd almost said "you."

So Weeghman had spies working for him, spying on his own players. Surprisingly, I wasn't bothered by it—it was just one more bit of craziness that fit in nicely with the way the whole season had been going.

"By the way," Weeghman added. "Don't tell Kaiser I said anything to you about it. This is just between us. As far as anybody's concerned, we never had this talk."

"You really think Willie was involved with those smoke bombs?" I asked.

Weeghman shrugged. "I don't know. I want you to find out. And make sure you keep him from going to any more of them meetings. Last thing I need is for somebody to find out I got a traitor on my team."

Right. As if Willie's going to listen to what I tell him to do. Weeghman didn't know Willie Kaiser. I wasn't sure I did any more either, but I was sure that he was no traitor. "If you think he's a traitor," I said. "Why keep him on the team at all?"

"What are you, crazy?" Weeghman squawked. "He's hitting .320. Where am I gonna find another shortstop like him?" No scowl this time. Instead his eyes rolled to show how appalled he was at my lack of business sense. The way Weeghman could express himself with his face, he could become a moving picture actor if Wrigley succeeded in putting him out of the baseball business.

Well, at least I'd learned something new: as long as you're hitting .320, you can sabotage your team, even be a traitor to your country, and some baseball owner will still want you playing on his club.

I suppose if Willie was batting .400, Weeghman wouldn't mind if he'd committed a murder.

Chapter Four

Game time was two o'clock. As usual, I was suited up and on the field before noon. What was unusual was that I didn't have to wait for my teammates to join me. All the Cubs players, as well as the visiting Cincinnati Reds, were going through their warm-up routines. We had to get practice out of the way early because of the pre-game ceremonies that had been planned.

It was Thursday, the Fourth of July, and Charles Weeghman was using the holiday to full advantage. He seemed determined to single-handedly demonstrate the patriotism of major league baseball, at least that of the Chicago Cubs. To this end, he'd scheduled enough speeches and music and marches for a political convention.

The Reds were helping ensure that the spectacle took place before a full house. They'd moved Fred Toney up in their pitching rotation to face our Hippo Vaughn in a re-match of baseball's greatest pitching duel. A year ago in this park the two men had pitched no-hit shutouts against each other for a full nine innings, until Jim Thorpe won the game for Toney and the Reds with a tenth-inning single.

The two big pitchers were warming up now, showing off, hurling bullets that smacked loudly in their catchers' mitts. Toney threw to Ivy Wingo in foul territory near the first base dugout and Vaughn to Bob O'Farrell along the third base line.

Kids outside the park were warming up, too, for the Fourth of July celebration, shooting off rockets and firecrackers that popped more harshly than Vaughn's and Toney's pitches.

The Reds were taking infield practice. The tall fellow hitting them easy grounders was Christy Mathewson, my old teammate with the Giants, now the manager of Cincinnati. He took care not to drive any up the middle to avoid hitting the carpenters working behind second base.

The workmen were putting the finishing touches on a small platform that had been built for the visiting dignitaries. Their hammering added to the percussive din in the park, making it almost impossible to hear the chatter of the crowd.

Already there were more people in the park than we'd had for the previous five games combined. They were here to see a ballgame, to enjoy a day of leisure, to forget about the war. For a couple of hours, the most important battle in the world would be fought between two teams of nine men each, with nothing more deadly than ball, bat, and glove as weapons.

Charles Weeghman strolled around near the backstop, cheerfully giving interviews to a clutch of reporters who trailed behind him. As he spoke, the beaming Weeghman kept his eyes on the stands, occasionally waving to individuals in the crowd.

There was a side to Charles Weeghman that I admired: he genuinely liked the fans. As much as he wanted their ticket money, he also wanted them to have a good time in his ballpark. Other men owned shares of the Cubs, but the park was really Weeghman's. He'd built it in 1914 for his Chicago franchise in the outlaw Federal League. When the Feds folded after only two years, Weeghman was allowed to buy the National League Cubs and move them into his North Side showplace. From the beginning, Weeghman catered to the wishes of the fans. He was the first club owner to build concession stands so that patrons wouldn't have their view blocked by vendors, and he was the only owner to let fans keep baseballs hit into the stands.

Then there was the side of Weeghman I had seen Sunday. I never did agree to help him, but I didn't refuse either. He'd never asked me for a direct answer, simply assuming that his threat would have the desired effect and I would do his bidding. It occurred to me after he'd left that it might have been Weeghman who'd had the water tank stolen from my cellar, just to show me how it felt to have my home sabotaged.

When the Reds left the infield, Shufflin' Phil Douglas shuffled out to the mound to throw batting practice for us. Douglas, a heavy-drinking pitcher whose specialty was the spitball, was stamped from the same large mold as Hippo Vaughn. Despite the prohibition on liquor, Douglas's spitters had enough alcohol on them that they could almost disable a batter by intoxication.

I picked up my bat from the ground in front of the dugout and went to join the Cubs lining up at the plate.

Willie was already there, first in line—until Wicket Greene elbowed his way in front of him. Greene was within his rights this time since the tradition was veterans before rookies. But it bothered me that Willie gave up his spot without a word.

I had to get some life in that kid. I also had to find out

what he'd been up to lately—not for Weeghman's sake, but for his own. I was going to help Willie whether he wanted me to or not. The problem was breaking through his shell of silence.

I suddenly dropped my bat and went to the bench for my glove instead.

After Greene took his hits, Willie stepped up to the plate. I walked to the mound with my mitt open. "Let me pitch him, Phil."

Douglas turned his blood-shot eyes to me. "Sure, what the hell," he said with a chuckle as he flipped me the ball. "Give him the spitter."

I didn't have a spitter. Nor a curve, nor a fastball. I wasn't a pitcher, and I hadn't thrown batting practice since I was in the minors.

Willie stepped away from the plate and lowered his bat, obviously disconcerted by my appearance on the mound.

"Get in there busher!" I barked at him. "Afraid you can't hit me?"

He gave me a vacant smile and took a tentative batting stance.

I wound up for the first pitch and let the ball loose—straight for his head.

Willie fell on his rear to avoid it. I didn't have a major league fastball, but I could throw hard enough and I could put it where I wanted.

Willie cautiously stood back up and took his stance again.

My next pitch went just behind his head, causing him to stumble forward. Angry rumblings came from the players crowded around the batting cage, and Fred Merkle hollered, "If you can't pitch, get the hell off the mound!"

After straightening himself, Willie slowly rubbed his

palms on the front of his jersey and eyed me with a mixture of anger and disbelief. I could see him thinking: *Brushbacks during batting practice?*

One more—at his chin.

He leaned back just far enough to avoid it. Then he pointed his bat at me and yelled, "Put one over the plate and I'll take your goddamn head off."

Yeah? Let's see.

I threw it down the middle, letter-high. He took an angry rip trying to kill the ball and tipped a weak pop up.

He got more of the next pitch, hitting a hard grounder to short. He came closer and closer to me on subsequent hits until he nailed a line drive that forced me to duck. It flew over second base and rattled onto the platform, sending the workmen scurrying for cover.

As I kept pitching, Willie got into a groove, hitting line drives up the middle that kept me hopping and the construction workers swearing. His face was alight now. None of the Cubs tried to oust him from the box, and their angry rumblings at me had turned to compliments on Willie's hitting.

Eventually I dropped the ball on the ground and announced, "That's it for my pitching career."

Phil Douglas pulled himself off the dugout bench, where he'd stretched out to "rest his eyes," and took the mound again to pitch to Fred Merkle.

Willie took Douglas's spot in the dugout. I followed him to the bench, leaving a few feet of space between us as I sat down.

"Pretty good hitting," I said, looking out at Douglas and Merkle.

Willie spat and kept his eyes on the field. "Hell, Edna could hit your pitching." A smile broke over his face. I couldn't remember the last time I'd seen such a grin on him.

I turned to him. "Felt good taking those rips, didn't it?"

He still didn't look at me. "Yeah," he conceded. "Damn good."

"Nice to see you fight back. You might try that with Wicket Greene sometime."

Willie's smile faded a bit. "I *am* fighting back. In my own way. You just don't see it."

"Okay." Should I push it? I decided no. I'd opened him up a bit; best to leave him that way for now and pry a little more later. "Well, let me know if there's anything I can do."

"Thanks," he said. "I might just. . . . uh, how 'bout we talk later?"

"Sure," I quickly agreed. Maybe then he'd tell me what the hell he'd been doing at Hans Fohl's meeting.

• • •

At one o'clock, a twelve-piece brass band led off the festivities with something by John Philip Sousa. I wasn't sure if it was "Stars and Stripes Forever" or "The Washington Post March." It sounded like the musicians didn't know either. They were playing for volume rather than accuracy.

The band stood near second base, in front of the platform that held the VIPs. Weeghman sat in the center of the stage, looking as rapturous as Rube with a bone. Attendance exceeded anything he could have hoped for: the grandstand was packed to standing room only and fans who overflowed the bleachers were herded into roped-off areas in foul territory. Since every square inch of space in the ballpark had been sold out, not even the freeloaders on the rooftops across Sheffield Avenue could spoil Weeghman's mood.

Seated to Weeghman's left was the mayor of Chicago, Big

Bill Thompson. The rest of the chairs were occupied by half a dozen of the city's most powerful businessmen, each of them a part-owner of the Cubs. Among them were J. Ogden Armour of the meatpacking family; Bennett Harrington, who owned the Dearborn Fuel Company; and William Wrigley, the chewing gum man. The Cubs' ownership had enough collective influence to get the lucrative Fourth of July game scheduled for Chicago's National League team. To Charlie Comiskey's chagrin, his World Champion White Sox were playing their holiday game in Cleveland.

After the noise from the band came to a merciful end, Weeghman rose and stepped up to a huge brown megaphone set upon a tripod. I hoped the speeches weren't going to last long. Holding a bat at "shoulder arms" was an uncomfortable position to maintain for any length of time. That's how the two teams stood, the Cincinnati players in formation at third base and the Cubs behind first.

I knew we didn't look like soldiers, but at least our home uniforms had a patriotic color scheme: *CUBS* spelled across the chest of our white pinstripes in red and blue letters and socks with bright bands of red, white, and blue. The Reds, in their road flannels, were limited to red and gray.

To his credit—and my relief—Weeghman made only a few brief remarks regarding "this great game of ours" before introducing the mayor.

Mayor Thompson was a large man with a large cigar clamped between his teeth. Before the U. S. entered the war, he'd been so openly pro-German that he was dubbed "Kaiser Bill." Since then, he kept a low profile, especially during patriotic events such as this. Thompson took the cigar from his mouth long enough to say a few words about "this great

game of ours" and quickly went on to introduce Bennett
Harrington.

Harrington was the ideal speaker for this occasion, a link
between baseball and the military. His Dearborn Fuel Company was one of the leading industries producing weapons
and ammunition for the war effort.

The other men on the platform were dark-suited and
looked every bit the businessmen and politicians they were.
Bennett Harrington, a tall slim man whose age was somewhere between thirty and sixty, affected the look of a Southern gentleman: white linen suit, black string tie, and a
Panama hat.

As Harrington started speaking, the wind picked up, giving ripples of life to the red, white, and blue bunting that had
been slathered around the park. Above the scoreboard, the
flag perked up and flew straight out.

Harrington's voice was different from the others, too. He
lacked their bluster, speaking softly and slowly. The content
of his speech was the same though—that of a politician. And
since I'd never heard a politician's speech that was worth
listening to, my attention quickly wandered.

I looked at moonfaced William Wrigley seated at the end
of the platform. I'd given a lot of thought to Wrigley and to
Weeghman's suspicions of him. I came to the conclusion
that it didn't make financial sense for Wrigley—or any of the
other Cubs owners—to try to hurt the club. Sabotaging the
team would only end up hurting themselves. There had to be
another explanation for the strange events at Cubs Park.

I was starting to juggle my bat and had to force myself to
stop. The pre-game practice had worn off long before and I
was starting to stiffen. With a glance over my shoulder, I saw
that my teammates were fidgeting more than I was.

Harrington's words caught my ears again, ". . . more than just a game. By allowing these fine young men to continue playing baseball, we will provide entertainment to boost the nation's morale *and* the training necessary to provide for the nation's defense. As General Pershing himself has said, 'The soldier who is best at throwing grenades is the one who knows how to throw a baseball' . . ."

Good thing Black Jack Pershing didn't see me throw batting practice, I thought.

Harrington came to his close. He paused to place his hat over his heart, then uttered the phrase of the day, "this great game of ours." The move looked insincere and the words rang hollow. Yup, he was a politician at heart. But if Bennett Harrington could help keep the War Department from closing down the season, he was all right with me.

After a few final words from Charles Weeghman, the band launched into a slow, cautious version of "The Star Spangled Banner." President Wilson had declared it to be the country's national anthem for the duration of the war, so the musicians gave extra care to playing the notes as written.

The anthem ended with a raucous burst of rockets and firecrackers. Our adolescent lieutenant ordered, "Forward . . . *march!*" and we began moving toward second.

The Cincinnati squad marched toward the same destination from their place behind third. Seeing the Reds squad, I realized what a ridiculous appearance both teams must be making. The knobs flaring at the ends of the bats made it look like we were armed with toy blunderbusses.

As the Cubs and Reds converged toward the VIP platform, Bennett Harrington stood. He put his hat over his heart again and lifted his right hand in salute. The rest of the dignitaries scrambled to follow his lead.

Our lieutenant squealed, "Right turn . . . *march!*" and Cincinnati's leader gave the same order for a left turn. Both squads executed the maneuver smoothly. The Reds veered off toward left field, while we marched toward the cheering fans in the right field bleachers.

I stole a look at Willie, tempted to congratulate him on the successful turn. I could tell from his satisfied smile that he'd sufficiently complimented himself on the feat.

Willie's face suddenly froze. A fountain of red erupted from his chest, spurting from the "U" in *CUBS*. He gave a soft grunt and blood bubbled from his lips. I dropped my bat and moved to catch him as he began to collapse. In the back of my mind, the sound of thunder registered. I threw my arm around his back to hold him up.

Teammates stumbled into us, then quickly stepped away.

Willie's eyes were wide, white, and sightless. He felt nothing as I laid him down on the grass, still supporting his head.

I never saw anyone die at such close range before. I didn't know how quiet death could be. Like turning off a gas lamp—a flicker, a hiss, and it's off.

That's how Willie Kaiser died.

• • •

The aftermath was fast and frenzied like a series of quick cuts in a moving picture. I watched, dazed, feeling as powerless and detached from the action as if staring at a movie screen.

Calls went up for a doctor, and one was ushered from the stands to the field carrying the traditional black bag. He took his time to do an examination before pronouncing the obvious: Willie Kaiser was dead.

The players of both teams looked on horrified. I spotted

Wicket Greene; his ugly mouth was agape, and he kept passing the back of his hand over his bulging forehead.

Mayor Thompson, J. Ogden Armour, Bennett Harrington, William Wrigley, and the other dignitaries quickly vanished from the scene.

I noticed blood on my right sleeve. Willie's blood. I absentmindedly began rubbing the spot with my thumb. I knew I couldn't erase it, but it was something to do. I wanted to make it all go away.

At the megaphone, Charles Weeghman announced that the game was canceled. He, too, looked distraught. I wondered if it was because he lost a .320 hitter or because he'd have to refund all of the day's ticket sales.

Fred Merkle and Hippo Vaughn were recruited to take Willie to the clubhouse on a stretcher. I watched as they carried his limp body from the field.

Stadium police swarmed about with no apparent purpose but to show that they were there. Nobody was taking charge. This just didn't happen at a baseball game. They could handle rain delays, fans running on the field, even a fire in the stands. For a shooting in the ballpark, they were at a loss what to do.

I approached a cop wearing sergeant's stripes. "Who's going to tell his family?" I asked.

"Damned if I know," he grunted.

I sighed. "I'll tell them."

I looked at my sleeve, at the blood spot I was rubbing. Edna and her mother shouldn't see that. As I walked to the clubhouse to change clothes, the cop called after me, "Who are you?"

Loudly and firmly, I answered, "His friend!"

Chapter Five

Accidental death from a stray bullet. That was the explanation printed in the *Chicago American*. Same in the *Tribune,* the *Herald-Examiner,* the *Journal,* and the *Daily News.* Chicago's Friday morning papers all came to the identical conclusion: some rowdy, probably drunk on illegal liquor, had carelessly shot off a gun in celebration of the holiday. The bullet had come down, purely by chance, in Willie Kaiser.

It was curious—and suspicious—how the newspaper stories matched each other almost word for word. This despite a conspicuous lack of specifics: no such drunken celebrant was identified, there was no mention of any witness who had seen someone wielding a gun, no make of weapon was specified—not even whether it was a pistol or a rifle. And each article ended with a sanctimonious sermon in favor of prohibition. The way the stories read, Willie's death amounted to nothing more than a useful morality tale on the evils of alcohol.

The other similarity in the reports was their location:

inconspicuous, single columns, no photographs. None of them appeared on the front pages, which were dominated by Independence Day observances and the war. The only baseball-related news to make a front page was in the *Daily News,* with a headline that read *Shoeless Joe a Slacker Says Comiskey;* it was subheaded *May Not Let Jackson Return to Sox.* I made a mental note to read that piece later.

I had to flip all the way to the inside pages of the sports sections to find the stories of Willie's death. The sports page. What a place to report a shooting. Why not summarize it in a box score: no at bats, one shot, one death.

The similarities in the stories were too similar to be coincidence. The news coverage had been coordinated by somebody. Most national news these days had to pass through the government's Committee for Public Information. Would they handle something like this?

Or was Weeghman behind it in an attempt to avoid bad publicity? A baseball player shot to death in a crowded ballpark—there couldn't be anything worse than that for scaring away fans.

I tossed the papers on top of the *New York Press* issues stacked next to my chair. After a few minutes' thought, I decided it wasn't Weeghman. He wouldn't have had the stories placed on the sports pages. That was the part of the papers his customers read.

Whatever the source of the tale, I didn't believe a word of it. I wasn't sure what I did believe, but I was certain that Willie's death was no accident.

I had no more solid evidence for my conclusion than the papers had for theirs. Except for the fact that I'd been next to Willie when he was shot, and I'd seen with my own eyes what the bullet did to him.

What bothered me most was where the bullet hit him: right in the "U" of "CUBS," dead center in his chest. I knew that an accidental shot would be as likely to hit that spot as any other, but it felt suspicious. I also knew that my logic was questionable, for if Willie had been intentionally targeted by a gunman with poor aim and struck in the foot, I could have easily believed the accident theory. Logical or not, the location of the wound was enough to get my instincts riled up, and I got to thinking.

About the path of the bullet, for another thing. I'd seen where the bullet had entered Willie's chest. Since I had blood on my sleeve from supporting his back, I also knew where it had exited. The bullet had traveled horizontally. If somebody shoots off a gun in celebration, he shoots it in the air. The slug would have come back down vertically.

Now I had something tangible that didn't jibe with the newspaper reports.

I thought a bit more and realized I hadn't seen the bullet actually enter. I knew where the two wounds were, but I couldn't swear as to which was the entrance and which the exit. Maybe the bullet had come from the other direction.

I pictured the way we were marching, Willie in the front row. The bullet couldn't have entered his back without first striking another player behind him. It had to have come from the front.

What was in front? I could see the crowded right field bleachers and the fans on the rooftops.

The shot hadn't come from the bleachers or somebody would have seen the gunman. Unless a pistol was used, maybe. But still somebody would have heard the sound.

From a roof, then? No, they had been packed, too. Again, somebody would have seen the shooter or heard the shot.

Heard . . .

The hollow thunder that I'd heard yesterday echoed in my ear. And I knew where the bullet had come from: one of the row houses on Sheffield Avenue. Not from a rooftop but from a window. No one to see the shooter, and four walls to give the sound a muffled resonance. A shot from outdoors would have cracked more like a bat hitting a ball.

Then it echoed again, more faintly, as I remembered a time when somebody had shot at me in a ballpark. Fenway Park. That shot had come from a tunnel under the stands and with the same deep, distant tone. I must have been about Willie's age then. And, like him, I was in my rookie season. There was one big difference, though: I wasn't killed. I was able to find out who shot at me, and I did.

For Willie to get justice, somebody would have to pinch hit for him.

• • •

Mrs. Chapman was slumped in her parlor chair, looking as though she had fallen into it hours before and hadn't moved since. A baggy black dress hung about her in folds and wrinkles like a pile of unironed laundry. She clutched a crumpled white handkerchief in her fist, holding it to her bosom as unchecked tears streaked her sagging cheeks.

I'd heard there's no worse pain than to lose a child, and from the look on her face I believed it. She had a far-off expression in her red, wet eyes as if staring at memories and noting every detail to keep them from ever fading.

"Mrs. Chapman," I said tentatively.

She didn't answer, didn't flinch.

I exchanged glances with Edna. She was dressed in the

same black as her mother, but she wore her mourning clothes with a kind of stiff defiance rather than resignation. Although Edna's narrow eyes were also wet, she refused to let the tears escape beyond her puffy lids, so her cheeks were dry. She gave a slight nod in the direction of her mother, suggesting I try again.

I did, twice more, before she noticed I was there.

"Ah, Mickey." Mrs. Chapman turned her head to face me without shifting her body an inch. There was faint pleading hope in her eyes. The same look that had been in them yesterday. By the time I'd gotten to their house, a neighbor had already phoned them with the news of Willie's death. But when I'd arrived, Edna and her mother had looked at me hopefully, perhaps expecting I would tell them it wasn't so. I'd have given anything not to have had to disappoint them.

"I, uh, I brought this," I said, holding out to her a carefully pressed Chicago Cubs home uniform.

"They gave you one!"

"No, ma'am, it's mine. But it should fit him fine." Willie and I sometimes had to borrow each others clothes on road trips; except for his neck being a little thicker, we were the same size.

"I asked the Cubs for a uniform to bury him in," Mrs. Chapman said in a choked voice. "They said no." She took the uniform and laid it on her lap. If she looked closely at the right sleeve she'd find a threadbare patch were I'd scraped off every trace of Willie's blood. "It's what he would have wanted," she said, tenderly stroking the fabric.

I doubted that she could know for sure how Willie would have wanted to be buried. He probably never gave it any thought. A rookie ballplayer doesn't think about his own funeral plans. I never did, not even when the occasion seemed imminent.

But it gave some comfort to Mrs. Chapman to believe she was complying with his wishes, so I was glad to have stopped at the park for my uniform. There'd been few people there: four or five maintenance workers dismantling the platform and half a dozen police officers strolling around the playing field. It would be three days until ballplayers would be on the field again. Weeghman had canceled all Cubs games until after Willie's funeral.

"My poor boy," murmured Mrs. Chapman.

The warm musty air of the room, dense with the aromas of sauerkraut, lamp oil, and perfume, started to close in on me. It was the same as the very first time I had entered the Chapman's home: heavy air, the kind found in the house of a stranger or an aged aunt, had tried to push me away. Then, after a few visits, the atmosphere no longer struck me as alien; it had become the agreeable scent of home. Now it was back, choking me, suggesting I was no longer welcome here.

I needed to get outside. "Think I'll take the dogs for a walk," I said to Edna.

"I just walked them," she said softly.

Figures. No matter what happened, she wasn't going to neglect the creatures who depended on her.

"Well, I'll take them anyway."

Her raised eyebrows asked if she could join me.

"You better take care of your mother," I said. Mrs. Chapman was running a fingertip over the front of the jersey, tracing the *CUBS* lettering. Fresh tears glistened on her face.

Edna nodded.

I took the leashes from where they hung on the kitchen doorknob and went to the dogs' room.

The dachshunds, who'd been sleeping off the earlier exercise, hopped up at the sight of the ropes and started bouncing around pretending they hadn't been let out in days. A convincing bunch of actors they were. As I attached the leashes to their collars, I could swear Rube was smirking at the way they were putting one over on me.

Taking our usual route, I started walking them north along broad Paulina Street through the Chapman's neighborhood of Ravenswood. Since the residents of this part of the city were predominantly German, no one objected to dachshunds.

It was slow progress, trying to walk four dogs who thought I was a maypole. I had to keep stopping to unwind their leashes from my legs.

Rube, oblivious to the death in the family, was in a playful mood, almost prancing. Although there's nothing more ungainly than a dachshund with a limp, I thought he was the best-looking dog of the bunch. And I wondered how many more times I'd get to see him.

I was part of the family when Willie was alive, a big brother, in a way. Now I felt like an outsider. With him gone, his family probably wouldn't want me around anymore. I'd serve only as a reminder of happier times that were permanently over.

Nothing was going to be the same without Willie.

We were on the corner of Lawrence and Hermitage when Edna came up at a brisk pace. Rube was tangled around my left leg, two others were around my right, and the fourth dog had his leg up to water a lamppost.

Edna answered my questioning look. "Hans came to visit.

He'll watch Mama." She bent down and unwrapped the two dachshunds from my right leg.

She took control of their leashes, and we headed south on Hermitage. I should have said something comforting but couldn't. All I could think was that before Willie was shot I had wanted to break up our dating routine, clarify it, stop seeing her. I felt inexplicably guilty now.

"That was nice of you to bring the uniform," Edna said in her little-girl voice.

"Oh, well. . . . It seemed important to your mother."

"You won't get in any trouble, will you?"

Probably, I thought. "No," I said. After all, what could the Cubs do to me—make me play in my underwear?

We paused while Rube tried to make use of the rear tire of a Model T. I tugged him away from the Ford to a Studebaker "Big Six" parked in front of it. In the back of my mind I was training him to a higher class of automobile in the event that he might run into Weeghman's Packard someday.

Edna asked evenly, "Who would want to kill my brother?" Her tone was of genuine curiosity; it wasn't an angry demand or a plaintive lament.

It was a question I couldn't answer. After some thought, I mumbled, "The papers say it was an accident."

She gave me a sharp look. I hadn't answered her question, and evasiveness wasn't going to work with her.

"I don't know why anybody would want to ki—uh, hurt Willie," I said. "He was a good kid. Never did anything to anybody. And a good ballplayer." After it left my lips, I realized how silly that last sentence sounded. Would there have been reason to kill him had he been a lousy player? "I don't know what happened," I said with more snap than I intended.

"Would you find out?"

Edna Chapman had a disarming way of asking things so simply and directly that her requests seemed completely reasonable.

We turned east on Sunnyside Avenue, past the Ravenswood Methodist Episcopal Church, and I mulled it over. I didn't know what I could do about it. There were too many things going on these days. How could I do any digging around when it wasn't even clear where to dig? The papers had obviously been censored by somebody, probably the government. The cops weren't revealing whatever they had found. And everything this year had political implications— not my area of expertise.

That might even be the reason Willie was shot: politics. I knew some of the usual motives for murder: greed, vengeance, jealousy. But politics? Could somebody have really felt so strongly about Willie Kaiser's name, or his heritage, that they killed him? It wasn't a motive I could understand, and if I couldn't understand it, how could I figure out what had happened?

At Paulina Street, the dogs tried to tug us forward; they knew a left turn meant they were going back home. They were too tired to do much more walking, but they made the effort to prolong it a little longer anyway.

Their effort failed, and as we made the final turn, I said, "I'm sorry, Edna. But I don't know what I could do. I mean, a bullet just came out of the air and . . . that was it. Nobody saw anything, heard anything . . ."

She ducked her head. "I understand." Not a trace of blame in her voice.

"I'm sorry," I said again. "If I knew where to start . . . anything . . ."

She nodded.

I felt like a complete heel and guiltier by the minute. I wasn't really reluctant to help—hell, I wanted to find out who killed Willie even if Edna hadn't asked me. I *wanted* to do something, I just didn't know what to do.

By the time we reached the Chapman home between Leland and Lawrence, frustration had supplanted guilt as the primary emotion running through me. It didn't feel any better.

Two small gatherings of people were clustered by the front steps of the Chapman's small two-story white clapboard house. The dogs perked up and pulled Edna and me along to join the crowd. Despite their near exhaustion, they weren't going to miss out on the possibility of some petting.

Rube went for the crowd of women gathered to the left of the steps. There were four of them, all generally in middle age. None of them was wearing black, so I assumed they were neighbors rather than relatives.

One of the women held a covered blue enamel dish that exuded a tempting smell of sausage. She was telling the others, "He was such a good boy. He used to play ball with my Johnny, you know. One time, must have been four, maybe five years ago, the two of them were playing and broke my bedroom window. Willie worked two weeks delivering ice to pay for it. Wasn't till a month later that Johnny admitted *he* was the one who threw the ball through the window. Ah, he was a good boy, Willie Kaiser was." She spotted Edna. "Oh, you poor dear." Holding out the dish, she said, "I brought a little dinner. You shouldn't have to worry about cooking at a time like this."

"Thank you, Mrs. Schafer," Edna said. She handed me her leashes and took the dish.

We moved to the other side of the steps where Hans Fohl and half a dozen other men were jawing heatedly with each other. Fohl acknowledged our presence with a solemn nod while the others continued arguing. A strapping blond young man said loudly, "Lucky shot for somebody. Celebrating the Fourth of July, shoots off a gun, and the bullet comes down in a German."

"Lucky my ass," Fohl growled. "He was—"

Edna blushed, and Fohl caught himself. Then he went on, "There was nothing 'lucky' about it. He was killed by the Knights *because* he was German."

I had some idea of what the Knights were: the Patriotic Knights of Liberty, one of a number of quasi-legal deputy forces around the country that were supposed to enforce patriotism. I had no idea how you could enforce something like that, but I'd heard that they had their ways.

"You can be damn sure," Fohl said with a defiant glance at Edna—he was going to cuss whether she liked it or not— "the cops won't do nothing about it."

If my experience with Mike the Cop was any example, Fohl was probably right about that.

"We're gonna take care of it ourselves," Fohl went on with a wag of his finger. "We'll get revenge for Willie Kaiser." Idle boasting? I couldn't tell.

The "we" again. That German group? The one Willie wouldn't meet with? The meeting Weeghman said he did go to?

I did have a starting point: was Willie really at that meeting, and if so, what was he doing there?

"We better bring them in," Edna said to me with a nod at the dogs.

"Yeah, okay."

She carried the food and I pulled the drooping dachshunds into the house. The air was no fresher than it was before, and I gagged on my first breath.

Two women were talking to Mrs. Chapman. She still had the uniform on her lap.

"Let me check on Mama," Edna said.

I touched her elbow and gestured to the back of the house. We were both somewhat startled by the contact. We'd never really touched before, never even held hands.

With puzzlement in her eyes, Edna followed me through the parlor and into the kitchen. She put the dish on top of the stove, then joined me in the dogs' room.

I dropped the leashes on the floor. The dachshunds plodded to their beds and collapsed in total contentment.

"The other night," I said. "Hans asked Willie to go to some meeting. Do you know anything about it?"

Edna paused. "I remember him asking," she said evasively. She bent over the dogs and began detaching the leashes from their collars.

"Do you know where it was?"

"I'm not supposed to know."

"But you do, don't you?"

She finished unhooking the leashes and straightened up. After a long pause, she nodded reluctantly.

If she was ever to be interrogated by the police, I pitied the officer who'd have to question her. "Well, where was it? Tell me."

"First Trinity Lutheran. It's off Division Street, near Humbolt Park. Not far from the movie theater."

"The" movie theater being the one showing *Tarzan*. "Okay. Thanks."

"Why do you want to know?"

"I'm going to find out—" I almost said "who killed your brother." But I wasn't doing it for her or for Mrs. Chapman. I wanted to know who killed my friend.

"I'm going to find out who killed Willie," I said.

Chapter Six

I don't know exactly what I expected to find at the church. Perhaps I'd absorbed enough newspaper propaganda that I thought I'd see men in spiked helmets devising plots to poison the nation's water supply or blow up the Palmer House hotel.

That's not what I found.

First Trinity Lutheran was a down-to-earth edifice, squat and solid, with a modest steeple that had no pretensions of reaching to heaven. The granite structure, impressive in its simple, clean construction, spread over half a block east of Humbolt Park.

I stood across the street from the church, talking with a barefoot newsboy while I kept an eye on the building.

Small red brick homes lined most of the quiet street, with a few churches, shops, and restaurants interspersed between them. The neighborhood was mixed: largely German, especially to the north, as well as a number of Poles and some recent Ukrainian immigrants.

Most of the shops had closed and daylight was waning. I

pulled my watch from my vest pocket: twenty past eight. Last week, Fohl had told Willie the meeting would start at nine. I assumed it would be the same today. If there was a meeting, that is.

From my vantage point, I could see nothing sinister developing at the church. A stream of people trickled into the front entrance, sometimes dawdling to greet acquaintances, with no sign of furtiveness. There were young families with small children in tow, older couples walking slowly together, groups of chatting women, and sullen-faced adolescent boys who would have preferred to be elsewhere. Everyone was dressed in what my uncle used to call Sunday-go-to-meeting clothes (he rarely wore such clothes and never attended such meetings). It could have been Sunday church in any town in America. Except that it was Saturday night in Chicago, the church was German, and America and Germany were enemies.

I was in church clothes, too: a stiff black serge suit that I'd worn for the first time to Willie's funeral this afternoon. A somber dark gray fedora, also new, took the place of the straw boater I usually wore. It was heavy attire for a warm summer night, and the cloth seemed to absorb moisture from the humid air, making it all the more cumbersome. The clothing didn't weigh me down nearly as much, though, as the memory of Willie lying in his casket.

Of course, with the funeral, Edna and I weren't going to be attending the movies this night. Instead, I was going to church to pay a surprise visit to Hans Fohl. After another twenty minutes of watching, I decided it was time to try getting in.

A family of five, a young husband and wife with two daughters skipping in front of them and a baby in the woman's arms, turned from Western Avenue toward First Trinity. I put a dime in the newsboy's palm and trotted across the street to join them.

A few quick steps drew me even with the tall young man. He was about twenty-five, with a proud bearing that I was sure came from being head of such a fine family. His clothes were far from new but clean and neatly pressed. "Hey, good to see you again," I said, offering my hand.

He shook it firmly. "Ah, yes," he stammered, "good to see you, too." His brow furrowed as he tried to remember me. He wasn't going to succeed.

His pale wife gave me a shy smile, and I tipped my hat in greeting. I noticed the baby was wrapped in a blue blanket. "My but he's getting big," I said. She smiled more fully and tilted the infant so I could see him better. Tapping the man on his shoulder, I added, "Soon he's gonna be as big as you."

He lit up. "Yeah, he's gonna be a strong one, all right."

By the time we walked up the steps to the church door, he was telling me that he planned for his son to be a pitcher "like Big Ed Walsh."

There were no guards at the door, no one checking the identity of those who entered. Whatever was going on at First Trinity Lutheran was neither secret nor exclusive. Not that I could see, anyway.

Still, having used this family to ease my way in, I wanted to minimize any possible trouble I might cause them. As soon as politeness would allow, I detached myself from them and strolled down a broad hallway, carrying my hat in hand. I tried to blend in, occasionally giving a familiar nod or a "How are you?" to people I'd never before met.

The tile hallway encircled the worship area of the church the way a corridor runs around the playing field of a ballpark to let people get to their seating sections. I looked in through the large open doorways. Instead of a green grass field were rows of varnished wooden pews. A large, plain wood cross took the place of a scoreboard. No services were under way, but a few pews were occupied by worshippers in solitary prayer or quiet contemplation—like pregame warm-ups.

Along the outer side of the hallway ran a series of smaller doors. All of them were open, and each led to a rapidly filling classroom.

A spindly, dark-haired young woman stepped from one of the rooms and placed her hand on the doorknob. After looking up and down the hall, she began to pull the door closed. This innocent act contrasted so sharply with the generally open atmosphere that it piqued my interest, and I quickly approached her.

She hesitated. "Were you coming in?" Her tone was surprised but hospitable.

I looked past her. The room was entirely filled with children. There was a piano, and many of the kids held violins and flutes. "Uh, no," I said. "Wrong room."

"Wrong church, if you ask me," a deep voice behind me said.

The woman pulled the door shut and I turned around. A muscular blond man had me fixed in his glare. Something about him was familiar. "What do you think you're doing here?" he demanded.

Caught. Not that I was caught really doing anything. "I was looking for Hans Fohl," I said.

"And who's Hans Fohl?"

I finally recognized the man. "You should know. You were with him outside Willie Kaiser's house yesterday." This was the fellow who'd said it was a "lucky shot" for some-body.

"You're . . ."

"Mickey Rawlings. Is Fohl here?"

The brittle screeching of violins came from behind the closed door.

He nodded. "Wait here. I'll get him." He started to walk away. Over his broad shoulder he added, "Wait *right* here."

As soon as he was out of view, I disobeyed the instruction. I strode the length of the hallway, looking into as many of the rooms as I could. I saw nothing unusual and returned to the music room.

Hans Fohl soon approached me, alone, his footsteps slapping loudly on the tile floor. Fohl's black hair glistened with something he'd applied in an attempt to slick it down, but it had sprung back up in spikes, giving him the appearance of an agitated porcupine. Like me, he was still attired in the dark suit he'd worn to Willie's funeral. "Looking for me?" he asked in his gritty voice.

"Yeah. I think we have something in common, you and me."

"And what's that?"

"At the funeral this afternoon, you were talking about how you were going to get even for Willie." That was putting it nicely. "Blood will flow" were the exact words he'd used.

"And you're planning to do the same?"

"Maybe not exactly the same," I admitted. "But I do want to know who killed him." Eerie flutes joined the scratchy violins in disharmony, producing something that sounded like a dirge. I pointed to the door. "This isn't what I was expecting to find here."

Fohl shrugged. "What were you expecting?"

"Some kind of meeting. Last Saturday you told Willie there was a meeting here. This looks like school or something."

"It is a school, in a way." After a moment, Fohl cracked something akin to a smile. "Come on, I'll show you around."

Fohl rapped twice on the door, then opened it and ushered me in. The music halted, and the woman I'd seen earlier looked at us.

"Please go on, Miss Reisdorf. My friend here just wanted to hear the music a little better."

No, really, I didn't.

She smiled at me, then nodded to the boys and girls, and the awful sounds picked up with more exuberance than before.

Fohl and I listened for several excruciating minutes. He said in my ear, "Those kids are breaking the law, you know." His voice was a welcome change from what the children were doing.

"What do you mean?" I asked.

He gestured to the door. I followed him out after we both thanked the teacher.

Once outside, he explained, "They're learning the music of Beethoven, Bach, Mozart. It's illegal to play music by those composers."

"Oh yeah, I read that all their music's been banned."

"Last year," Fohl said with rising outrage, "Dr. Karl Muck was fired from the Boston Symphony Orchestra and put in jail. A harmless old man, a symphony conductor, a scholar—and they put him in jail for playing 'German' music." His face flushed with anger.

"That's lousy," I said, and I meant it. I let Fohl settle down a bit, then added, "By the way, what exactly were they playing in there?" Whatever it was, I wanted to avoid it when it became legal again.

"Damned if I know. One of those classical guys. I can't tell one from another. I like ragtime," Fohl admitted. "But I'm not going to stand by while this government tries to wipe out our culture. That's what we're doing here: keeping our heritage alive."

We stopped outside the open door of the next room. A group of children were reciting German words in high-pitched tones. "The language has been banned in schools," Fohl said. He spoke flatly now, the anger gone from his voice, letting the facts themselves carry the weight of his argument. "We keep it alive here."

I didn't see anything wrong with what I was finding at First Trinity Lutheran.

The next room was quieter; a group of elderly women were doing needlework and chatting amiably in German. "Some of the older folks don't speak any English," Fohl said. "And the *Staats-Zeitung*—that's a German-language paper— has been closed down. What are they supposed to do? Not talk or read until the war is over?"

We passed to the next room, this one filled with old men talking in the same guttural tones. It appeared to be a crafts shop, some of the men doing leatherwork, others woodcarving. One wizened little man spotted us at the door and waved at Fohl. "Ah, Henry," he called. The man pulled himself from his chair and a brown paper parcel from under his seat.

"Henry," he said to Fohl. "I want to show you." He pulled open the wrapping and exposed a pair of new high-button ladies shoes. He held them out for Fohl's inspection.

"That's nice work, Mr. Doscher," Fohl said. The shoes

had shiny black vamps and cream white tops that looked to be almost knee-high.

"Feel. Soft as butter."

Fohl hesitated, then poked at one of the shoes. "Yes, very nice."

The little man grabbed Fohl's arm and squinted up at him through tiny spectacles. "Bless you Henry Fohl. You're a good man."

Fohl pulled away. "It's okay. *Don't* mention it." He dismissed the man with a nod and ushered me back into the hallway. Fohl looked embarrassed.

"Why'd he call you 'Henry'?" I asked.

"That's my real name," he answered with a shrug.

"I thought it was Hans."

"That's what I go by now."

Fohl was obviously uncomfortable. Maybe he realized how foolish it was. And he looked enough off balance that I thought I'd try to throw him further off.

"Why did Willie come here last Saturday?" I asked point blank.

He pulled up short. "What makes you think he was here?"

I stared him in the eyes. "I know he was."

Fohl clenched his teeth so sharply that his jowls rippled. He ran a hand over his black hair, causing more of it to pop to attention. Then he decided to talk. "Yeah, okay, he was here. He wanted to know about the smoke bombs that day. And he warned us that the Knights were going to come after us."

"How would Willie know what the Knights were planning?"

"He wouldn't," Fohl said with a shake of his head. "He

just wanted us to keep low and not do anything. I think he was bluffing about the Knights. Needed something to try to scare us. Like we're going to be scared of the Patriotic Knights of Liberty. Bunch of—"

The big blond fellow lumbered down the hall toward us. Before he arrived, I quickly asked, "Did you plant the smoke bombs?"

Fohl tried to laugh off the question. "Oh yeah, we had those kids smuggle them into Cubs Park in their violin cases."

"Hans, you done with this guy yet?" the blond asked.

"I think so, Gus." Fohl said. "Anything else on your mind?" he asked me.

"No, not for now."

Gus asked me, "Where you from, anyway?"

"Lake View," I said.

"No, no. Originally."

"Oh. New Jersey."

He gave a scowl that would have done Charles Weeghman proud. "Before that."

Now I caught on to what he meant. I chose to pretend that I didn't. "I wasn't anywhere before that. I've always been from New Jersey." I like aggravating people who ask pointless questions.

"Rawlings," he growled. "That don't sound German to me. If you ain't German, you don't belong here."

Actually, I did have a German grandfather, but I chose not to mention it. I didn't need Hans and his friend to approve my background. It shouldn't matter. Once you're here, you're American. It's like a baseball team that way. Probably a simple way of thinking, but that's the way I saw it. Although it might have been easy for me; without a deep sense of national identity of my own, I didn't know how strong the ties of heritage or culture could be.

Fohl put an end to Gus's interrogation, and the two of them escorted me out of the church.

I had the feeling I'd missed something. While I tried to figure out what it was, I strolled through Humbolt Park, enjoying the cool air and the smell of the greenery. Softly glowing gas lamps provided just enough light for me to see my way.

Fohl wasn't straight with me, I thought. Or maybe the classrooms were a little too innocent. Or perhaps because I agreed with what they seemed to be doing at the church there were things I'd chosen not to see. Something was missing.

I emerged from the park on North Avenue and headed east. Near California Street was the Crystal Theatre, where I'd been sitting with Edna Chapman one week ago at this time. One very long week ago.

In front of the theater, I caught a street car for Lake View. It wasn't until the ride home that I realized what I hadn't seen at First Trinity: young men. Other than Fohl and his friend Gus, everyone in the classrooms had been children, young ladies, or old folks.

Where were all the young men I'd seen entering the church? Like the fellow whose boy was going to be the next Ed Walsh. There were rooms Fohl didn't show me and maybe a basement. The men were somewhere in the building, and I'd bet they weren't taking music lessons.

Chapter Seven

Sunday morning, half past nine, halfway into my second cup of coffee, Charles Weeghman phoned. "What the hell are you trying to do to me?" was his greeting.

"Uh, I don't know what you mean."

"You see the morning paper?"

"Which paper?"

"Any of 'em, for chrissake." He projected his scowl through the telephone wire. "Every goddamn one of 'em has it plastered on the front page."

"No, I haven't read the newspaper yet. What's on the front page?"

"That I'm pro-German!" He paused. "And do you know why they're saying that?"

"No." But I had a feeling he was going to tell me.

"Because I let your friend Willie Kaiser be buried in a Cubs uniform!"

Oh, jeez. "Well, actually, Mr. Weeghman, that was my doing. See—"

Weeghman roared, "I know goddamn well it was your

doing! It sure as hell wasn't mine!" He must have been thoroughly peeved to take the time to yell at me over the phone. In a couple of hours I'd be at the ballpark and he could have the pleasure of bawling me out in person. Of course, this could be just a preview of what he'd be giving me at the park.

I tried to explain. "See, Mr. Weeghman, his mother said that's what he would have wanted. Of course, I don't see how she could have known that, but hey she's his mother, so if anybody should know she would, right?" Picking up steam, I said, "Anyway, it made her feel better to do it, and I figured at a time like that it's the least I could do. Did you know she lost two husbands?" Without giving Weeghman a chance to answer, I continued, "She told me you wouldn't give her a Cubs uniform. So what I did was I gave her mine. But I didn't know there might be a good reason why you wouldn't give her one, like that the papers might take it the wrong way or something. See?"

His lengthy silence told me he didn't see. Finally, Weeghman said, "Well, the uniform is just one thing you screwed up on. The other is First Trinity Lutheran. What the hell were you doing there last night?"

I'd forgotten that Weeghman was watching his players. "Uh, well—"

"You already knew I was pissed about Kaiser going there. What makes you think it was all right for you to go?"

"Well, because you told me to."

"I *what?*"

"You told me to see what he was up to."

"That's when he was alive. What do I care about him now?"

I didn't like the way he said that, but I let it pass. Sometimes I don't word things so good either. I groped for another explanation that might satisfy him about my presence at the church and came up empty.

"Look," Weeghman said. "Stay away from that place. Stay away from anything German. I don't need no more front pages like today. Find out who's trying to put me out of business. That's all I want you to do."

"That's what I was doing at the church," I said. It wasn't really, but I didn't want Weeghman closing off any options. I intended to go wherever I pleased.

"What—you think Kaiser was involved in something there?"

"No, but he might have known people who were. Other people who were at the church when he went there last Saturday."

"Huh." It sounded like he was coming around. "So did you find out anything?"

"Not yet, but—"

"No buts. You keep working on it. I worked too hard to get what I got. I ain't gonna have it taken from me."

"Okay, Mr. Weeghman." I figured I owed him something after getting him bad press for the uniform.

He clicked off without saying good-bye. I wondered if before buying a baseball team a prospective owner has to sign an agreement that he'll treat his players like something you'd scrape off your shoe.

Then I decided that I did not need to make up for getting him in trouble over the uniform. All I owed him was to play good baseball. No, I did that out of pride and for the fans. I didn't owe Charles Weeghman anything at all.

• • •

This year began with such promise.

In my second season with the Cubs, I was a starting player for the first time in my career. I earned a starting player's salary: $3,800, enough to carry me through the winter without taking an extra job. And a couple of other firsts, long-standing goals of mine, appeared to be in easy reach.

One was to end a season over the .250 mark in batting. With so many of the National League's best pitchers in France, that looked easy to achieve.

More important was getting to play in a World Series. When Grover Alexander, who'd averaged more than thirty wins a year for the past four years, joined the Cubs' pitching staff, we were heavy favorites to win the pennant.

After the initial scare when Alexander joined the Army, things settled down nicely and still went pretty much according to plan. The Cubs kept rolling to the pennant, and I kept hitting. As of today, the Cubs were five games ahead of the Giants in the standings, fourteen games ahead of the third-place Pirates, and I had a batting average of .274. Even allowing for the fact that it was inflated by the low-caliber pitching, I figured it wasn't inflated by more than twenty points and therefore was a legitimate .250. So I'd convinced myself, anyway.

I was settling into life as a citizen, too. For years, I'd moved from team to team, city to city, boarding house to hotel to apartment, and I'd gotten tired of it. On my arrival in Chicago last year, I'd decided no more boarding houses or cheap apartments for me. I rented this nice cottage and bought furniture that matched—mission-style furniture of white oak, clean and new and fully paid for. I used to assemble it years ago when I worked in a furniture factory; now I could afford my own.

Life was about as stable and normal as it could be for a ballplayer. I even voted in elections—though, breaking with Chicago tradition, never more than once. And I had a regular Saturday night date for the movies.

Everything was cozy and comfortable. Until the fates decided they didn't like for me to be content.

Now my roommate and friend was dead. I no longer wanted to see my Saturday night date. Charles Weeghman was threatening to drop me from the team unless I helped him find out who was trying to put him out of business. Secretary of War Newton Baker was threatening to shut down baseball so that I could have the pleasure of being gassed in trench warfare, protecting censorship and persecution at home.

And I couldn't even take a hot bath. My landlord still hadn't agreed to get me a new hot water tank.

I decided if the big things were all going against me, at least I was going to have one little thing taken care of. Putting in a call to my landlord, I agreed to pay for a new one. "You're right," I told him facetiously. "It was my fault. I must have just misplaced the darn thing."

Then I left for the ballpark to see if Charles Weeghman was going to chew me out some more.

Walking from my front door to the street, I saw my next-door neighbor sitting on her porch, knitting something brown and tangled. "Good morning, Mrs. Tobin!" I called with a wave. "Heard from Harold lately?"

The clicking of her knitting needles stopped momentarily as she held up a piece of paper. "Got a letter Friday!"

I walked up the flagstone path to her front steps. Mrs. Tobin was an attractive, petite woman with long chestnut hair and glittering green eyes; she had no husband and was rumored to be a divorcee. She sat in a bare wood rocking chair that was almost motionless. Piles of light and dark brown yarn rested in her lap contrasting with the blue calico of her dress. Hanging in the window behind her was a red and white service flag with a single blue star representing her one son in the service.

"What does he say?" I asked.

"Oh, he's excited to be in France. Hasn't been to Paris though. And he hasn't seen any battle yet. That's fine by me. He's my only child. Harold's raring to fight though. What is it about men and war, anyway? For some reason, they just love to fight."

Was she implying that I lacked something because I wasn't eager to go to war? "I don't know, Mrs. Tobin. That a sweater?"

She held up the knitting. About half a sleeve was completed. "I want to send this off to him by fall. Winter can get cold in those trenches, I expect."

"Expect so," I agreed. "Tell him hi from me next time you write him." I turned to go, then turned back. "Say, Mrs. Tobin, about a week ago did you by any chance see somebody move a water tank out of my place?"

The needles stopped. "A tank of water?"

"No, a water tank. You know for hot water. It was in my cellar and somebody took it."

She shook her head emphatically and the clicking resumed.

"Well, I better get to the park. That's going to be a real nice sweater."

She smiled. "If you decide to go over there I'll make you one, too."

Was that a suggestion that I should enlist? "Thanks," I said, and I walked back to the street.

Mrs. Tobin called after me, "Have fun at your game!"

She sounded like she meant it. But within two steps, my ears translated her words to, "Go play your game. Harold's going into no-man's-land to be cut down by machine guns."

This damned war was making me crazy.

• • •

It was a relief to be in Cubs Park again.

Strange. Despite Willie being killed the last time I was on the field, I still looked forward to being in this ballpark. It was still a sanctuary for me.

With a doubleheader to play against Christy Mathewson's Reds to make up some of the lost games, I'd have eighteen innings to concentrate on nothing but hitting Fred Toney's fastball and Hod Eller's shineball. And on turning double plays with our new starting shortstop, Wicket Greene.

Greene got what he wanted: Willie's job. He at least had the good sense not to gloat about it. In fact, he wasn't saying much of anything. Winning a starting job by replacing a dead man is nothing to brag about. Nor is taking the place of one who's off at war, I suppose.

I slammed my bat on the locker room floor at the thought and garnered surprised looks from my teammates dressing nearby. Okay, so I hadn't really earned my job either. But I was going to keep it, dammit. I liked playing baseball, playing every inning of every game if I could. That's what it came down to: I wanted to keep playing baseball. After the number of innings I'd spent on the bench in my career, I deserved it. But I hadn't earned it, any more than Wicket Greene had.

After picking up the bat, I resumed honing it with a dry ham bone. I sat in front of my locker, wearing only my summer underwear, while I waited for our clubhouse man to bring me a new uniform to replace the flannels that Willie would be wearing forever. I looked into the locker next to mine. Willie's street clothes still hung there from his last day in the park, his last day alive.

I was itching to get out on the field and into the throes of a game because so far it didn't feel like I was escaping from thoughts of Willie or the war.

At least we wouldn't be repeating Willie's final march today. With the four-day layoff, both teams needed extra practice. However much the owners wanted to convince the War Department that we were ready for war, shagging flies and taking batting practice took priority over close-order drills.

Our manager, Fred Mitchell, walked up to me with a cherubic boy in tow. Mitchell was a modest, square-jawed former pitcher and catcher who'd played for seven teams in seven years. As a pitcher, he'd relieved Cy Young in the first game in Boston Red Sox history and got credit for the win. Now in only his second season at the helm of the Cubs, he had us heading for the World Series. "Mickey," he said, laying a hand on the boy's shoulder. "I want you to meet our newest Cub. This is . . ."

Cub? Jeez, they're getting younger all the time. The war could go on for another five years and he still wouldn't be draft age. Maybe that was the owners' latest plan: fill the rosters with children.

". . . played shortstop with the Oak Park Stars. He's a little green yet though. Figured you could show him a few things."

Like what? How to dress himself? The kid couldn't have

been wearing long trousers for long. He was going almost directly from wearing short pants on the schoolyard to knickers on the baseball field.

"You two will room together on the road."

I wasn't a babysitter. "Your mother know your here?" I said.

The kid—I'd already forgotten his name and didn't care enough to ask—bobbed his head up and down. "Yup. Sure does. My father, too. Heck, my whole neighborhood knows I'm gonna be playing for the Cubs. I told everybody I know, and my mother told the rest of them."

This busher doesn't even know sarcasm when he hears it. The bench jockeys are going to have a field day with him. I chuckled, imagining the first time he'd have to endure the verbal stings of John McGraw.

I gave the kid a closer look. He had fine blond hair and an eager pink face that had never experienced or needed the scrape of a razor. Sixteen years old, probably. Seventeen at the most.

Mitchell sent the kid to find the clubhouse man for a uniform and sat down next to me. "Don't take it out on him, Mick," he said softly.

"I'm not. It's just . . ."

"Yeah, I know." Mitchell slapped my thigh. "Look, I got some more bad news for you: you're playing in your road uniform today. Weeghman's orders. He didn't tell me why, but I read the papers so I think I know." He rose. "Oh, and clean out Kaiser's locker."

"Don't give it to the kid," I blurted.

"Can't make a shrine of it."

"Hell, Fred. We hardly got a full team. There's plenty of empty lockers. Don't give him Willie's."

Mitchell scratched the back of his neck. "Yeah, okay. But clear it out anyway. His family should get his things."

"Thanks. I'll bring them his stuff."

Left alone, I proceeded to clear out Willie's locker. His uniform, spikes, and cap were already gone, taken away with his body. I took his straw boater and turned it upside down to throw in the few other things from the shelf—a celluloid collar, cuff links, clean socks, and garters. Then his old seersucker suit hanging on a hook. I folded the trousers neatly and put them on a stool. I was folding his jacket when a comb fell out of a pocket. I threw the comb in the hat, then quickly checked the other pockets for anything else that might fall out. I added a handkerchief, a small clasp knife, a few coins, and, from an inside breast pocket, a folded green paper. I had one like it at home—a draft registration card. Why did he carry it around with him? I wondered.

The new kid returned with a Cubs cap perched on his head. He hugged a white home uniform to his chest with his right hand and held a brown road uniform in his left. "The guy with the uniforms told me to bring you this," he said. I took the road flannels from him. They were solid brown with black pinstripes. The ugliest design since the plaid violet uniforms I'd worn with the Giants in 'sixteen. Those uniforms had done a lot to soften the blow of leaving New York.

I laid the brown flannels on my stool.

The kid proffered his right hand. "I'm real happy to be playing with you, Mr. Rawlings," he said.

Mister Rawlings? What am I, an old-timer? I shook his hand firmly. "It's Mickey, kid." I got a lot of years to go before being "mister."

"Okay, Mickey. My friends call me Wally."

"Uh-huh. And what do your enemies call you?"

"They call me kid."

The muscles of my mouth relaxed into a smile. It was the first one since Willie had made that right turn last week.

He was going to be a scrapper, this kid. I suddenly found myself looking forward to seeing what he could do on the diamond.

I pointed to Willie's locker. "I got your locker all cleared out. Stow your gear and suit up."

The green paper was still in my hand. I unfolded it and gave the paper a glance. It wasn't a registration card.

Willie Kaiser had been an employee of the Dearborn Fuel Company, the one that Bennett Harrington owned. According to the ID card, Willie worked in the chemical plant.

Chapter Eight

I brought a dozen pink carnations for Edna, a box of chocolates for her mother, and four large soup bones for the dogs. In a leather satchel I carried Willie's clothes, cleaned and pressed, fresh from a Lincoln Avenue laundry.

When Edna let me in, I noticed immediately that the atmosphere was no more inviting than it had been last time. The air was dense, and the rooms seemed to have contracted in size. The Chapman home had all the ambiance of a crypt.

I quietly placed the satchel under a small hallway table and handed her the gifts. She accepted them with a smile that was less than ecstatic. Leaving the chocolates in the parlor to avoid disturbing her mother sleeping upstairs, she took the flowers and bones into the kitchen as I followed. She left the soup bones in their brown butcher paper wrapping on the kitchen table. "For after their walk," she said, then filled a porcelain vase with water for the flowers.

I'd given particular attention to the choice of blossom. I'd asked the florist for something that wouldn't have the romantic implications of roses nor the funereal connotations of lilies; she'd suggested carnations as sufficiently neutral.

I picked the time of my visit—mid-morning on Monday—carefully, too, so that I would have an excuse to leave early: the last games, another twin bill, of the series with Cincinnati. Despite Hippo Vaughn being out with a bad shoulder, we'd won both games the day before. To my surprise, and I'm sure Weeghman's delight, the games were near sellouts. Willie's death didn't keep the fans away. I hated to think it, but his murder might have added to the attraction—maybe people came to the park for the same reason they stop to look at a traffic accident.

Edna carefully arranged the flowers in the vase so that they looked full and symmetric. "They're lovely," she said. "Thank you."

"You're welcome." Even about bringing flowers, I felt guilty. I hadn't had dinner with the Chapman family since Willie died. Edna and I had been to no more movies, and I hadn't come by to walk Rube. I'd been neglecting them, so I'd brought presents. Not for them, really, but to make myself feel better.

After getting the dogs from their room, Edna and I took them out for their exercise.

We spoke little on Paulina Street, less on Lawrence, and we walked Hermitage and Sunnyside in total silence. When we returned to the house, I suggested we stay outside—for the fresh air, I thought to myself.

Edna and I sat on the steps to the front porch. The dachshunds frolicked around us unaware of the treat that was awaiting them inside. Otherwise, they would have dragged us through the front door.

I held a bent forefinger to Rube. He gnawed on the knuckle with gentle bites, his tail flicking the air.

"I went to that church," I said. I waited for Edna to prod

me with a question but wasn't rewarded with any word or gesture. "Willie did go there that night," I went on. "Don't think there was much to it though."

Edna nodded and remained silent. She was controlled and tight, even in appearance. Her hair was raked back from her face, kept in place by amber combs. It made her skin seem taut and her cheekbones higher.

I straightened my finger and Rube's teeth grabbed hold of the tip. We started to play tug-of-war, with my finger as the rope. He emitted a determined, high-pitched sound that was closer to a whine than a growl.

I went on to what I really wanted to ask her. "I brought Willie's things from his locker. They're in the bag." Fishing in my jacket pocket with my free hand, I drew out the green paper I'd found. "This was with his stuff, too. I kept it out so your mother wouldn't see." Unfolding the paper with one hand, I held it out so that Edna could read it. She scanned it without comment.

"Did you know he was working there?"

Edna nodded.

"Did your mother know?"

She shook her head.

"Speak," I said with diminishing patience. I hadn't meant to sound harsh. In a kinder tone, I tried to persuade her, "Please. I'm trying to find out what happened to Willie. If you know anything that can help, please tell me."

Edna hesitated. A sheen of water coated her narrowed eyes, and I could see her fighting back tears. She won. "Willie told me," she said calmly. "He wanted to do something for the war effort. So he worked in the plant at night."

He'd told her but not me, his teammate. "He told you?"

I repeated, not quite believing he'd confide something in her that he wouldn't tell me.

"It was a secret," she explained. "You have to share a secret with somebody, can't keep it to yourself."

"Your mother still doesn't know?"

She shook her head, then promptly added, "No. A secret's a secret."

"Do you know any other secrets about Willie?"

"If I told you, they wouldn't be secret anymore."

I was exasperated to the point where I knew I'd better drop it for now.

Edna stood up. "I better go inside in case Mama calls. She hasn't been well lately."

"Anything serious?"

She gave me a look that could have come from Charles Weeghman. Stupid question, it said. "Yes," said Edna. "Somebody killed her boy."

I followed her into the house. While Edna took my satchel to Willie's room, I took the dogs to theirs.

I gave the dogs their bones but found little satisfaction in their gratitude. They were too easy. They didn't need support. They'd have licked the hand of anyone who gave them a pat or a bit of food. That's one of the joys of dogs, I suppose: they're reliable in their affection. But not particularly challenging.

I went to Willie's room. Edna was laying Willie's clothes out on his bed, smoothing the folds with her hand. "Mama wants you to have his books," she said. "You can take them now if you want."

"Oh. Well, thank you." I didn't like the idea of getting something because somebody had died. It was too much like Wicket Greene getting his job. "Are you sure you don't want to keep them?"

A negative shake of her head.

"I have to go to the park from here. But I could take some of them with me."

"Okay," she said, still concentrating on the clothes.

I grabbed four volumes of the Mark Twain books to put in my satchel. Then I put three of them back. "How about if I take one each time I'm here?"

"If you like."

"I was thinking. . . . How about we go to the movies Saturday? I think *Tarzan* is still playing."

Edna bit her lip and nodded.

• • •

It was a windy day in Cubs Park last year, I remembered, the end of August, when Fred Mitchell had brought a skinny kid to me after a game with the Dodgers. "This boy thinks he's a shortstop," the manager said. "Find out if he is. Name's Willie Kaiser. Oh, and we're taking him on the road with us next week. You're gonna be his roomie. Take care of 'im."

The Willie Kaiser of 1918 was a different fellow from the eager rookie I'd first met in the summer of '17. He'd become a better player with time, but less fun, more secretive, more burdened.

When Willie had first joined the Cubs, he'd been eager to see the world, his definition of the world being any city east of Pittsburgh. On our first train ride to New York, Willie had climbed into the upper berth of the Pullman sleeper, leaving me the coveted lower berth. Willie's arrival in the big leagues coincided with my becoming established as a veteran.

In the city, I kept him under my wing, away from saloons and brothels. Nothing stronger than beer to drink, and no female temptations other than the burlesque houses of Union Square and the dance halls of Coney Island. The kid threw himself into these pleasures with the same passion he had for baseball. He grew so fond of the girlie shows that I often let him go alone while I went to the movies, my own preferred form of entertainment.

The signs of change started to appear in him last fall, as war fever gripped the country; but they were slight, manifested mostly in brief periods of brooding. Then, when the season was over, Willie went back to his job in the Union Stockyards and I went to play winter ball in California.

By the time Willie and the rest of the Cubs came to Los Angeles for spring training in February, the change in him was visible and complete. I couldn't drag him to a burlesque show, and I could hardly drag a word out of him.

The problem I faced now was that there were two Willie Kaisers: the enthusiastic kid of 1917 and the new somber model of 1918. Actually, there were more than two. There were two this year alone: the one who played baseball and the one who worked nights in a munitions plant. I barely knew the one who played ball this year and didn't know the secret life of Willie Kaiser at all.

He'd been keeping secrets from me, and I was only starting to discover what some of them were. Mostly what I was discovering were questions: Why did he go to Fohl's church? What, if anything, did he know about what the Patriotic Knights of Liberty were planning? What was going on at Harrington's plant? And why would a war make him lose interest in burlesque shows?

I decided the only way I could figure out what was going

on with him was for me to *be* Willie Kaiser for a while. The secret Willie.

• • •

Wednesday morning, the earliest that I could get an appointment, I was in Bennett Harrington's third-floor corner office on State Street. The furnishings of the airy, sun-washed room were modest and spare, with white wicker chairs and several healthy green potted plants situated about the parquet floor. The office had the feel of a verandah; all that was missing was a porch swing.

Harrington sat in a high-backed chair behind a gleaming, uncluttered white desk. A black candlestick telephone, a brass tray with two glasses, and a pitcher of water were the desk's only accessories. Through the windows behind him, I could see the Masonic Temple across the street and Marshall Field's on the corner of Randolph, confirming that I was still in Chicago, not Mississippi. The cross-breeze that blew through the open windows provided further evidence—a plantation would smell more like magnolias and less like the Chicago River.

"Thanks for seeing me, Mr. Harrington," I began. I was seated in one of two small chairs placed a good ten feet from his desk. It made him seem more imposing to have to view him from a distance. And with the empty chair next to me, it felt like he had me outnumbered.

Harrington nodded as though fully aware of his generosity in granting me some of his valuable time. Dressed in his white linen suit, he looked like he belonged on a verandah, too, sipping a mint julep. All he needed was a white goatee and a matching mane of hair to make the image complete.

With his Panama hat off, I could see his hair was dark and trim, though graying at the temples, and he was clean shaven. He had a gentle face and a sleepy left eye that appeared to be perpetually in mid-wink. I narrowed my estimate of his age to late forties, early fifties.

"The reason I came," I went on, "was to ask about Willie Kaiser. I just found out that he worked for you."

"Did he?" The question was noncommittal.

I plucked Willie's identification paper from my jacket pocket, stepped up to the desk, and handed Harrington the evidence of Willie's employment with the Dearborn Fuel Company.

He gave the paper a cursory glance. "So he did." His thin lips showed a hint of a smile.

I sat back down. "Why was it a secret?"

Harrington paused to take a sip from his water glass. "Well, I suppose there's no reason not to tell you," he drawled softly. "Young Kaiser preferred it that way." The winking left eye made it seem he was sharing a confidence. He leaned back in his chair. "See, I've given jobs to quite a few ballplayers. That way they can contribute to the war effort and still play baseball. I let them work whatever hours will fit in with the baseball schedule." He smiled fully. "Truth is, I love baseball—"

Please, I hoped, don't say "this great game of ours."

"—and I don't want to see the War Department shut it down. If we can show that baseball players can do both, play ball and help win the war, maybe we can keep everybody happy."

Meanwhile, I thought ungraciously, you make money from both. "If that's the purpose," I said, "don't people have to know about it? Nobody knew about Willie working in the plant."

Harrington nodded. "That was his choice entirely. I respect him for that. Respect-*ed,* I suppose. Most of the players are eager to publicize the fact that they're working in the plants. Not young Kaiser. He didn't want any credit for it. Just wanted to do his bit to help."

And keep his mother from finding out.

Harrington added, "Some of the players are taking a beating in the press for not fighting or doing war work."

"Joe Jackson's taking a beating and he *is* working. Comiskey says he won't let him back on the Sox if he doesn't enlist."

Harrington chuckled. "That's just The Old Roman's way of negotiating. He'll take Jackson back but at half the money he was paying him before. You'll see." Harrington suddenly caught himself. The art of negotiating isn't something for an owner to reveal to a ballplayer. He changed the subject completely. "The Giants are coming in tomorrow, aren't they?"

I nodded.

"John McGraw . . ." A relaxed smile developed on Harrington's face. "You played for him before you came to the Cubs didn't you?"

"Yup. Three years."

"That must have been great."

"Sure was," I agreed, though it often hadn't seemed so great at the time. McGraw was not an easy manager to play for. I'd heard, and didn't doubt, that he breakfasted on warm blood and gunpowder, then cleaned his teeth with barbed wire.

"I used to love the old Baltimore Orioles," Harrington

said wistfully. "McGraw at third base, Hughie Jennings at short, Wilbert Robinson behind the plate . . ."

"Joe Kelley and Wee Willie Keeler in the outfield," I joined in.

Harrington lit up. "Did you see them play?"

"Not at their best." I wished I had. Ned Hanlon's Baltimore Orioles of the mid-1890s may have been the best baseball team ever.

"John McGraw, he was the best of the bunch," Harrington said with admiration. "Smartest ballplayer there ever was."

Smart was one word for John McGraw. Opponents and newspapers had other words for him—"hooligan" and "ruffian" were among the few the papers could print.

"The tricks he came up with," Harrington went on. "He had one where he used to hold back a runner trying to tag from third on a fly ball. While the umpire's looking at the outfielder to see if the ball is caught, McGraw would hook his finger under the runner's belt. By the time the ump turns around and McGraw lets go of the belt, he's cost the runner a couple of steps."

Harrington was off in a baseball reverie now. "I was at the game the time he got caught pulling that trick. Big Ed Delahanty, playing for the Phillies, hit a triple with nobody out. Next batter—might have been Sam Thompson—hits a towering fly ball to left. Delahanty's ready to tag up from third when John McGraw moves up behind him and loops his finger through the back of Delahanty's belt. So what does Big Ed do? He unfastens the buckle. The ball drops into Joe Kelley's glove, Delahanty takes off for home, and John McGraw's left holding a dangling strip of leather—looked like a dead snake! Delahanty runs all the way home holding his pants up with one hand and scores!"

We both laughed. I'd heard the tale before, but never from someone who'd been there.

"McGraw told me another one where they got caught," I offered.

Harrington nodded for me to go on.

"The Orioles used to have their groundskeeper keep the outfield grass real high so they could hide extra balls in it. The other team hits a ball that looks like it's going through for extra bases, and hey, the Oriole outfielder just picks up one of the planted balls and throws it in."

Harrington roared, "That's a good one!"

"Here's the best part—I think it happened against Louis- ville. Joe Kelley usually played left field for the Orioles, but this game he was playing center and Willie Keeler was in right. A Louisville batter hits a low line drive that goes right between Kelley and Keeler. Both of them ran in the general direction of the ball, both of 'em pretended to field it, and they each picked up a different ball stashed in the grass. So what happens? Two balls are thrown in to second base when only one was batted out. Umpire forfeited the game to Louis- ville."

"That's what you call getting caught red-handed!"

"Sure is. And you know why McGraw told me the story?"

"Why?"

"Not because he thought it was funny. He still didn't forgive Keeler and Kelley for costing them the game!"

Harrington shook his head. "That's McGraw all right. I remember the tall grass in the outfield. Right field was really tough. Know how Fenway has that hill in left?"

"Yeah, I played there."

"Orioles Park went *downhill* as you went back. And it was just about always wet. There was a crick—Brady's Run it was called—that ran behind the fence. Water would overflow into right field. Keeler played it well, but I saw more than one visiting player take a header in that swamp."

"Are you from Baltimore?"

"Born and bred."

Funny, from his clothes he looked like he was from Georgia or Mississippi or somewhere. I never really thought of Baltimore as southern.

We swapped a few more stories about the old Orioles. The cracker barrel baseball talk was nice, but I still wanted to know what Willie was doing at his plant. The next time he paused for a sip of water, I said, "Say, Mr. Harrington, do you think you can give me a job, too?"

His face turned businessman. "What can you do?"

A little bit of everything, after working for industrial leagues. But the only thing I was good at was baseball.

"Chemistry?" he asked.

I shook my head no.

Of course, Willie couldn't have known much either, I thought.

"Plumbing?" he tried.

"I can do anything Willie could," I said. "You must have an opening for his job. Can I have that?"

Harrington smiled. "I have more than a thousand employees. I don't know if Kaiser's job has been filled yet. But if you want it, you've got it. I'll check with the foreman."

"Thanks Mr. Harrington. Oh, and I don't want it publicized either."

"Very well. Of course, it wouldn't help as much with you as it would have with Kaiser anyway."

"What do you mean?"

"Kaiser. A 'Kaiser' working for the American war effort? It would have been great publicity. Not just for baseball. It would have shown that Americans of all backgrounds are united. We're fighting the Germans 'over there,' not here. Anyway, how about starting Monday?"

"That would be great. We're going on the road end of next week though."

"No problem. Like I said, baseball comes first."

I stood to go and offered my hand. "Thanks Mr. Harrington."

Harrington took it without rising. "It's a shame about Kaiser getting killed like that. That's really going to hurt gate receipts."

Hurt gate receipts. Just when I was starting to like the guy, he shows he really is an owner at heart.

Chapter Nine

Saturday afternoon, hours before the final game of a three-game series with the Giants and long before my teammates would be joining me, I strolled about the infield of Cubs Park. Always the first player on the field, I was earlier than usual today. My punishment was over. I was wearing white home flannels again and was eager to show them to the fans already sprinkled throughout the stands.

Contrary to Bennett Harrington's prediction that attendance would be down, we'd had packed crowds for both of the previous meetings in the series. For a game against the Giants, the fans will always come out—no matter that a player was shot and killed in the park not ten days before. Part of the attraction was John McGraw; fans throughout the country delighted in taunting him, giving him the same verbal abuse that he dispensed so profusely.

The other draw was simply that the opposition was a team from New York. There were plenty of rivalries in baseball—Giants and Dodgers, Red Sox and Yankees, Cubs and Cardinals—but those were for local bragging rights, like being the toughest kid on the block. A series between Chicago and New York was a battle between different parts of the country, different cultures almost. The frontier spirit of the Midwest versus the big-city pugnacity of the Northeast.

The papers had lately been playing up the rivalry, reminding fans that this was the tenth anniversary of the contentious 1908 pennant race that had ended with the Cubs beating the Giants in a play-off game to take the championship.

What the papers didn't say was anything more about Willie Kaiser's death. They'd reported nothing at all after that initial nonsense about the gunshot being an accident.

As I gave the second base bag a kick, I looked beyond the right field bleachers to the row houses on Sheffield Avenue, then at the spot on the outfield grass where Willie had last stood. It occurred to me that since the bullet had passed through his body, it might still be on the field someplace.

I picked one of the second-floor windows near the middle of the row and mentally drew a line from the window to where Willie's chest would have been. Extending the line to the ground, I assumed that to be the most likely spot for the bullet to have landed.

Between the pitcher's mound and first base, I began sweeping my right foot over the grass. I combed several square yards with my cleats, unearthing nothing but somebody's front tooth, probably from a pitcher who'd caught a line drive with his mouth.

Stopping to take another look at the houses, I realized the shot could have come from any of them. That meant the angle could have been wider. And what if the bullet had ricocheted off a bone in Willie's body and changed direction on exiting? I had enough trouble with arithmetic, never mind geometry.

I revised my estimate of where the slug had landed to somewhere in the infield and methodically resumed sweeping my spikes along the grass.

"Whatcha doin'?" a high voice behind me asked.

I turned around, surprised. It was still too early for other players to be out. But here he was: the baby-faced new kid, Wally Dillard, a ballplayer badly in need of a nickname. "Checkin' out the field," I answered.

"For what?" He apparently didn't know that rookies aren't supposed to pester veterans. Lucky for him, I wasn't a stickler about that particular custom. I liked to share what I knew with other players. Maybe it was team spirit, maybe it was that I enjoyed a chance to demonstrate that I did indeed know something.

Of course I didn't give him the exact truth. "You have to check out the field to see how to play a ground ball," I said. "Got to see if it's hard or soft or rocky, how thick the grass is, all that. You know how an outfielder plays a fly ball, judging the wind and how heavy or dry the air is?"

"Yeah."

"Well, he's got it easy compared to us. He can feel the air and the wind without trying. Playing infield, you gotta take the time to check out the ground and map it out in your head beforehand. Once the ball's hit, it's too late."

"Huh. Makes sense."

"Why don't you go check out the field around short? Maybe Mitchell will put you in the game."

"You think so?" he said eagerly.

Not a chance, I thought. "Never know. You always got to be ready."

"Okay, thanks!" He trotted off to follow my example on the left side of the infield. I wished I could have asked him to let me know if he found any bullets.

I went back to searching for the slug on my side of the field. While I scratched the turf, I tried to think of a nickname for Wally Dillard.

Neither effort produced results.

•   •   •

It was a good game. A crowd of at least fifteen thousand saw us beat the Giants 5–1 to sweep the series. I went three-for-four with a stolen base and two RBIs. Shufflin' Phil Douglas easily slipped his spirituous spitballs past the New York bats to ring up a dozen strikeouts. Wicket Greene booted two easy grounders at shortstop and made one throwing error. Wally Dillard maintained a steady stream of encouraging chatter from the dugout bench.

After showering and changing, I left the clubhouse with Fred Merkle. "I was talking to Larry Doyle before the game," Merkle said. "How about the three of us get together for dinner tonight?"

"Sure, sounds good." Doyle, Merkle, and I had been teammates on McGraw's 1914 Giants. Last year, the three of us had all been playing for the Cubs. Now Doyle was back with the Giants.

A few fans stood at the exit gate waiting for autographs. We stopped while Merkle obliged them and I held his bag. I was thinking that baseball's a strange business: your team-mate one year can be your enemy the next. Then I tried to imagine what would happen if countries could do that—

maybe France trades a lieutenant to Germany for a sergeant and two privates to be named later . . .

When Merkle finished giving out his signature, he said, "Gimme a call. I'll set it up with Larry."

We split up and I started walking west on Addison. I'd turned south on Racine, heading for home, when a sniffily voice behind me said, "Good to see they're letting you wear the home uniform again."

Slowly, I turned around. "I know they're desperate to sell tickets, but I can't believe they let *you* in."

Karl Landfors grinned. "They made me pay extra for the privilege."

I dropped my bag on the ground. We shook hands hard and long. The best I was hoping for was that his name would appear in the newspaper again; I never expected him to show up at a Cubs game. "Jeez, Karl. Where the hell you been?" Before he could answer, I gave him a playful punch to the shoulder and said, "You're looking good." Another thing I never expected of Karl Landfors. He used to resemble a skeleton, in both color and physique. Now his angular face was tanned, he'd put on a few pounds of muscle, and he'd abandoned his customary black undertaker's suit and stiff black derby for a casual khaki sack suit and an oversized brown driving cap.

"Hey, I got a place not far from here," I said. "Come on over."

"Sure."

During the walk to my house, Landfors gave me a cursory rundown on his three and a half years in Europe. He'd covered the war for the *New York Press* during most of it, then quit the paper to drive an ambulance. And he'd gotten married to a Belgian girl, who'd died of the influenza this spring.

When he related that last part, I glanced at him from the side of my eye. He didn't look quite as good as he had on first appearance. Behind the horn-rimmed glasses on his long bony nose, I could see his eyes looked weary, as if they'd seen everything and would prefer to forget most of it.

In answer to his question about what I'd been up to, my report was less remarkable. Not getting into the World Series was what I'd been doing. I'd spent three years with McGraw's Giants and we'd lost the pennant every year, to the unlikeliest teams: Boston Braves, Phillies, and the Brooklyn Dodgers. The *Dodgers*—that one really hurt. I left New York for the Cubs in 1917, and the Giants won the pennant that year.

By the time we walked through my front door, I was thinking that Landfors had certainly had the more interesting time of it. And that I was probably never going to get to play in a World Series.

Once inside, Landfors removed his cap to reveal a head that had gone almost completely bald. "Not bad at all," he said approvingly, as he ran a finger over the same oak sideboard where Charles Weeghman had sat.

I headed off the joke I was sure would follow. "I know, almost as nice as some of the trenches you been in."

He smiled. "No. This is a really nice place."

Maybe Landfors had changed.

"You know," he said. "Baseball's really big with the doughboys. I impressed quite a few of them by telling them I knew a big league ballplayer."

"Me?" I was flattered.

"Well, no. I told them I knew Ty Cobb and Casey Stengel. I figured you knew them and I knew you, so that was close enough."

"You haven't changed a bit," I said.

Landfors walked around, inspecting the place. I thought he might be needing a place to stay. "Say, Karl. I got plenty of room here. You can stay if you want. Uh, no hot water though. Somebody stole the tank."

"Huh?"

"Somebody stole my water tank. But other than that, it's okay. Good location, nice neighbors. And quiet. There's a cop who keeps the kids away."

"Thanks," he said. "But I'm staying with a fellow I met in the ambulance corps. Another writer. Got a place down in Roseland."

"How long you been in town?"

"Not long. A couple weeks." Spotting the issues of the *New York Press* stacked next to my chair, he picked one of them up. "What are you doing getting the *Press?*"

"Is that what that is? Hell, to me a paper's a paper. As long as they print the box scores right, I don't care where they're from."

Landfors chuckled. I don't think he was entirely sure I was pulling his leg.

I pointed him to the sofa. He sat down on the edge of the couch while I took the armchair.

Landfors leaned over and picked up a ten-day-old Chicago paper from the coffee table. It was opened to the story about Willie's death. Frowning, he proceeded to spread out the other papers on the table; they were from the same date, also opened to that story. "I heard about this," he said. "You knew the guy?"

"Of course I knew him. He was my teammate. Roommate when we traveled."

"Huh."

I gave him a few more minutes to read before saying, "You been reporting on battles a little too long, Karl."

"What do you mean?"

"A major league ballplayer getting shot and killed in Cubs Park on the Fourth of July should be a pretty big story. Look at what page it's on."

He quickly shuffled through the papers. "They buried it," he said.

"Exactly. Why do you think they would do that?"

"Don't know."

"I thought it might be the censors."

"Could be." Landfors pondered a minute. "Willie Kaiser. . . . There could be a lot of angles to something like that. A German baseball player—"

"American," I corrected.

Landfors nodded and continued, "A baseball player of German heritage, named Kaiser, playing America's national game, marching in a military drill, killed on the Fourth of July." He thought some more. "The government censors wouldn't know how to present something like that to the public—hell, either side could have wanted to kill him. So they bury the story. The Committee for Public Information likes to manufacture propaganda, but sometimes they don't know how to handle reality."

Either side could have wanted to kill him? That was crazy. Nobody should have wanted to kill him.

"Hey, look," I said. "It's been years. Let's not talk about this stuff. How about dinner? There's a place in the Loop I been wanting to try."

"Great. I'm famished."

We walked out the door, then I ran back in as I remembered to call Fred Merkle and tell him I couldn't make the reunion with Larry Doyle.

• • •

"Whaddaya gonna have?" demanded the sullen-faced waiter.

"A couple of your best steaks," Landfors promptly answered.

The waiter frowned at him.

"No beef on Saturdays," I explained to Landfors. To the waiter, I said, "Anything but whale meat."

He nodded. "An' to drink?"

"Ginger ale," I ordered.

"Oh, wine, I think," said Landfors. "Red. Burgundy, if you have it."

He earned an angry glare from the waiter.

"Prohibition, Karl," I said. "Hell, I'd have ordered a beer if I could." I turned to the waiter. "He's been in the war the last few years. Just got back."

The waiter nodded approvingly. "Army?" he grunted.

"Ambulance corps," Landfors said. "Make mine ginger ale, too."

"Comin' right up."

As the waiter lumbered away, Landfors looked around the place. "Nice," he said. He seemed to think everything was "nice" today—maybe I should introduce him to Edna Chapman.

T.J.'s, wedged between a pawn shop and a music store on South State, wasn't an elegant establishment, but poor lighting helped conceal its true dinginess. The joint was cramped, with the dining tables packed closely together to leave space in front of the bandstand for dancers. There were no tablecloths on the tables, and the straight-backed chairs were uncomfortable enough to encourage you to eat quickly and either leave or dance. People didn't come for the decor but for the food and the music. In fact, that's all the signs outside the restaurant mentioned: *FOOD* and *JAZZ*. The place had no official name; it was known only through word-of-mouth as "T.J.'s."

"Hey," I suddenly blurted. "You said it was 'good to see they're letting me wear the home uniform again.' So you must have seen me when I played in my road suit. Why didn't you tell me before today you were in town?"

He stammered, "Well, it's been a long time. I didn't know what you'd be up to. It just . . . took a while for me to feel up to it, I guess."

I tried to rest my elbows on the table, but it was too small and too round. "Why Chicago?" I asked. "Why didn't you go back to New York?"

"I did. Just long enough to clear out my things from the *Press* office. They weren't happy to see me again." He laughed. "I left them without a war correspondent."

"Why'd you leave them?"

"How many ways can you describe kids dying?" He shook his head and his whole body shuddered. "And they didn't even print all of it. When the rains came, the trenches turned to quicksand. You be surprised how many soldiers drowned in the mud, but you won't read about that here, doesn't sound like a glorious enough death. You won't read about the rats that live in the trenches, either, and how they grow fat eating the corpses of the doughboys."

He was right. I hadn't read any of that. "Sounds like hell," I said.

"Exactly what it was. So I decided to do something to help those kids instead of writing for the newspaper and joined the ambulance corps. A lot of writers did. Met one named John Dos Passos who's from here. He told me Chicago's a good city for socialists. If anything will make you a socialist, it's war." Landfors had already been a member of that party long before the war. "Industrialists make money by selling the weapons. Politicians and generals get the headlines and the glory. And the kids, they go into the trenches and come out on stretchers—if they come out at all." It sounded like he was already composing a pamphlet. "So I decided to come back and work for the socialist cause."

"Things have really changed here while you been gone, Karl. It's crazy. This might not be the best time to be a socialist. Not openly. You can go to jail for it. Eugene Debs did, under the Espionage Act, just for giving a speech." Debs was the Socialists' perennial candidate for president and something of a hero to Landfors.

"Then this is the time I should be speaking up. You can't let other people decide when you can or can't exercise your rights."

The waiter arrived. "Your coffee," he announced, putting a large white mug in front of each of us.

I started to protest, "But we ordered—" Then I looked into my mug. Coffee doesn't have a head on it. Neither does ginger ale.

When I looked back up, the waiter was gone.

"Cheers," said Karl. He took a sip from his mug. It left a purple smudge on his lip.

Oh well, no sense letting it go flat. I took a sip of the beer, my first in many months. It was as good—better—than I remembered.

I tried again to warn Landfors about what was happening in the country. I repeated some of the things Hans Fohl had told me about books and music being banned and a symphony conductor being imprisoned.

"Land of the free," Landfors said derisively.

"Even pretzels can get you in trouble."

"You got to be kidding."

"No. Somebody put pretzels in the concession stands at Cubs Park. The papers crucified Charles Weeghman for it."

The waiter whisked up to us again, almost throwing our dinners in front of us. "Today's specialty: whale steak." He winked and hurried away. The T-bones were still sizzling and had sliced potatoes heaped around them.

We started cutting into our steaks. "Actually," I said. "Weeghman is convinced that somebody's trying to put him out of business."

"Really?" Landfors sounded no more than mildly interested.

"Yeah. And he wants me to investigate."

"You going to?"

"Just enough to keep him off my back. He thinks one of the other Cub owners, William Wrigley, is trying to take over the club."

"And you don't." Landfors had caught the skepticism in my tone.

"No."

"You talk to Wrigley?"

I swallowed a piece of steak. "Uh-uh. No need to. There might be somebody trying to hurt the club but not one of the other owners. If fans don't come to the park, they all lose money. No, if one of them wanted to hurt Weeghman, they'd go after his restaurants."

"He has restaurants?"

"About twenty of them, a whole chain. 'Weeghman's Cafes' is the name. That's where he made his money. You remember the Federal League?"

"Sure. Outlaw league. Nineteen-fourteen, right?"

"And 'fifteen, but you were in Europe by then. Anyway, Weeghman was one of the big shots behind the league. Helped finance the operation with money from his cafes. The sporting papers called the Federal League 'the flapjack circuit' because of it. He owned the Chicago Whales in the new league, got Joe Tinker to manage and play shortstop, Three Finger Brown to pitch." In answer to Landfors' blank look, I explained that Tinker and Brown were star players. "And he built Cubs Park—it was Weeghman Park then—for the new club."

"Yeah, so?"

"So, anyway, if somebody wanted to take over the Cubs, they'd sabotage his cafe business, not the team. The restaurants aren't doing well anyway. Not many people can afford to go out to eat anymore."

That wasn't a problem at this restaurant, nor for the others that were sprouting up in the area. It was the music that brought people. A new music, called jazz, that was quickly winning converts from those like myself who used to be ragtime fans.

The band, which according to the name painted on the bass drum was King Carter's Dixieland Jazz Band, consisted of five colored musicians in white dress clothes. They started warming up and I said to Karl, "You're going to like this. They're from New Orleans. A lot of musicians have been coming up from New Orleans lately."

"The Navy closed down Storyville," he said.

"What's Storyville?"

"Red light district in New Orleans. Jazz and whorehouses. I heard a lot of sailors complain about it being shut down. And, actually, I like opera."

"Oh." I'd never known that about him. The band started to play, with a wailing cornet and a pulsating piano. "Well, then I'm going to like it."

The waiter came by and our empty plates and coffee cups vanished. The mugs then reappeared just as quickly, freshly filled.

After a couple of tunes, which Landfors seemed to enjoy well enough, I said, "There's another reason I'm not bothering about Weeghman's problem. I'm trying to find out who killed Willie Kaiser."

He smiled wryly. "Why doesn't that surprise me?"

Through the rest of the band's set, we talked about Willie's death. It was just like old times. I told him about the way Willie had died, about Edna and her mother, that I figured the shot had come from across the street, and everything else that I'd found out or suspected.

While we talked, couples started dancing. They were dressed in the latest fashion, which is to say drab. With German dyes no longer available, colors were duller, mostly hues of brown and gray. And there were fewer styles to choose from, so the dresses looked like uniforms. War-time economy had one positive effect on the ladies' clothes though: skirts were shorter to save cloth and shoes were lower to save leather, thereby leaving a nice expanse of exposed leg all the way from ankle to mid-calf.

"Why don't you get the autopsy report?" Landfors asked.

"Yeah, why not. And how do I do that?"

He laughed. "Let me see what I can do about it. I need

to get back into things anyway. Might take me a while though. I don't have a lot of contacts in this town. I'll try to get the police report, too."

"Thanks Karl."

"What about this?" he said. "Could your friend getting shot be part of that sabotage you were talking about?"

I shook my head. "No, I thought about that. But it doesn't fit the pattern. The other stuff was minor—sawing seats, smoke bombs. More like pranks. Big difference between pretzels and murder. It doesn't fit."

"Hmm. Makes sense."

I changed the topic. "What was her name?"

He didn't have to ask who I meant. "Aileen."

"How'd you meet her?"

"She worked for the Red Cross." He then turned the questioning around on me. "So, this Edna, is she your latest?"

"No."

"You're trying to find who killed her brother. You sure she isn't the reason you're doing that?"

"No. And not to avenge a friend, either," I confessed. In one long swallow, I downed the rest of my "coffee." "I'm doing it because whoever killed Willie killed the one thing that was fun about this season. Turning a double play with Willie Kaiser was perfect. The kind of perfect you can't get by yourself. Like when you know somebody so well, you start a sentence—"

"And the other one finishes it." Landfors smiled.

Jeez, I was glad to see him again. "That's it. And when Willie was killed, that little bit of perfection in my life was killed, too."

Maybe that's why I'd been feeling so strange about Edna

lately. I wasn't doing this for her or for her mother or for Willie. I was doing it for me.

Edna. *Damn.* I was supposed to take her to the movies tonight.

Chapter Ten

I didn't know much about my new job or what exactly was expected of me, but I was pretty sure that setting the place on fire wasn't the way for me to make a good first impression.

I ran a metal rake through the peach stones in the hope of quenching the flames. They died down briefly, then flickered up again and were soon blazing.

This should have been a simple assignment. So said the supervisor who spent a full two minutes explaining the task before leaving me on my own. All I had to do was shovel the pits into a wire mesh tray, slide the tray into a furnace similar to a pizza oven, and rake through the pits periodically as they slowly burned to charcoal. That was it. Simple enough even for baseball players like Willie Kaiser or Mickey Rawlings to do.

The problem was that the flames kept flaring too intensely. They licked at the open front of the furnace and sent tight coils of black smoke spiraling up to the ceiling. The concrete block building, which had a high roof and a disproportionately small floor area, was of recent construction but poorly ventilated. There was only one door in the place and no windows.

I turned away from the furnace and looked through the smoky haze to see if I could spot the supervisor.

About twenty other employees of the Dearborn Fuel Company were hard at work. They were all dressed in baggy olive-green coveralls, and many wore goggles or masks as protection from the soot and cinders being spit out of their own furnaces and ovens. I couldn't identify any of them as the supervisor.

This was my first day of work. Night, really—I was on an eight-to-midnight shift. And if I didn't get the fire under control, it could be my last.

The worker at the station next to mine had his back to me. He was using a cutting torch on an elaborate old piece of boiler equipment that had copper pipes twisting in and out of it. The torch was in one gloved hand; the other held the tin handle of a protective shield that he kept pressed to his face. The face shield, which looked like the device my aunt used for viewing stereoscopic photographs, had dark glass set in it for the man to see through. A striped brakeman's cap was on his head, with the visor turned backward like a catcher's.

I didn't want to tap him on the shoulder—instinct told me that's not the thing to do to somebody holding a blowtorch. "Excuse me," I said, quietly enough to avoid drawing attention from the others but hoping it was loud enough for him to hear over the hissing of the torch.

No response.

I glanced back at my oven. The flames were roaring brighter. I yelled louder at the fellow, "Hello!" I followed up with a light tap on his back and quickly stepped away in case he spun around.

He turned a knob on his torch, reducing the flame to the size of a candle's, then turned and faced me through impenetrable slate gray glass. "What?"

I pointed to the furnace. "I think it's burning. I don't know how to stop it."

The face shield came down. "It's a fire. It's supposed to burn."

I took a closer look at the man. It took a minute for me to realize that it wasn't the face of a man. This was a woman.

He—*she*—put her torch and shield on a small workbench and stepped over to my furnace. "Not this hot though." Her voice was low-pitched and rough. "You got to cut back on the gas." She turned a valve on the side of the apparatus. "Low heat is what you want. Otherwise you get ash instead of charcoal." The flames soon retreated from the oven door.

A woman, dressed like a man, working in a factory, doing a man's work—using a blowtorch of all things.

She tugged off her leather gloves and removed her cap. With a red handkerchief, she wiped her brow. There wasn't a trace of femininity in her appearance: dark eyes were deeply set above a pug nose; coarse short dark hair twisted in a dozen directions. I was no better at determining women's ages than I was at deducing anything else about them, and the masculine clothes made it tougher, but I put her age at about thirty.

"What are you staring at?" she demanded sharply.

"Uh—no—I wasn't . . ."

With a snort she went back to her work station. The baggy clothing hid her figure, but I guessed her height to be an inch or two taller than Edna's and her build a little broader. Before resuming work, she reached into a deep pocket of her coveralls and pulled out a sack of tobacco and a package of cigarette paper. She tugged the drawstring open with her teeth, deftly rolled a cigarette, stuck it between her thick lips, and used her torch to light it.

A woman, dressed like a man, working in a factory, who smokes cigarettes.

After I recovered somewhat from the series of shocks, I stepped over to her. "Thanks for the help," I said. "I wasn't sure what to do."

She sucked hard at the cigarette.

I extended my hand. "My name's Mickey Rawlings."

A stream of smoke was exhaled into my face.

My lungs halted in mid-breath, but I didn't blink.

After pulling her cap back on, she finally said, "Agnes O'Doul," and gripped my hand in a firm shake.

"Nice to meet you Miss O'Doul."

Agnes O'Doul looked taken aback. After another drag on the cigarette, she removed it from her lips and blew the smoke to the side. "Call me Aggie."

"Hey! It ain't break time!" The belligerent voice came from a man with the size and bearing of a bantam rooster. He was dressed the same as us, except for a leather aviator's helmet pulled tight on his skull. He also had a nightstick that he waved at us with the same enthusiasm as Mike the Cop chasing kids from Wolfram Street. "Get back to work," he ordered.

Agnes flicked her half-smoked cigarette on the concrete floor. She ground it out with her heel while she stared angrily at him. I had no doubt she was pretending the butt was his face.

The man had bulging eyes, a beak of a nose, and an upturned chin. The tip of his nose and the point of his chin looked like pincers struggling to meet in front of his small mouth. His head looked more like that of an insect than a human being.

He poked me on the chest with his stick. "If you think you get some kind of special privileges just 'cause you're of one Harrington's Cubbies, you got another think coming."

I grabbed the end of his stick and yanked it down. "I don't expect nothing."

He pulled the club from my grip and wound back to swing. Then he held up and a smile crept over his face. A smiling wasp. "Good," he said, apparently having decided to declare victory instead of fight. "Get back to work."

Agnes donned her gloves and picked up her torch.

I picked up my rake and stirred the peach stones in the oven. They glowed dull red now, without burning.

With a satisfied look, Waspface turned and walked away, twirling his billy club by its leather thong.

I put down the rake. As Agnes was about to open up the flame on her torch, I asked her, "He the foreman or something?" He wasn't the same supervisor I'd met earlier.

"Something," she grunted. "He's Curly Neeman. A rat turd." With that explanation, she twisted the knob on her torch until the flame burned blue and went back to work.

I returned to my job also and soon got the hang of it. I even started to feel I was doing something important: helping to keep doughboys' lungs from being seared by chlorine gas.

My task was but one in a long process. It started with thousands of housewives all over the country who'd saved tens of thousands of peach pits and brought them to government collection sites. In another building of the Dearborn

Fuel Company, the pits were cracked open to remove the kernels inside, and the shells were dumped in the bin next to my oven. After I'd cooked the peach stones into charcoal—the usual result no matter what I attempted to cook—the charred shells were brought to yet another building, where they were crushed and put into filter cans. The cans would then be shipped to France, where they would be attached to gas masks and distributed to the soldiers.

I liked the idea that what I was doing was helping prevent people from getting hurt. I didn't know you could contribute to a war effort that way.

At ten o'clock, a whistle blew to signal break time.

Curly Neeman, the wasp-faced rat turd, passed by twirling his club. He opened his pincers enough to say, "Now you two can do your sweet talking."

Agnes pulled away her face shield and shot him a lethal glare as he walked off.

"What's he do here?" I asked. So far, it looked like his job was even easier than shoveling peach pits.

"Security," she said derisively.

"A cop?"

"Something like that. But unofficial. Spying is more like it. He'll report anybody who doesn't work hard enough as a German agent. Neeman checks for smuggling, sabotage, things like that. Harrington has guys like him all over the place."

This wasn't the building where the real munitions were made or stored. "Big problem with smuggling out peach pits?" I joked.

Agnes let out a belly laugh. "Not that I know of. But that doesn't stop Neeman from playing Sherlock Holmes." She rolled and lit another cigarette.

The Dearborn Fuel Company was a massive complex on Western Avenue between Twenty-Second Street and the South Branch of the Chicago River, near the McCormick Reaper Plant. There were clusters of small buildings; one of these clusters was designated the Chemical Plant. It was cheerfully explained to me when I arrived that the small buildings were to help limit the damage in the event of an explosion. One of the things that surprised me about the plant was that security seemed lax. I'd expected armed military personnel, but none were visible. The use of "unofficial guards" explained the lack of uniformed ones.

Agnes grabbed a couple of tin buckets from near her workbench and upturned them on the floor for us to sit on.

"Neeman called you a Cubbie," she said.

I shifted my bottom, trying without success to get comfortable on the low pail. "Yeah, I play for the Cubs. Second base." It reminded me why I was here: to find out about the Cub who used to play shortstop. "You work here long?" I asked.

"Just over a year."

"Did you know the fellow who had this job before me?"

"About as well as I know you. Just some guy working at the station next to me."

"How did he get along with the others here?"

Agnes shrugged. "He stood there, did his shoveling and raking, didn't talk much to anyone." She took a final deep drag on her cigarette, then ground it out. "Why you ask?"

"He was my teammate. Friend."

"Huh."

"His name was Willie Kaiser," I said.

"I know. Neeman wouldn't let the poor kid forget it."

From what I saw of Curly Neeman, that didn't surprise

me. I stood up from the cramped sitting position and flexed my knees.

"So what was he really like?" Agnes asked in a strained voice. She hastened to add, "I was just wondering. All I ever saw was the back of his clothes. That kid shoveled and raked like it was gonna win the war. I'm kind of curious what he was like."

The whistle blew again before I could answer. Break over.

Curly Neeman came by to check that we were back on the job and we were.

I worked two more hours, steadily and in silence. Agnes did the same at her station.

Neeman didn't appear again until midnight, when my shift ended. Agnes, since she wasn't on a baseball player's schedule, had four more hours to go.

"They tell me your name's Rawlings," he said.

"They're right."

"Good American name," Neeman said approvingly. "That's what we need here is more good American white men. All we got now is foreigners and coloreds and women."

I glanced around the room. In their coveralls and masks, everyone looked the same to me, each working as hard as the next.

Neeman pointed at Agnes and added, "If you can call that one a woman."

Her back stiffened and I knew she heard.

I was determined to be on good behavior until I learned everything I could about Willie. But I was pretty sure that someday I would end up punching Curly Neeman right in the pincers.

"You know, we got an organization for patriotic Ameri-

cans," Neeman said. "You might want to join. It's called the
Patriotic Knights of Liberty. Maybe you've heard of us."

Fortunately, with age, I'd developed the ability to refrain
from always blurting out whatever went through my head. I
still did it too often, but not this time. "Go to hell," was the
impulsive answer that ran through my head. Fast on its heels,
though, was the memory that Willie had warned Hans Fohl
about the Knights getting revenge for the smoke bombs. How
would Willie know what the Knights were planning? "Sure,"
I said in my most agreeable voice. "I'd love to join a patriotic
group."

Agnes's back twitched again.

"Good!" Neeman tapped me on the shoulder with his
stick. "We got a meeting Wednesday night. Eight o'clock."

"I'm supposed to be working Wednesday night."

"Don't worry about it. Somebody will fill in your time
card. Same as being here, except you don't have to work."

"Hey, that's great," I said. "Special privileges."

Neeman looked blank.

An audible snort came from behind Agnes's face shield.

Chapter Eleven

Today's topic: "What *You* Can Do to Enforce the Sedition Act."

One of President Wilson's Four-Minute Men, a gawky boy with an earnest face, stood alone on the stage of the Crystal Theatre. The crimson drapes behind him cloaked the movie screen. Before the evening show could start, the audience would have to listen to his spiel.

The Four-Minute Men were a homefront army who delivered patriotic messages composed by the Committee on Public Information. To encourage the maximum number of appearances for these speakers, the government guaranteed that their talks would last no longer than four minutes each. Though brief, the messages were numerous. Every picture show, play, concert—almost every public event with a captive audience—was preceded by such a speech.

This boy was explaining the Sedition Act that had recently been passed by Congress in an effort to curtail those exercises of free speech that the Espionage Act didn't already prohibit. According to the new law, any "disloyal, profane, scurrilous, or abusive language" about the war, the U. S. government, the flag, the draft, Liberty Bonds, or a dozen other sacred things would result in a twenty year prison term and a $10,000 fine. The broadest possible interpretation of the sedition law was encouraged. From what I gathered, simply muttering "this damn war" would and should land somebody in jail.

As far as "What *You* Can Do," the Four-Minute boy urged us to spy on neighbors, coworkers, and relatives and to report any "unpatriotic" language to the authorities.

Ending his talk within the allotted time, the kid finished to rousing applause from the audience. The noise of the clapping and cheering drowned me out as I muttered, "This damn war."

Edna Chapman was the only one who heard. Her head twitched a warning look in my direction.

This was the first time Edna and I had attended a motion picture show since Willie had been killed, and it was four days later than I had promised her. I'd called her after my dinner with Karl Landfors and apologized profusely, feeling truly awful about having forgotten her. She'd graciously deemed Landfors's unexpected return from the war to be a satisfactory excuse but then claimed to have unspecified "other plans" that prevented her from accepting a rain check until now, early Wednesday evening.

When the Four-Minute Man stepped off the stage, the red curtains drew away from the movie screen and the house lights dimmed. We still had to endure a few more reminders that this was wartime. First, the newsreels, purportedly shot at the front lines. They showed rousing scenes of Allied soldiers marching cheerfully off to battle—always as they were going off to fight, never as they returned. Not once was the aftermath of battle revealed on the screen. Then there was a publicity reel from Mutual Films showing their star actress Margarita Fischer as she changed her last name, which was written on a huge blackboard: with a thick piece of white chalk, she crossed out the "c" to make it a less Germanic-looking "Fisher." Another patriot doing her bit for America.

"Stupid," I muttered.

"Ssshhh," urged Edna.

Next was a short film encouraging the purchase of Liberty Bonds. In the uniform of a doughboy, Douglas Fairbanks boxed with another actor, who was made up as a villainous Kaiser Wilhelm. A tall, gaunt actor dressed like the Uncle Sam of the recruiting posters cheered Fairbanks on as he pummeled the "Kaiser." The actor playing Uncle Sam used to be Gustav von Seyfertitz until his name changed to G. Butler Clonebaugh, a moniker that might be more acceptable politically but that I didn't find to be all that much of an improvement.

Finally, the main feature began with an opening title card that announced *TARZAN OF THE APES.* Edna visibly relaxed and her lips softened into a small smile.

The last time I'd talked to her at length—if any conversation with Edna could be considered "at length"—was on her front steps when she'd said something about Willie having secrets.

Later tonight I was going to the Patriotic Knights of Liberty meeting that Curly Neeman had invited me to. Tomorrow the Cubs were traveling to Philadelphia for a road series. Since I was pressed for time, I decided to ask Edna a few more questions during the movie. We'd seen the picture often enough to have it memorized anyway.

The introductory scenes flashed on the screen: Lord and Lady Greystoke set sail from England; mutineers took over the ship and abandoned the couple on the edge of the African jungle; there, Lady Grey gave birth to a son. The noise in the theater grew as scores of moviegoers read the explanatory title cards aloud in a dozen accents. Some people were trying to learn English on their own; others were reading and translating for those who understood no English at all. This multilingual buzz was one of the things I found appealing about nickelodeons when I'd first started going to them; no matter what town I was in, I always felt I had company at the picture show.

I knew I'd better talk to Edna while Tarzan was still a boy. Once beefy Elmo Lincoln appeared in his leopard skin loincloth as Tarzan the man, Edna tended to become absorbed in what was happening on the screen.

As the words *And Kala, the Ape, nursed the son of an English nobleman* were haltingly read by the crowd, I said to Edna, "I was hoping you could tell me some more about Willie."

She hesitated. "You knew him."

"Not like a sister would. And only for the last year." And, as I'd recently been discovering, not very well at all.

She nodded. When the screen flashed *Happy with Kerchak's tribe, Tarzan did not dream he was different from the apes* and others around us starting reading it aloud, Edna said, "What do you want to know?"

A chorus recited, *Until one day in the mysterious depths of the pool he glimpsed a vision that set his little English brain to wondering.* "Did he really want to be a soldier?" I asked. "Was it because of his father? Did he think he had to fight to be an American? What was it?"

Like me, she timed her response to coincide with the next title card. The chatter of people reading enabled us to speak in virtual privacy. "His father died in the Philippines," she said. "Of malaria. There wasn't anything glorious about it. Willie knew that. He never wanted to be a soldier."

"Malaria? But what about those medals on the wall. They give medals for malaria?"

"Those are campaign medals. Everybody got them. My father got one for the Mexican campaign."

Mrs. Chapman must have remarried soon after her first husband's death. "What about your father?" I asked. "When did your mother meet him?"

She let a few title cards go by before getting synchronized with them again. "She'd known him since she was a girl. Both their families were from Slovakia. I think they were sweethearts before she met Willie's father. They married just a year after Otto Kaiser died."

"Your father was a soldier, too?"

She nodded. "He joined the Army when I was ten. Couldn't find any other work. It shouldn't have been dangerous. There wasn't any war on."

"What happened?"

"He was with General Pershing on the expedition in Mexico, going after Pancho Villa." She paused. "He was shot and killed two years ago."

"I'm sorry," I said.

We watched the sad scene of the boy Tarzan discovering the jungle hut in which he was born and his parents died. Then I started again. "What did—"

Edna suddenly moved her arm to my side of the armrest and lightly slid her hand under mine. She wanted a date, not an interrogation. Her fingers were loose. I was supposed to take hold of her hand, interlock fingers, give her hand a squeeze—something to show I was receptive. I wanted to but couldn't. Our hands just lay there, limp. There was nothing I could do about it. I couldn't feel what I didn't feel.

"Uh, I know Willie used to play ball for the Union Stock-yards," I said rapidly. "How long did he work there?"

Edna bit her lip and took a deep breath before answering in a strained voice. "Nineteen-fifteen he started. First in a packing house, then Hans Fohl got him a job in the tannery."

"Was he close to Fohl?"

She shook her head no.

"Was there trouble between them?"

Another negative shake.

"Did—"

"Could you pass the popcorn please?" Her voice was barely audible.

"Of course." I picked up the box at my feet and passed it to her.

She took the box with both hands. "Thank you." After slipping a single kernel in her mouth, she handed it back to me then folded her hands in her lap.

The "graceful disengagement." I'd used it myself more than once when a date didn't respond to my overtures. It can be a risky thing to offer one's hand sometimes.

Edna knew now that there was never going to be anything between us. I felt bad, but that's all I felt. I had no romantic intentions toward her and couldn't force myself to pretend that I did.

We continued to watch the movie in silence.

I still had a couple of questions to ask, and asking them sure wasn't going to make things any worse than they already were. During the scene of Tarzan burning down a native village, I leaned toward Edna and it seemed I had to lean far to bridge the chasm between us. "Did Willie say anything about his night job at the chemical plant?"

A head shake.

"Did he ever say anything about the Patriotic Knights of Liberty?"

An even fainter shake. I wasn't going to be getting any more words from her.

So it came as a surprise when the movie ended, the lights came up, and Edna turned to face me with red eyes. "Willie was a wonderful brother to me," she said. "I will do anything to get the man who killed him."

• • •

Frank Timmons spoke with greater intensity and more elaborate gestures than had the Four-Minute Man earlier in the evening.

The meeting hall, an abandoned ramshackle garage really, just over the Cicero border on Twenty-Second Street, was filled with men paying rapt attention to his every hysterical word.

Timmons, Grand Knight of the Patriotic Knights of Liberty, had the burly build of a butcher, the clothes sense of an insurance salesman, and the bluster and thunder of a faith-healing evangelist.

In a rich bass voice, Timmons boomed, "I want to make this clear: the good white men of the Patriotic Knights of Liberty are not at odds with the Illinois State Council of Defense. No sir. Not at all. The Council of Defense was set up by the state, and it would be wrong to say anything against it."

Not to mention seditious, I thought. I also thought it unfortunate that there wasn't a four-minute time limit on all speeches. Timmons had been speaking for half an hour and appeared to be only warming up.

"There's some other folks," he went on, "who might tell you that the Illinois State Council of Defense isn't being run by a real American. Well, of course, that's true. Samuel Insull wasn't born in this country. He's an Englishman. But you'll never hear me say anything against him for not being a true-blue American. A lot of other folks might say that they don't trust him on account of he's a foreigner, but not me. *No* sir. The way I see it, we're over there saving England's country for them, so it's only fair that we should have an Englishman here helping us do it."

Cheers and a burst of applause greeted this statement.

"We *support* the Council of Defense," he proclaimed. "But we support it through *action.*"

So far there'd been only talk, lots of it, issued solely from the tireless mouth of Frank Timmons. But on the tables behind him, under a large American flag nailed to the wall, was a variety of weapons and ammunition. All for sale at reasonable prices, as Timmons had pointed out several times during his speech.

I was uneasy, and not only because of the firearms. Even though I was with the supposed "good guys" in this place, I felt as much an outsider as I had at the German church. Maybe there's just something about secret societies of any kind that makes me uncomfortable.

Timmons continued to rant and appeared to come apart as he threw himself into the effort. His baggy gray jacket came off first, then his polka-dot bow tie. He brushed his sweating forehead, and the long lock of light brown hair that had been pasted over the top of his head fell across his eyes. Finally, he detached his collar and flung it on the floor.

He reached to the table behind him, grabbed a newspaper, and held it out for all to see the banner headline on the front page. From my sixth row seat, I could read the bold black type easily: *QUENTIN KILLED.*

A chorus of angry *damns* came from the crowd. Everyone knew who Quentin was: Quentin Roosevelt, Lieutenant in the U. S. Army Air Corps, Teddy Roosevelt's youngest son.

"His plane was shot down behind enemy lines," Timmons said.

The crowd elaborated their curses to "Damn Germans."

With the Knights riled by the news, Frank Timmons spoke with renewed vigor. "A year ago, 'preparedness' was the word of the day. Then it was 'mobilization.' I say we *still* have to be prepared! Prepared to mobilize!"

More cheers. I wondered if the others understood what Timmons had just said. I sure didn't.

Timmons waved an arm. "German agents are in this country. They're in *America,* on *our* soil. And they're putting ground glass in our food."

Cries of outrage from the audience.

"They're poisoning Red Cross bandages!"

More angry yells.

"The next thing you know, zeppelins will be sneaking in over our skies and bombing our cities. Are we going to let that happen?"

"No!" the chorus cried.

"Then we better be prepared to stop them, shoot them right out of the sky! Are you prepared for that?"

"Yes!"

"I can't hear you!"

"Yes!"

"Are you prepared?"

"YES!!" There were also a few *amens* and *hallelujahs*.

Timmons ended his speech by encouraging the men to stock up on the arms for sale at the table. He also passed the hat, and everyone, including myself, threw in a dollar. I promised myself that I'd give ten dollars to the Red Cross to make up for it.

Most of the audience broke up, with many of the Knights going to the merchandise tables. Others stood and talked in small groups. Some remained seated in the folding chairs that were arrayed in the center of the garage and spoke to their neighbors in hushed whispers. I was left completely alone. I'd come at Curly Neeman's invitation, but he'd remained close by Timmons's side and hadn't said a word to me all night.

Sitting by myself, I started to feel conspicuous and thought it must be obvious to everyone that I didn't belong. And this group was not one that had a lot of tolerance for any kind of outsiders. Would they think that I'd come to spy on them? What did they do to people they suspected of being spies?

I gave an anxious look about the place. Around the walls of the garage were remnants of the building's previous incarnation: rusted engine parts, stacks of bald tires, and a variety of body segments from both carriages and automobiles. Standing near a pile of mangled fenders was somebody I knew. Unfortunately, it was Wicket Greene.

Greene was in conversation with another man. It seemed he was listening closely to the man, but it was hard to tell for sure; with his jutting forehead and weak chin, Greene's head always appeared to be tilted down.

Wicket Greene would have to do, I decided, as I rose from my chair. As much as I detested him, I disliked feeling so alone in this crowd.

I approached him and we exchanged curt nods. Greene had been on pretty good behavior lately, never gloating about Willie's death, but we were still far from being on friendly terms.

"You know Lefty Rariden?" he asked, indicating his odd-looking companion. The lanky, horse-faced man had a frightening shock of frizzy red hair and wide spooky eyes that might have resulted from seeing his reflection in a mirror. The black sateen shirt he wore made his pale skin seem whiter and his fiery hair brighter.

"No, I—Oh, yes. Yes I do." Lefty Rariden. A right-handed pitcher who was called "Lefty" because he was as screwy as a left-hander. "How you doing, Lefty?" I greeted him.

As we shook hands he grunted, "I know you?" His eyes dilated even further, and he made a show of scrutinizing my face. It was the look he gave batters when he was on the mound, a goofy look of perpetual surprise that kept hitters off balance trying to figure out what he was up to.

"We played against each other a few times." I also remembered that Lefty Rariden tried to be colorful; he wasn't a natural character like Rube Waddell or Casey Stengel.

"Federal League?" Rariden asked.

"Nope. When I was with the Red Sox. You probably don't remember, but there was a game in Comiskey Park, August of nineteen-twelve, and you were pitching for the White Sox. You threw me a low and away curve that I hit for a triple just inside the right field foul line."

"Hope I put you on your ass next time you came up."

"Uh, no. No, you didn't."

"Then I owe you one."

I shot a wary glance at his right hand. A major part of Rariden's concept of "colorful" was to get into brawls. "I'm sure you would have," I said, hoping it would console him, "except you got yanked. Eddie Cicotte went in to finish up."

He smirked. "Then I owe you two."

Wicket Greene laughed. I was sure he hoped to see it when Rariden administered the payback.

"What are you doing now?" I asked Rariden, trying to keep things civil.

"Dearborn Fuel Company," he answered with some pride. It was a better job than many former ballplayers were able to get.

Before I could ask if he knew Curly Neeman, Neeman's insect face was looking up at me. Ignoring Greene and Rariden, he tugged at my sleeve. "You can meet the Grand Knight," Neeman said. I was clearly supposed to feel honored by the invitation; it was equally clear that I was expected to accept it.

I reluctantly followed Neeman to the front of the room, where Timmons was conducting transactions at the weapons table. Neeman slithered between a couple of Timmons's customers and with the manner of an agitated puppy tried to get his attention. I looked at the materials spread out on the table: rifles and revolvers of various makes and ages; an equally broad variety of ammunition; and some hand-to-hand killing implements, including bayonets and trench knives, which were basically brass knuckles with short triangular daggers attached. There were also spiked helmets and other German equipment brought back as souvenirs and a number of patriotic pamphlets which went largely ignored. I don't think Timmons's clientele did much reading.

When Frank Timmons could no longer ignore Neeman's demands for attention, he came over to me with a meaty hand extended and a practiced grin on his face. "Mr. Neeman tells me he's brought us a new recruit," he said in a voice that was deep and resonant. "Welcome, Mr. Rawlings!"

"Uh, thanks," I said, shaking his hand.

"Are you *prepared,* Mr. Rawlings?"

"Well, I thought I was. But tonight I'm starting to realize just how *un*prepared I really am." I gave him a smile that I hoped would look self-deprecating.

"Well said, Brother Rawlings!" Timmons adopted a jolly tone. He reminded me of a minister who could threaten a man with eternal damnation one minute and the next be glad-handing him in the spirit of brotherhood. "We can certainly provide you with everything you need to protect yourself *and* your country."

"Yes, I was just looking at these things. Uh, very, uh, nice."

"And affordable." Timmons turned to Curly Neeman. "Fine new man you've brought us, Brother Neeman. Well done!"

Waspface beamed at the words of approval, his pincers twisting into a smile.

Facing me again, Timmons lowered his voice. "I understand you play for the Cubs. I imagine you must have known that German boy who got shot."

I stammered something to the effect that I did know him and tried to guess where this was heading. Had I been brought here so they could find out if Willie had told me anything? Had Willie known something about the Knights they didn't want him to know?

I was saved by a customer. A well-dressed older man

asked Timmons, "How much for the Browning automatic?"

Timmons's face lit up. "Ah, a man who knows quality!" He dismissed Neeman and me, quickly saying, "You'll excuse me for a minute." Before the sentence was finished, he was already huddling with the new customer.

The question about Willie Kaiser really threw me. I'd come to find out about him, not be asked about him. I wasn't prepared for it and decided to bail out while I had the chance.

"Damn," I said loudly.

Curly Neeman asked, "What's wrong?"

"Forgot I have a date tonight," I lied. "Hate to leave, but. . . . Well, you know how it is."

Neeman leered.

"Tell Mr. Timmons I'm sorry I had to go. I'll come again though."

"Sure," he said, still leering. "Have fun. Give her some for me."

"Uh, yeah, I'll do that."

He guffawed. "As long as it's not Aggie O'Doul you're seeing!"

"Hell, no," I said, forcing a laugh at Neeman's idea of a joke. But I'd have much rather been on a date with Agnes O'Doul than spend another minute with Curly Neeman and the Patriotic Knights of Liberty.

Chapter Twelve

As the Cubs' train rumbled eastward through Ohio, the news rippled from seat to seat, from car to car. Secretary of War Newton D. Baker had made his decision: baseball was not an essential industry.

My gut reaction was, "Hell yes, it is," but I knew that in the context of world affairs it very likely wasn't. Actually, if I had the power to make the ruling, I probably would have rendered a split decision: that the national game was not an industry but was essential.

I sat in an aisle seat, pondering silently the potential impact of the news. Wally Dillard—I really had to come up with a nickname for him—was in the window seat next to me. I'd swapped seats with him while passing through Indiana in the hope that he'd be distracted by the view and quit his jabbering. It turned out that he had the ability to watch scenery and jabber at the same time.

On hearing the news, Dillard shifted topics without pausing for breath. Instead of listing all the things he wanted to see and do in Philadelphia and New York, he began worrying aloud about Secretary Baker's ruling. "What's gonna happen, Mickey?" he asked for the fourth time in five minutes.

"Wish I knew."

He rattled off a succession of questions that paralleled the ones running through my own mind: Is the season now over? Are players going to be drafted? Can we play the World Series first?

I barely listened and didn't answer him at all. The idea that major league baseball could be shut down had me almost immobilized.

I knew the war was more important than baseball. Deep down, I knew there were probably several things more important than baseball. But not to me. To me, there were four seasons in a year, and each was essential to the annual cycle of life: spring training, with its renewal of hope; the summer games, long and leisurely; the fall classic, to crown the new world's champions; and the hot stove league in winter, to revisit glories of seasons past. To interrupt that exquisite sequence seemed a violation of nature.

Eager to sustain some hope, I tried to convince myself that the news about Baker might be mere rumor.

Fred Mitchell interrupted my deliberations with a tap on the shoulder. "Mr. Weeghman wants to see you," the manager said.

I pulled myself up and followed Mitchell to the crowded club car at the rear of the train. With the war-time restrictions on travel, we were lucky to get passage on any kind of train, and Charles Weeghman had to forego his customary private car. Even baseball magnates had to endure some hardships this year.

Weeghman motioned me into an armchair opposite his.

He was nervously smoking a long thin cigar and his sunken eyes smoldered. A folded newspaper was in his lap.

Fred Mitchell left us alone and joined Phil Douglas, Hippo Vaughn, and a couple of other Cubs in a poker game. The card players were at a table as far from Weeghman as they could get. I wasn't sure if it was to accord him some degree of privacy or because nobody liked to sit too close to the boss.

"See the paper?" Weeghman asked the instant my posterior touched down on the seat.

"No. Heard about it. About Baker—"

"Got this at the last water stop," he interrupted, passing me an *EXTRA* edition of the *Cleveland Plain Dealer*. Most of the front page was covered by a headline that read *Baseball Not Essential Says War Secretary*.

So it was true. "Is that it?" I blurted. "Is the season over?"

"Not yet. We'll appeal. Try to get an extension." Weeghman sounded like he was trying to convince himself more than me. He paused to peel a shred of tobacco from the tip of his tongue. "That's what I want to talk to you about," he went on. "Don't think you're off the hook on that matter we discussed. In fact, you better work harder in case the season does end early." The threat he'd made before was still there, unspoken: get results or I'll cut you from the team and you'll be drafted.

"I've been working—"

"And have you learned what Wrigley's up to?"

"No," I admitted. "Not yet."

"What have you done to find out?"

"Well, I started with Willie Kaiser, like I told you before. Turns out he did have something going on in secret."

"What?"

"He was working for Bennett Harrington in his chemical plant."

"Why didn't anybody tell me about that?" Weeghman demanded. "It would have been great publicity for us!" Great publicity—same thing Harrington had said. Baseball owners must all go to the same magnate school. "Would have taken the heat off Kaiser, too," he added.

"He wasn't doing it for publicity. He just wanted to do his part to help."

Weeghman thought for a few minutes. I could tell he was thinking by the slow scowl that bloomed on his face. "You sure he was working for our side?"

"What do you mean?" I tried to control my anger. I knew exactly what he meant but was giving him a chance to retract it.

He passed up the opportunity. "Kaiser. That *is* a German name."

"And 'Weeghman,' that would be?"

"Never you mind," he roared. "I'm an American!"

The clatter of poker chips ceased and conversations broke off in mid-sentence.

"So was Willie," I said quietly.

There was one appealing aspect to canceling the baseball season: I wouldn't have to put up with Weeghman's crap anymore.

Shufflin' Phil Douglas broke the silence in the club car. "It was two bits to you, Fred," he said. The game continued and the chatter resumed.

"Okay," Weeghman finally said. "So your buddy Kaiser was a true blue patriot. What else have you done? You find out about the smoke bombs?"

I shook my head.

"The pretzels?"

"No. But I think I'm getting close," I lied. "You know, you're the one who's holding me back in all this."

"What do you mean?"

"Stop having me tailed."

Weeghman shot me a defiant look. I wasn't the one to be giving orders.

"It's for your own protection," I explained. "I might have to go places, see people, that you wouldn't want any connection with. See?" In reality I couldn't care less about protecting Weeghman, but it seemed a plausible reason for him to leave me alone.

He paused. "Nobody's tailing you."

"What about seeing me go to the church? You said—"

"The *church* is being watched, not you."

"Who's—"

"The Patriotic Knights of Liberty. They keep an eye on any gatherings of Germans, socialists, pacifists, whatever. And they sell— And they offer reports to interested parties such as myself."

I wondered if there was anything Grand Knight Frank Timmons didn't sell. "So you'll let me do things my own way?" I asked.

Weeghman nodded. "Just get results. Soon."

"You know," I said. "It could be that Mr. Wrigley has given up. There hasn't been anything bad happen since Willie was killed."

"Not yet," Weeghman sighed.

· · ·

Eager to see Philadelphia, Wally Dillard went out on the town after our Saturday game with the Phillies. I let him go alone. There weren't enough temptations in this city for him to get into any trouble.

I sat in the plush lobby of the Bellevue-Stratford Hotel, examining the newspapers for more details on the Baker decision. From what I read, seventeen-year-old Wally Dillard would still have a job playing baseball. At thirty-six, so would Wicket Greene. The National League owners had decided to play out the season using only players who were below or above draft age. Along with Fred Merkle, Hippo Vaughn, and most of the other Cubs regulars, I would be going to war.

At least I wouldn't be missing out on a World Series. American League president Ban Johnson had decreed that today's games were to be the junior circuit's last of the year. The 1918 American League season was now over.

This wasn't the only baseball news in the papers. Workers at Philadelphia shipyards had gone on strike. The reason: baseball players. Ballplayers who were on shipyard payrolls but didn't work. Instead, they played on industrial league teams while avoiding the draft. No doubt about it, the image of baseball players as heroes was taking a beating this year.

Other articles reported that Shoeless Joe Jackson was coming to Philadelphia tomorrow to speak at a Liberty Bond rally. He was working, really working, at a Delaware shipyard during the week and giving up his Sundays for the war effort. It was reassuring to know there were still some good guys around.

I folded the papers and leaned back in the leather wing chair. Over the past few years, with ballplayers getting to stay at better hotels than in the old days, I'd developed a taste for the leisurely pastime of lobby sitting—watching travelers come and go, swapping stories with other players and the occasional fan, reading the papers to see what was going on in each of the cities we visited. But even this simple pursuit was less enjoyable this season, for gamblers were starting to infest the hotel lobbies. Needing horses for the war, the government had shut down the racetracks a year ago, so the sporting types were turning their attention to baseball. It was only a matter of time, I thought, until there was a fix. A major one, more than the occasional games that Hal Chase had been throwing throughout his notorious career.

There was a crowd of gamblers in the Bellevue-Stratford, at the other end of the lobby. They were dressed in the bright plaids of their trade, the flashy clothes identifying them the way uniforms identify a baseball team. The reason they were here was to try to get inside information from the players; they wanted an edge, something to increase the chances that they'd make money on their bets.

I started thinking about what they did and why. Their objective wasn't to harm the losing team but to profit from the winning team. Perhaps the motivation for the strange doings at Cubs Park was along the same line: not to hurt Charles Weeghman, as he thought, but because whoever was behind the sabotage had something to gain.

I'd dismissed his partners as possibilities because they would be hurt as much as he. The question I should have asked was: Who would gain if the Cubs went out of business?

There was one obvious choice, obvious but unimaginable. With two major league teams in the city, if one team folded the other would pick up its fans and its gate receipts. The Chicago White Sox. Charles Comiskey.

• • •

The crowd at the Liberty Bond rally was large enough to fill Baker Bowl, and if Sunday baseball weren't illegal in Philadelphia, they might have been there to watch the Cubs play the Phillies. With no ballgame to entertain them, they thronged in front of Independence Hall to see and hear Shoeless Joe Jackson.

Jackson spoke through a hand-held leather megaphone, gently urging people to buy war bonds. His voice was similar to Bennett Harrington's, soft and slow and southern. The similarity ended there; Joe Jackson didn't have Harrington's natural affinity for speaking in front of crowds. He shifted and fidgeted, and at times he was barely audible as he recited what must have been a painfully memorized speech filled with baseball metaphors.

I paid little attention to his words as I elbowed and sidled my way to the front of the mob. As I drew closer to him, I could see that Jackson was dressed in an expensive gray suit of conservative cut. A well-shaped charcoal fedora was on his head, and on his feet were the best wing-tip black oxfords that money could buy. In the minors he'd played one game wearing only socks, and ever since he got to the big leagues he spent a good part of his annual salary trying to live down the "Shoeless Joe" tag.

It sounded as if Jackson was coming to the end of his speech by the time I reached the line of policemen who had the speakers' platform cordoned off.

I asked one of the officers to give Jackson a note for me.

"Get lost," he said.

I tried another who offered to bust me over the head with his club. City of Brotherly Love indeed.

Finally one agreed to do it for a dollar. "That's a long way to walk," he explained. It was a reminder that prices are high in the East—a Chicago cop would have done it for two bits. I agreed and the cop promptly jacked it up another fifty cents "because I'm gonna have to read it to him, too." I forked over the money.

It was well spent. After Jackson stepped off the back of the platform, I could see the cop reading the message to him and Jackson nodding.

A minute later, the White Sox slugger approached me. He was tall and handsome, with friendly eyes and an awkward smile. "Mickey Rawlings," he drawled, holding out his hand. "I reckon we're just about neighbors, you playing for the Cubs."

It suddenly hit me that this was *Joe Jackson,* talking to *me.* I stammered something about being honored to meet him and returned his grip. No matter how many years I play major league ball, I'm always going to be star-struck by the game's real champions. After indulging in a minute of silent hero worship, I jerked myself out of it to say, "I was wondering if I could talk to you for a minute . . . when you're done here."

"I'm done," he said. "How about now?"

"Sure, great."

The next speaker went into his sales pitch for Liberty Bonds.

"Let's move out of here," Jackson suggested.

I followed him as he worked his way to the fringe of the crowd, past admirers who called out his name and reached out to touch him. Although obviously uncomfortable, he accepted the attention graciously.

The two of us turned north on Sixth Street. With fewer people about, Jackson began to walk briskly with long strides. I half-trotted to keep up with him. He didn't slow down until we crossed Market Street. "Never did like this town," he said quietly.

"Yeah, I know. I came here to see you when you were with the Athletics, in ought-eight." A decade before, back when they played in Columbia Park, in the aromatic part of Philadelphia known as Brewerytown.

"I only played a couple games that year."

He'd played in five. After his first game in Philadelphia, he'd gone back home to South Carolina without bothering to tell anyone that he was leaving. After a ten-day absence, Connie Mack had talked him into coming back. He lasted four more games before going home again. But I watched him play in one of them. "Saw you hit against Walter Johnson," I said.

"I didn't get any hits," Jackson said glumly. "Oh-for-four that game." Most good hitters, most bad ones for that matter, could recall every game in which they'd faced Walter Johnson.

"Yeah, but you swung real good."

He laughed. "With Johnson, sometimes that's about as much as you can hope for."

"Too bad it didn't work out with the Athletics."

"I felt bad about letting Mr. Mack down," Jackson said. "But I couldn't live in this here city. And my teammates weren't exactly what you'd call hospitable to me." A Southern rookie playing in a Northern city wasn't going to be treated kindly by his teammates.

"Ever think it might be better playing for Connie Mack than Charlie Comiskey?"

"Hell," he snorted. "A load of buckshot in the ass is better than playing for Comiskey."

"Say, I saw today that the American League is going to keep playing, no matter what Ban Johnson says." The league owners were rebelling against their iron-fisted president, one more example of how the world had gone crazy.

"Comiskey's probably behind it," Jackson said. "Him and Johnson hate each other."

We turned west on Race Street. On a vacant lot, between a warehouse and a boarded-up saloon, a group of boys were playing baseball. Jackson and I automatically drew to a halt to watch them.

The weedy plot of land was littered with broken bottles, bricks served as bases, home plate was a mud puddle, and they were playing with only four boys on a team. But they were clearly having great fun, and their mud-spattered legs testified that it was a high-scoring game.

"Starting to look like soon that might be the only baseball left," I said.

"Be just as well," said Jackson. "As long as kids are still playing the game, it'll go on just fine."

As I watched the boys scampering with abandon around the base paths, I concluded that Joe Jackson was right. This was baseball, and there will always be baseball whether or not it's played by major leaguers. People don't have to pay to watch it, and it doesn't have to be played by men getting paid to do so. As long as there's a bunch of kids, a long round piece of wood, and something that passes for a ball, there will be baseball.

"Hey Joe," I said, "Why don't you show them how it's done? Give 'em a thrill."

He smiled mischievously. "Now that you mention it, I reckon I could do with a little batting practice."

When the boys found out that Shoeless Joe Jackson was going to hit them a few, they happily broke up their game. So would most major-leaguers, I expected.

Jackson, in a pearl gray silk vest and white starched shirt, stepped up to the mud puddle gripping the heavily taped handle of their little bat. I held his hat and coat and was proud to do so. The biggest boy of the group started pitching to him, and Jackson lifted easy fly balls to the rest of the kids, who clustered at the furthest end of the lot.

Even holding himself back, there was magic to the way Joe Jackson could hit a baseball. He was unique. A perfect swing, no extra movements, smooth and graceful with an explosion when the bat contacted the ball.

Maybe Joe Jackson and Ty Cobb and Babe Ruth shouldn't ever be sent to war. They were national treasures. Irreplaceable.

Then I remembered my neighbor, Mrs. Tobin. Her son Harold was as much a treasure to her as Joe Jackson was to these boys. Was it fair for Harold to face death in the trenches while other men were exempted because of their ability to hit a baseball? A pang in my gut answered no.

Jackson called an end to the exhibition with one last shot, a long towering drive that would have been a homer to dead center in the Polo Grounds.

The boys scrambled to retrieve it while Jackson brushed himself off and donned his coat and hat. Before we could leave, they came back to mob him and pepper him with questions. Jackson was trying to make a graceful good-bye when the boy who recovered the ball ran up breathlessly. He rubbed the dirty baseball on his shirt to clean it off and panted, "Would you sign it, Joe?"

"Sorry, son," he said, "I ain't got a pen."

"I'll get one!" the boy volunteered. He ran into the warehouse and came back with a pencil. He handed the ball and pencil to Jackson.

"Well," he hesitated, "I'll sign it if Mickey here will sign it, too. Mickey Rawlings—he plays for the Cubs."

The boy agreed. He didn't mind having his ball messed up with my signature in order to get Joe Jackson's.

Jackson held up the ball and flourished the pencil, then handed it to me. "Sign it right below mine," he said.

I looked at the ball. There was nothing on it. Then I remembered: Joe Jackson couldn't read or write enough to sign his own name. I quickly scribbled *Joe Jackson,* then wrote my own name in smaller letters below.

The boys ran away to show their prize to the rest of the neighborhood kids.

"Better head back," Jackson said. "Gotta catch a train for Wilmington."

Retracing our route, I came to the reason I wanted to talk to him in the first place. "You know Comiskey pretty well," I said.

"Better than I'd like to."

"There's been some accidents . . . and things . . . happening at Cubs Park. Weeghman thinks somebody's trying to put him out of business. You think Charlie Comiskey could be behind something like that?"

"I wouldn't be surprised by nothing Comiskey did," he promptly answered. "You know what he's been saying about me in the papers?"

"Yeah, I've seen."

"I thought I was doing what I was supposed to. I work six days a week for the Harlan and Hollingsworth Shipbuilding Company, and on Sundays I play benefit games or do appearances like today. And he says I'm a slacker, says he's not letting me back on the Sox."

I decided to let Jackson in on what Weeghman had told me. "It's just negotiating, Joe. Comiskey figures he can get you back for less money that way."

"Damn skinflint." He sounded disgusted.

"You know, sometimes I think baseball would be a better game if you didn't make money at it."

"I don't. I play for Comiskey."

"He does. That's the problem. Him and Weeghman and the other owners."

We walked in silence back to Jackson's hotel. By the time we got there, I had an idea. "Why not work in Chicago?" I asked. "Bennett Harrington's got these munitions plants. He'd give you a job. You could keep playing for the Sox that way. And Comiskey would have to get off your back."

"Harrington? No."

"You could—"

"No. I wouldn't work for Bennett Harrington. No way." Jackson clamped his lips like Edna.

I tried to go back a step. "So about Comiskey—"

"Like I said," Jackson snapped, "nothing he did would surprise me." That was the last he would say on the matter.

Chapter Thirteen

Trains are good for thinking. Even on a brief journey, like the one we were taking now from Philadelphia to New York. Maybe better on a short trip—long ones tended to lull me into a stupor. Since I didn't play cards and couldn't read on a train without feeling queasy, sleep and contemplation were the only activities left for me to pursue.

I was becoming confident that I might finally be on the right track about who could be after Charles Weeghman. The idea was to see who would benefit if he lost his baseball team.

And then I realized that the same logic could be applied to a subject of far more importance to me than Weeghman's business: Willie Kaiser's murder.

I'd been looking at it almost solely from the angle that somebody might have something against him, either personally or because of his heritage. But there are more motives for murder than revenge or anger or prejudice. Greed, for example. Did anyone benefit from Willie's death?

At first, the answer seemed an obvious no. There was one

person, though, who came out ahead because of it: Wicket Greene. He inherited Willie's job at shortstop.

Greene's gain was the Cubs' loss. He simply could not play a ground ball cleanly. He made a fielding error in each of the four games with Philadelphia and, as a bonus, two throwing errors in the final contest; his bad throws cost us the game and left us with a split of the series.

The question was: Did Wicket Greene want to start so badly that he killed Willie Kaiser? The notion seemed far-fetched, but I couldn't dismiss it entirely.

Wally Dillard returned from the club car with a soda pop and interrupted my daydreaming. "Hey, Mickey!" he said excitedly. "The guys are setting up a poker game, and Hippo Vaughn says they'll let me play!"

I stifled a laugh. I also stifled the urge to warn him about getting into card games—telling him not to play would only make it more appealing.

"That's great," I said. "How much money you got on you?"

"Twenty-eight dollars. . . . Why?"

"Let's see."

He pulled out a roll of bills. I took it from him, peeled off a ten, and handed the rest back to him. I stuck the ten in my vest pocket. "I'll keep this so you won't be completely broke when we get to New York."

"What if I win?"

I couldn't hold back the laugh this time. Rookies.

He went off to join Hippo and the others. Hippo . . . Maybe an animal nickname. Wally Dillard didn't have the bulk to be "Hippo" of course. Rabbit? No, Rabbit Maranville had that one taken. Possum . . . Muskrat . . . Doggie. Doggie Dillard. That had a ring to it.

Having solved that problem, at least temporarily, I went back to mulling over Willie's murder. I'd been working under the assumption that his death and the sabotage at Cubs Park were unrelated because they seemed so different. Again, I'd been thinking the wrong way. I should have been looking for similarities.

It didn't take long until I found one. A possibility, anyway.

There might have been sabotage that Weeghman wasn't aware of and that I hadn't caught onto either. Until now. When I told Weeghman there hadn't been any additional incidents, he'd said "not yet." I now revised that to "not that we knew of."

Wally Dillard came back to his seat before we were half-way through New Jersey.

"How'd you do?" I asked, though I could see the answer in his face.

"Pretty much broke even," he said with a taut smile. I never heard a card player yet admit that he did any worse than break even. After a couple of minutes, Dillard added, "Uh, I can use that ten back."

I forked it over and he quickly changed the subject. "Can't wait to play in Ebbets Field and the Polo Grounds," he said.

I couldn't either. Because when we did, I'd be keeping an eye on Wicket Greene.

• • •

I love being booed. Well, I don't love it exactly, but it's a hell of a lot better than being ignored. There's nothing worse than being announced to the crowd and hearing dead silence in response.

That wasn't a problem for me in the Polo Grounds. After playing three years for John McGraw's Giants, I was sure to be jeered every time I returned to the park in an enemy uniform. Especially this year, as a member of the Cubs, when there was so much publicity about it being the tenth anniversary of the 1908 pennant race between the two clubs.

Fred Merkle didn't feel the same as I did about being heckled. But then, the taunts thrown at him were downright vicious. And why? Because ten years before, as a rookie with the Giants, he'd made a base running mistake in a critical game of that fabled pennant race. Some claimed his blunder had cost New York the pennant, and Fred Merkle became known thereafter as Bonehead Merkle.

The chants of "Bonehead! Bonehead!" rocked the Polo Grounds when Merkle took his position at first base for infield practice. I wanted to go over and say something to him—"Don't let it get to you" or "You'll show 'em." Merkle's face was steeled, though; he was pretending not to hear the crowd. I decided it would be kinder to let him maintain the pretense.

As an added attraction for the final game of our road trip, Fred Toney and Hippo Vaughn would finally face each other in the rematch that Willie Kaiser's death had postponed.

When Fred Toney came out to pitch for the Giants, he was cheered by the fans. It was his first appearance for New York, having been recently acquired from Cincinnati. The Reds were eager to deal Toney away because he had become too much of an embarrassment for them. First, he was arrested for draft evasion—he'd exaggerated the number of his dependents in order to be granted an exemption. Then, he was indicted for violating the Mann Act, the white slavery law (the newspapers referred to his transgression as "traveling with a woman not his wife"). When Cincinnati made Fred Toney available, New York didn't hesitate to add him to their pitching staff. It would take more than an immoral draft-dodger to embarrass John McGraw.

It bothered me, though. I couldn't get over the unfairness of Toney being cheered and Fred Merkle ridiculed.

As the innings rolled on, my thoughts were barely on the game. I was thinking that baseball has a cruel side. Despite the illusion that a ballpark is its own little world, it really is not a sanctuary. The baser aspects of human behavior can manifest themselves as easily at a ballgame as they can anywhere else. People just naturally have a mean streak in them, and baseball is one more avenue for them to vent that meanness. Whether it's in the name of nationalism or team spirit, label the fellow in the other uniform "the enemy" and then you have free license to make his life hell.

Hippo Vaughn ended up outpitching Fred Toney to take the contest 6–3. I paid enough attention to playing the game to pick up one single in four at bats. Wicket Greene set a record for wildest overthrow by a shortstop in a National League park.

And Fred Merkle was the star of the game. He went three-for-four, including two doubles and four runs batted in. He also stole two bases.

Sometimes there is justice. And I felt better being reminded of that fact.

•   •   •

The time was somewhere between late Saturday night and early Sunday morning. The Cubs team was somewhere between Pennsylvania and Indiana. I was between the sheets of my berth, a lower berth, in the Pullman sleeper car.

The rhythmic rocking of the train failed to rock me to sleep. I was reviewing everything that had happened over the ten-day road trip.

Some of it was fun. Brooklyn, for example. Between games of a three-game sweep of the Dodgers, I'd taken Wally Dillard—he'd declined the "Doggie" moniker—to Coney Island and a number of the borough's other attractions. I even gave him a tour of the Vitagraph Motion Picture studios, where I'd once made a few movies. Dillard took to big-city life the same way Willie had on his first visit.

Beating the Giants two out of three in the Polo Grounds was fun, too, and it left us with a full three-game lead over New York in the standings.

And of course there was the thrill of meeting Joe Jackson in Philadelphia.

There were also some frustrations. Neither the Brooklyn nor the New York City libraries carried the *Spalding Baseball Guides,* which caused me to question what good was a library like that. It wasn't until the last day of the trip that I was able to look up the records I wanted. To get them, I visited Karl Landfors's old employer, the *New York Press.* Their sportswriter, Fred Lieb, let me use his back issues of the *Guides,* and I was able to obtain all the information I needed.

On the national and international fronts, events of the past week and a half were bewildering.

Some was encouraging: Secretary of War Baker gave baseball an extension until Labor Day and would allow the World Series to be played immediately thereafter. Only one month of the season would be lost.

Some was frightening: a German U-boat fired on Cape

Cod, sinking two tugboats. The attack made me want to run out and enlist. My country was under attack, and I would defend it. The war wasn't just "over there" anymore.

Some was disheartening: in Detroit, a man named William Powell was sentenced to twenty years in prison under the Sedition Act; his crime was that he had said he thought some of the stories of German atrocities might have been exaggerated, like the one about German planes dropping poisoned candy onto French streets in order to kill off France's children. It saddened me that my country could do such a thing to one of its citizens.

I'd concluded several things by the time the Cubs boarded the train to go back home. One was that I would no longer read any part of a newspaper except the sports page. Another was that no human being could make as many errors as Wicket Greene had this season unless they were intentional.

And I was starting to have an idea of who killed Willie Kaiser and why. The question that remained for me was: Who else was in on it?

Chapter Fourteen

I was tired and cranky by the time we arrived in Chicago and more than half-tempted to take a taxicab home from Grand Central Station. Going along with the war-time austerity program, I resisted the temptation and opted for the El with a transfer to a Lincoln Avenue street car.

From Lincoln, I trudged on foot to my house, with a satchel in one hand and a small suitcase in the other. It was a dry, hot summer morning; I was soon tired, cranky, and thirsty. My shoes kicked up little dust clouds that floated up and danced on shimmering waves of simmering air. I began to visualize a tall frosty glass of ginger ale. Then I figured since it was only imagination I might as well go all the way, and I changed the object of my fantasizing to an enormous glass of beer, dark amber with a thick head of foam.

As I turned from Herndon Street onto Wolfram, I spotted Mrs. Tobin on her front porch knitting away at the piles of yarn. I hoped to get by with only a quick greeting and go into my house. I liked coming home from road trips and had a regular routine: check the mail, dump the dirty laundry from my bags, and sprawl out in the comfort of my own place with something cold to drink.

Not to be. Mrs. Tobin halted me by crying, "Mickey! I have something for you!"

Leaving my luggage to fry on the sidewalk, I approached her porch with as big a smile as I could muster. "That's a fine-looking sweater, Mrs. Tobin. If they give a medal for best-dressed soldier, Harold will win it easy."

With a beaming smile, she said, "Well, so long as he's warm is all I care about." She paused from her knitting to point one of the needles at a wooden crate on the other end of the porch. It was the size of a block of ice. "That come for you."

After the minimum number of words necessary to be polite, I said good-bye and lugged the heavy crate home and into my parlor. I had no idea what was inside but was tremendously excited by the prospect. This was even better than mail! Before retrieving my bags from the sidewalk, I got a hammer from a cupboard and pried off the loosest-looking board. Inside the box, neatly lined up with their spines facing me, were Willie Kaiser's Mark Twain books.

There was no note, no return address. Edna Chapman apparently had as little use for written words as she had for spoken. Her message, however, as always, was clear: she didn't want me coming to their house to pick up the books. Nor for anything else, I was sure.

My spirits considerably dampened, I went to the kitchen, where I guzzled a glass of tepid tap water, then retrieved my bags from the sidewalk.

Back inside, I checked the mail and found a note from Karl Landfors. The letter said he'd be out of town for a week, but he thought he was close to getting the autopsy report on

Willie Kaiser. There was no date on the note—Landfors must still be rusty in his reporting skills. The envelope was postmarked two days ago.

I'd completed my homecoming routine—read the few pieces of additional mail, dumped the contents of my bags on the bedroom floor, and collapsed into my Morris chair with a cold ginger ale—when the phone rang.

Grumbling about having to get up again, I went to the phone and picked up the receiver. "Hello?"

"Hello. May I speak to Mickey Rawlings please?" The light feminine voice was familiar.

"This is me."

"This is Edna Chapman."

Ah, she was going the formal route. At least she was still talking to me in some manner. "Uh, hi Edna. Thanks for the books."

"You're welcome. My mother wanted you to have them." Sudden silence. I could picture her lips clamping shut.

I thanked her again and received more silence in response. Was she nodding or something? It was hard to get a read on Edna Chapman without being able to see her expressions.

She suddenly blurted, "Did you find out who killed my brother yet?" It came out sounding like, "Why is it taking you so long?"

"No. But I did make some progress, I think." I added apologetically, "I wish I could tell you more, but it's not easy to find out what happened."

"You asked me about secrets . . ."

"Yes."

"If Willie had any secrets . . ."

"Right." This was more arduous than talking with her in person.

"There was one: he was seeing a lady."

Willie? I didn't believe it. I would have known. "He was?"

"Yes. He didn't tell you because he thought you might tease him."

Of course I'd have teased him. What are teammates for? Still, he should have told me. "Do you know who he was seeing?"

"Her name is—was—*is* Aggie."

Jeez. Aggie O'Doul? "Did you ever meet her?"

"No."

"Did he tell you anything else about her? Last name?" Not that I expected there could be very many girls named Aggie.

Silence.

I'd bet she was shaking her head. "Helloooo," I prodded.

"No."

"Okay. Well, thanks for letting me know. I'll see if it leads to anything."

"Are you still going to tell me when you know who killed Willie?"

"Yes."

"Promise?"

"Yes."

Satisfied, she ended the conversation and hung up.

Willie Kaiser and Agnes O'Doul. I couldn't believe it, couldn't picture it at all. Might have been serious, too, if he didn't want to be kidded about it.

I looked into the box of Mark Twain books, my only tangible mementos of Willie. Then I cleared space for them in my small bookcase, pulling out movie magazines and baseball guides to make room. Careful to maintain alphabetical order, I put the books on the shelf one volume at a time. I liked the way they looked—having books in the house really made it seem like a home.

It was about time to wash the dust of the road from my body, so I went to draw a bath. There was still no hot water. I called my landlord, who informed me that plumbing supplies were hard to get. "There's a war on, you know," he explained. I settled for a cold bath; it was more refreshing anyway.

Afterward, feeling fresher and cooler and wearing a clean robe, I scanned the titles of my new library. I picked out *Pudd'nhead Wilson.* I once knew a catcher by that name who played in a North Carolina textile league, with the Byerly Bobbins, I think it was.

Settling back in my chair to read it, I took another look at the title before opening the book. Pudd'nhead. That could be a name for the new kid: Pudd'nhead Dillard. Hmm. Then again, maybe not. Piano Legs Dillard . . . Peanuts . . . Pepper . . . Pickles . . . Pickles Dillard. I decided I'd try that one.

•   •   •

Monday night I was back at work in the chemical plant of the Dearborn Fuel Company. I was even getting proficient at my job. By using smaller loads of peach stones in the oven and stirring them more frequently, I improved the product considerably. The pits charred more evenly and I was able to do a larger total amount in less time.

Between shoveling in fresh loads, emptying the charcoal, and running the tines of my rake through the stones, I was kept hopping. Still, every chance I got, I kept glancing back over my shoulder to steal looks at Agnes O'Doul.

Her body was cloaked in the same baggy coveralls as before, with the safety mask held close to her face as she worked her cutting torch. I couldn't really see her, but I remembered how she looked. And it wasn't anything like the kind of girls Willie went to see in the burlesque houses. I knew, though, that the girls you prefer to look at aren't often the ones you get to date.

During our ten o'clock break, I studied her up close as we sat next to each other on a couple of overturned buckets. No matter how hard I tried, I couldn't picture her with Willie Kaiser.

Agnes rolled a cigarette, lit it with a match that she'd struck on the sole of her boot, and inhaled deeply. "How was your road trip?" she asked in her gruff voice.

"Good. Won seven out of ten. You a Cubs fan?"

She shook her head. "White Sox. Ever since the Hitless Wonders in ought-six."

Well, better a Sox fan than not a baseball fan at all, I figured.

Agnes pulled off her striped cap and ruffled her short dark hair. "Must get kind of lonesome, traveling like that," she said.

"Well, no. Not for me, I guess. Maybe for some of the guys who have wives and kids." Or sweethearts. Reading women wasn't my strong suit—is it any man's?—but I thought I was starting to see where she was going with this.

"So what do players do when they're on the road?"

I gave her an expurgated list: "Oh, play cards, go to the picture shows. Talk mostly. Just sit around in lobbies and talk baseball." Yup, a regular bunch of boy scouts we were.

Agnes took another deep drag on the cigarette and exhaled slowly. "That kid that used to work here, Willie Kaiser,

you said you and him were roommates. Was *he* married
. . . or anything?"

"No, not married." She waited for me to answer the "or
anything." "He was a real quiet kid," I said evasively. "Kept
his thoughts pretty much to himself."

I had no doubt now that Aggie O'Doul had more than a
passing interest in Willie Kaiser.

That was all I wanted to know for now. Before I ended up
revealing to her that I was aware of their relationship, I
changed topics. "What is that you're building anyway?"

"I ain't *building* nothing," she snorted. "I'm salvaging.
Taking that piece of crap apart for parts. Materials are hard
to get with the war on."

"Yeah, I heard."

With half a minute left in the break, Curly Neeman joined
us. He was chewing something that made the pincers on his
face look like they were opening and closing. In silence he
stood, staring at us, using his nightstick to tap out the passing
seconds on his palm.

Agnes and I said no more to each other and nothing to
Neeman. We stared back at him until the break was over and
then went back to work.

Willie Kaiser and Agnes O'Doul. It was true.

What else had that kid been hiding from me?

Chapter Fifteen

One month ago Willie Kaiser had been alive and I'd thought I knew him. Now he was dead and I was finding out all sorts of things I never expected.

The latest surprise was that he had a secret sweetheart. This revelation alone opened up several questions: What if Aggie had another suitor who was jealous of Willie? What if there'd been a lovers' quarrel between Willie and Aggie? Not that I seriously suspected Agnes O'Doul of anything or that Willie had much competition for her affection, but it made me realize that I needed to be thorough, to explore all possibilities, if only to eliminate them. I had to be open to investigating all aspects of Willie's personal history.

There was one chapter in Willie Kaiser's past that I hadn't yet given any consideration: the Union Stockyards. He'd worked there for several years, as recently as last winter, and had played ball for them last summer. Was there anyone there who'd had something against him? Could his murder have been the result of a long-standing grudge that had developed there?

First thing Tuesday morning, after another cold bath, I called my landlord again and asked if he had any houses that weren't currently rented. On hearing his answer that he had many such vacancies, I asked him to give me a water tank from one of them. He agreed, for double the price. By now it was worth it.

The second thing I did was endure more than an hour on various segments of the Chicago transit system, working my way down Halsted Street. The final leg was the South Side El, which spit me out at Exchange Avenue.

This was a different part of Chicago: the South Side. Earthy and bold. Home of Charlie Comiskey's White Sox, the University of Chicago, and thousands of recent immigrants, many of whom worked in Packingtown and lived in the dilapidated shanties "back-of-the-yards." It was also a land inhabited by vast herds of livestock. More than ten million animals made a one-way trip to the stockyards each year.

Treading my way over a maze of railroad tracks, I couldn't help but be impressed by the scale of the Union Stockyards' operation. More than a square mile of Chicago real estate was taken up by the Yards, with most of the space being used for an endless sea of pens to temporarily house the hogs, sheep, and cattle brought there for slaughter and packaging. A steady stream of trucks and railroad cars transported the animals, other cars carried loads of hay to feed the creatures, and still others brought out their manure to be sold as fertilizer. I couldn't help but be nauseated by the operation, either, for permeating everything was the worst stench imaginable, worse even than that of Brooklyn's Gowanus Canal.

At Peoria Street was the imposing limestone portal that marked the main entrance to the Yard. It looked like a medieval castle, complete with turrets and archways. Chiseled into the stone above the central archway were the words: *Union Stock Yard Chartered 1865.* Above the inscription was a massive stone steer's head projecting over the entrance; the head hung there like a hunting trophy on a wall. It detracted from the otherwise majestic image of the place. I couldn't see why anyone would be so proud of killing a cow.

I had a story prepared for the friendly guard who halted me at the gate. I explained to him that I was on a scouting expedition for the Cubs. We were short of players, and I wanted to see if there were any hot prospects on the Union Stockyards' team.

"Team?" the guard chuckled. "We got a whole league. There's a hundred thousand people working here! I expect you should be able to find a decent ballplayer or two among them."

"Oh. Well, let me start with whoever Willie Kaiser played for," I said. "It worked out good with him, maybe there's others on that team."

"And who did he play for?"

I didn't know. Neither did the guard, who seemed eager to be helpful if I could give him a starting point.

"Where did he work?" the guard asked.

"In the tannery. That was the last place he worked here, anyway."

"Then he probably played for the Tanners. We go by departments here. Cattle drivers got a team, slaughterhouse got a team, tanners got one, and there's a bunch of teams for the meatpackers." While I waited outside, he stepped into a small office and made a couple of phone calls. He emerged with the information that the Tanners' manager was Bill

Pines and gave me directions to the tannery building, where I could find him.

Heading west on Exchange Avenue, I approached Packingtown, the processing section of the Stockyard. Here were the factories where Armour, Swift, Libby, and the other meatpackers turned cattle and hogs into corned beef, canned hams, and sausage. There were adjacent buildings for the manufacture of soap and glue, using those few parts of the animals that didn't make it to the sausage grinders. The packers liked to brag that the only part of the hog they didn't use was the squeal.

The tannery consisted of a group of large brick buildings near Packingtown. Their doors and windows were all wide open. It would have been futile to keep them closed—the smell of death and excrement penetrated everything and couldn't be shut out. The best that could be done was to let the putrid air circulate, prevent it from collecting in any one place.

One of the buildings housed a collection of enormous metal vats and exuded sharp scents of chemicals, which added their own caustic quality to the atmosphere. Another contained rows and rows of skins hanging from hooks while workers scraped them clean. And in an adjacent structure, finished hides were being cut into strips.

I located the tannery warehouse where Bill Pines was a supervisor. Cowhides, sorted by color, were piled nearly to the ceiling. Thinking of all those living wide-eyed animals I'd seen in the pens being reduced to this was disturbing. It gave me the creepy feeling of having walked into a morgue.

"Got a call from the main gate," Pines said, after introducing himself. "Hear you're scoutin' ballplayers."

Still distracted by the surroundings, I said, "You got a whole lot of shoe leather in here."

He shook his head. "Two years ago, it would've been shoe leather. Now it all goes to the damn government. Harnesses for army mules, Sam Browne belts for officers . . . and we don't get paid nothing like we used to—" He caught himself. Complaining about the government, long a cherished American tradition, was no longer allowed. "Anyway," he said quickly. "What about them ballplayers you're looking for?" Pines could have been a player himself twenty or thirty years ago. Third baseman probably. He looked a bit like a gray-haired gorilla, built low to the ground with long muscular arms that poked out of his turned-up shirt sleeves.

"Well," I said, sticking to my fabricated story, "you probably know that the Cubs are short of players. Keep losing them to the army. We figured since you're the fellow who discovered Willie Kaiser, you must have a keen eye for talent. Thought you might have a couple more like him."

"To give to the Cubs, huh?" He rubbed his chin thoughtfully. "Well, our season ain't over yet. And I gotta say my team ain't nothin' like it was a year or two ago. Too many boys going off to France." He shook his head. "Nah, I don't think I got anybody you'd be interested in. Hell, we're barely hanging in there. Right now we're only in third place." He added in a gruff whisper, "And I got twenty bucks riding on us taking the championship."

So that's how it was. Allowing his players a chance at the big leagues wasn't one of Bill Pines's priorities. "Hmm. I would bet," I said, after a little thought, "that your eye for talent can see all the way across the field to the other dugout. Maybe there's somebody on the first or second place teams you think I might take a look at." I gave him a hint of a smile.

His return smile confirmed that we understood each other. "Now that you mention it, there are a couple of players on those teams I think would do real well on the Cubs."

Pines gave me a couple of names, which I jotted down in a small notebook, and directions on where I could find them.

"Before I go to see about these other prospects," I said, "tell me about Willie Kaiser. Did he get along with his teammates?"

"Yeah, sure. He wasn't one to go out for beers after a game, but he wasn't a problem either. Quiet kind of kid. Kept to himself mostly."

"None of the other players gave him trouble?"

"Nah. Thanks to Kaiser, we took the championship. Everybody on the team gets a bonus for that. Why you ask?"

"Just curious. No trouble in here either? His coworkers didn't object to him playing ball while they had to work?"

"Hell, no. They were kind of proud of him, if anything."

"His cousin works here, too, doesn't he? Hans Fohl."

"Fohl, yeah. He's back . . ." Pines turned about, then pointed to Fohl piling hides in a corner of the building. "Over there."

"Does he play on the team?"

Pines laughed. "Nah. I don't think he knows nothin' about the game."

"Okay." I offered my hand. "Thanks for the tip about those players. I'll see they get a tryout."

• • •

There aren't a whole lot of improvements that can be made to the process of burning peach stones. After my innovation of using smaller loads, the job again became mechanical.

My arms shoveled and raked while I thought about Agnes O'Doul and Willie.

During tonight's break, I would tell her that I knew about the two of them. And, since he'd been telling other people things that he'd neglected to mention to his roomie and double play partner, I'd ask Aggie if Willie had said anything to her about someone who might have had a grudge against him.

The load of pits had charred to a uniform black, with only some of the edges burnt to flaky white ash. I pulled the tray from the flames and let it rest a minute on the edge of the oven door to cool. Once the wire mesh no longer glowed red, I picked up the tray in my gloved hands and dumped the coal into the bin at the left of the furnace. Then I shoveled up a fresh load of stones from the bin on the right side of the furnace to start all over again. It was as monotonous as the toe-touching exercises we had to do in spring training.

After sliding the newly filled tray back into the fire, I spread out the stones to make a thin even layer, then rested on my rake handle and looked back at Agnes O'Doul. I couldn't picture Willie telling her anything that would prove helpful. Hell, he hadn't been much for saying anything at all. But sometimes things slip out when you're talking to a sweet-heart.

I turned back to the oven. Poking the tines of the rake into the oven, I stirred the peach pits.

They suddenly exploded with a bright blinding flash. The oven boomed, sounding like the report of a cannon. The force of the blast sent me flying backward, my feet completely losing contact with the floor.

My tailbone was the first part of my anatomy to land on

the concrete floor. The pain of that impact caused another explosion to rip along my spine.

When I was no longer in motion, I mentally took an inventory of body parts: it felt like everything was where it was supposed to be, though my smarting backside made it difficult to feel anything else. My right hand was up, palm out, to shield my eyes. But I couldn't see it, couldn't make out any shapes. And the only image my brain conjured up was of me standing in the batter's box against Walter Johnson, totally blind. Then I realized I couldn't hear, either. Only the roaring sound of a waterfall in my ears.

My hearing came back first. I hoped it was only the first of my senses to return. I heard the crackling sounds that still echoed from the oven like bursting popcorn and people shouting fragments of sentences that all started with "What the—"

Then the sense of touch returned to the rest of my body, mostly a tingling sensation in the limbs. I didn't know if it was caused by the explosion or the shock of the landing.

Next, the feel of liquid in my right eye. I couldn't yet see, though. I brought my hand slowly to my face, hoping desperately that there would still be an eye there.

There was. They were both there. My lids were closed, and my right lid was covered with something wet. I brushed it away; the wetness returned and I wiped a few more times, then gave up when it was immediately moist again.

"Are you all right?" I heard. It took a moment to recognize the voice as Agnes O'Doul's.

"Don't know. Think so." Except for my eyes. They were wide open now and seeing nothing but sparkles.

I blinked a few times and got liquid in my right eye; it stung, causing me to blink more rapidly. I wiped at the eye and looked back up. Just as suddenly as the blast, Aggie's face was in front of me. I don't remember ever seeing anything so pretty.

"You look okay," she said. "Just some cuts, I think."

Curly Neeman's voice was the next I heard. "What the hell happened here?"

Agnes O'Doul answered him, "Mick— Rawlings here almost blew himself up."

Her words made it sound like I'd caused the explosion, and I didn't think it was true. I forced myself to sit up, then stand. I was unsteady, but all the moving parts seemed to be in working order. To Neeman, I explained, "I put a load in the oven, started to rake it, and *ka-boom!* It just blew up on me."

"Musta been rigged somehow. Sabotage!" He glared accusingly at the other workers who'd gathered around. "So which one of you is workin' for the Germans?"

They hustled back to their work stations. Neeman looked satisfied, though why I couldn't imagine. "You're supposed to be in charge of security," I said to him. "Why don't you do your damn job?"

Neeman's eyes bugged and his pincers started chewing the air.

Agnes, the only worker who remained near me, said, "Yeah. Ain't that why you're here, to keep this kind of thing from happening?"

His only answer was to order Agnes back to work and tell me I could go home early if I wanted to.

I did.

Chapter Sixteen

The following night, Wednesday, I was squirming in my seat at the weekly meeting of the Patriotic Knights of Liberty. The fidgeting wasn't solely due to the length of Frank Timmons's speech; it was primarily because my back still hurt from getting knocked on my ass in Bennett Harrington's chemical plant.

The soreness and lack of mobility kept me from playing in the afternoon game against St. Louis. I had the urge to play anyway, and in my younger days I would have stubbornly kept quiet about the injury rather than give up playing time. Now that I was wiser, I knew I had to put the interests of the club ahead of my desire for a few more at bats. A second baseman who can't bend over to field ground balls isn't an asset to his team. I didn't want to end up costing us a game by letting a grounder through my legs. Fred Mitchell, though he appeared skeptical at my story about having fallen down the cellar stairs, readily gave me the day off. Wally Dillard, who'd vetoed my "Pickles" Dillard suggestion, took my place at second base. He played it so well that I knew my back would be better by tomorrow. I don't mind sitting out one game for the benefit of the team, but I'm not about to lose my starting job to a seventeen-year-old.

Although Frank Timmons wasn't the sole cause of my discomfort, he was certainly adding to it. He'd been on an interminable tirade, ranting about yellow-bellied men who left the fighting to others. He did it with such conviction that it took a while until I realized that every man in the room, himself included, fell into that category.

Just when I was certain that I would never be able to stand again, Timmons came to a thundering conclusion. His audience, which never came to the realization that the "yellow-bellied" description could apply to them, applauded him enthusiastically, then left their seats to examine the weapons for sale and to talk in small groups.

I was the last out of my chair, painfully forcing myself to straighten up. I kept my head down, self-conscious about my appearance. The blast had singed off both of my eyebrows, then put one back in the form of a scab left by the cut over my right eye. I probably should have gotten it stitched but hadn't. Flying peach stone fragments had left several other cuts and scratches on my face, none of them deep but none of them attractive, either. I wore a straw boater tilted forward as far as it could go without falling off and kept the hat on indoors. The good news was that none of the fragments had penetrated my eyes, and my vision had completely cleared up.

From under the brim of my hat, I looked around the room. Wicket Greene was standing alone near a rusted engine block. I expected him to be with Lefty Rariden again, a couple of decrepit ballplayers commiserating together and talking about past glories that were largely fiction. Rariden's red hair was nowhere to be seen though.

I walked stiffly over to Greene; it occurred to me that the way I looked and moved qualified me for honorary status as decrepit. "Lefty not here tonight?" I asked.

"Ain'tcha heard?"

"Heard what?"

"He's gonna be pitching for Pittsburgh. They signed him this morning."

The Pirates' fans had my sympathy. "What they want him for? His arm's deader than—" Willie Kaiser came to mind. I searched for another way to end the sentence and came up with "the Federal League."

Greene shrugged. "He's over draft age and he can reach the plate. That's good enough these days."

If the pitching standards got any lower, I could end up batting over .300.

"How's the back?" Greene asked. There was no note of genuine concern; the question was merely to make conversation.

"It's getting better. I think."

"I heard about what happened at the plant, the bomb or whatever it was. That's sure lousy luck."

How did Greene know about that? "Nobody's supposed to know I'm working there," I said. Bennett Harrington had promised to keep quiet about it. Trying to maintain the pretense that my employment was for purely patriotic reasons, I added, "I just want to help in the war effort. I don't want any publicity."

"Then you better tell Curly Neeman to shut up about it."

Neeman. Of course. I spotted him near the weapons table, regaling a couple of other Knights with some loud story. "I think I'll do that." With a dismissive nod at Greene, I hobbled off to give Curly Neeman a few well-chosen words to the effect that he'd better shut up.

I'd almost reached him when a meaty hand clapped me on the back and sent a searing tremor along my spine. "Brother Rawlings! Are you *prepared?*"

I twisted to face Frank Timmons's sweating visage and issued an affirmative groan.

He touched my arm and indicated that he wanted me to join him at a vacant end of the room. I followed until my slow pace caused him to stop short of the destination. He lowered his pink round head. Maintaining a toothy grin, he said in a low voice, "I wanted to talk to you about your position at the Dearborn Fuel Company."

Curly Neeman must have told everyone I was working there. "What about it?"

"I have a proposition for you, Brother Rawlings. I need your help. The Patriotic Knights of Liberty needs your help. Your *country* needs you."

Warning bells in my head were pealing loudly. "To do what?" Please note the lack of enthusiasm in my voice, I silently hoped.

He didn't. "I'm glad you asked!" Timmons rested a hand on my shoulder and drew me toward him. "You remember that incident with the U-boat attacking Cape Cod?"

I nodded.

"Well, ever since then, the good men of the Patriotic Knights of Liberty have been arming themselves to the teeth. Acquiring a considerable number of weapons and a great deal of ammunition, and, uh, other materials." In other words, business was booming. "Demand has been so high,

I'm finding myself unable to satisfy it. That's where you can help."

"How?"

"In your position at the Dearborn Fuel Company, you surely have access to materials. Specifically gunpowder. If you can acquire such material for me—for us—you'll be doing a great service."

I didn't answer.

"And, of course, you will be generously compensated."

I ducked my head, not knowing what to say. The wasp-faced Curly Neeman was looking up at me. Somehow he'd weaseled himself into our conference. Timmons didn't seem disturbed by Neeman's presence. I suspected that Neeman was probably privy to many of Timmons's business dealings.

"The place I work in doesn't have that stuff." I addressed myself to Timmons. "All we got is peach pits."

Neeman piped up, "You could get a transfer."

"Fine idea, Brother Neeman!" Timmons transferred his hand from my shoulder to Neeman's. If Curly Neeman had a tail, the possibility of which I didn't entirely dismiss, it would have been wagging to show his pleasure at Timmons's approval.

"Might even be safer for you to move someplace else," Neeman added. "We found there was explosives in them peach stones. Maybe you should be working in a different building."

Instead of somebody bringing in a load of explosives I'd be right in the middle of where they made them. It didn't sound safer to me. "I'll see about that tomorrow," I said, trying to sound agreeable.

With the excuse of needing to rest my back, I left the meeting early.

By the time I reached my house, the trolleys had jostled my spine until it felt like I was impaled on a hot steel spike. When I got home, I made straight for the bathroom and a bottle of hot liniment.

I'd had a few thoughts about Timmons's proposal. One was that he must have had a previous source for gunpowder, but for some reason that source had dried up. The reason could be that the source was no longer at the Dearborn Fuel Company but pitching for the Pittsburgh Pirates instead. Lefty Rariden.

The other idea I came up with had to do with Willie Kaiser. If somebody at the plant had been smuggling out munitions, Willie could have stumbled onto it, and the reason for killing him might have been to keep him quiet.

Chapter Seventeen

Mickey!" The high-pitched cry came from behind the third base dugout.

I backed out of the three-way catch I'd been having with Fred Merkle and Wally Dillard. While Merkle and Dillard continued warming up for the opener of our series with the Braves, I ambled over to the front row seats to speak with Karl Landfors.

He was starting to look like the Landfors of old, which to my eyes was going in the wrong direction. His clothes were black and white and stiff and somber, and the tan was fading from his face. A new black derby was perched daintily on his head.

When I reached the railing, it was my appearance that received comment. "Somebody spike you in the face?" he asked.

"No. I'll tell you about it later."

"Okay." Landfors paused in a way that he intended to be dramatic. "I have something." He opened his coat far enough for me to see the tip of a brown envelope in an inside pocket.

I laughed. "You look like a man with an autopsy report." It wasn't the first time Karl Landfors had brought an autopsy report to a baseball game. I hoped it wasn't going to become a habit.

"Police report, too," he said with a self-satisfied smirk.

With all the things that had changed in the world, it was almost comforting that Landfors was reverting to his old familiar ways.

An attractive young brunette in a white shirtwaist and navy blue skirt asked Landfors for his ticket. The white straw hat pinned to her hair had *USHER* written on the hat band. Another recent change due to the war: for the first time, women were serving as ballpark ushers and, perhaps not coincidentally, attendance was starting to rise again.

"Meet me outside after the game," I said to him.

Landfors raised his hand in mock salute and followed the usherette back to his assigned seat.

It took several hours, and a couple gallons of saliva, until the game was over. Shufflin' Phil Douglas and Boston's Dick Rudolph, both spitballers, pitched twelve superb innings of shutout ball. Rudolph's spitter wasn't much—his own catcher once conceded that the most that could be said for it was that it was wet—but his control was terrific. After the Braves scored twice in the top of the thirteenth, Rudolph shut us down again in the bottom of the inning to take the win. I managed to play the entire game at second base with my back almost entirely free of pain.

I quickly showered and dressed and hustled out of the park to meet Landfors.

"Dinner?" he greeted me.

After a great game like that, his first thoughts are about food? Talk about un-American. "How 'bout if we grab a couple sandwiches and head back to my place," I suggested. "I gotta leave for work soon."

"I thought baseball was what you did for 'work'."

I explained about my job at the Dearborn Fuel Company and the explosion that left my face looking as it did.

"Accident?" he asked.

"If you can tell me how a pile of peach pits can accidentally explode."

Landfors actually pondered it for a while before he answered, "Beats me."

Then I told him about Curly Neeman's claim of sabotage.

"People are seeing saboteurs everywhere," he said. "If a fellow gets a flat tire, he thinks German agents are responsible."

I thought that what had happened to me was a little more severe and unusual than a flat tire, but I dropped it.

We stopped at a cafe for sandwiches and ginger ales. Landfors ordered roast beef. I opted for peanut butter. My visit to the Union Stockyards had killed my appetite for meat.

As the sandwiches were being prepared, he said, "I estimated some distances during the game. From your description of where Kaiser was marching when he got shot, I'd guess it was about seventy-five yards from where he was to across Sheffield Avenue."

I pictured the scene in my own mind. "Mmm . . . about two hundred fifty feet, I'd say."

Landfors peered at me over his spectacles. "Nearly the same thing."

"Oh." I'm a baseball player; I measure things in feet. Roughly three hundred feet from home plate to the outfield fence, ninety feet between bases, sixty feet from the plate to the pitching rubber. Sixty feet six inches really, but I can't see to that fine a resolution. Anyway, those are my references for distance.

We carried the dinners to my house. During the walk, Landfors filled me in on the information he'd obtained. "The autopsy report confirms what you told me. The bullet went through him at a horizontal angle, not vertically."

"They find the slug?"

"No. But according to the police report, they did find the rifle."

"Where?"

"Where you suspected. Second floor of one of the houses on Sheffield Avenue. The gunman left it there."

"Huh."

"It's a Mauser 'ninety-eight. Uses spitzer bullets."

"Ninety-eight caliber?" That sounded awfully big.

"No. Eighteen ninety-eight. The year that model came out."

"Oh. 'Mauser', 'spitzer'—those sound German."

"They are. Actually, there's an interesting story about that rifle. When the British brought out their first tanks, the Germans found that if they turned the bullet around, with the blunt end forward, it could blast right through the tanks' armor."

"That's what happened to Willie?"

"Well, no. It's just something I learned when I was over there."

I figured Landfors was entitled to show off some of his hard-earned knowledge, as long as it didn't distract us from determining what had happened to Willie.

I waved to Mrs. Tobin as we approached my house. "Nice lady," I said. "She got a boy in the army. Been working on a sweater for him for weeks now."

I opened the door and let Landfors through first. "It's funny," he said. "I know there's a lot of folks here knitting sweaters for the doughboys, but in three years I never saw a soldier wearing one."

"What difference does it make? As long as it makes her feel she's doing something to make her boy more comfortable."

Landfors's attention had already wandered. He pointed to the Mark Twain collection in the bookcase. "Finally decided you're going to learn to read?"

"Yeah. Might come in handy—in case you ever learn to write."

He grinned and sat down on the sofa.

After taking the soda bottles into the kitchen to open them, I brought them back to the parlor and sat down in my chair. Landfors was already nibbling at his sandwich; I ripped open the wrapping of mine and proceeded to catch up.

"The rifle being German," I said. "Could that be why the papers didn't know how to report the shooting?"

"Probably," he said, spitting crumbs on the floor. "He could have been killed by German-Americans angry that he wouldn't join them."

"Or by an American, like the kind who used to heckle him from the stands, who wanted to kill a German."

He nodded. "Or German saboteurs out to damage the American national pastime."

I rolled my eyes.

"I'm just saying what the papers could be thinking," he explained. "Not what I think."

Landfors talked between mouthfuls of roast beef. My responses were slightly delayed by the peanut butter.

I cleared some sandwich stuck to the roof of my mouth. "Or it could have been somebody wanting to cast suspicion on Germans."

"German-Americans angry at being persecuted," he suggested next.

"Why was he shot while marching?" I asked. "Maybe Germans who objected to the military drills?"

We ran out of guesses about the German connection. The sandwiches devoured, we worked on finishing the sodas.

"I don't think it had anything to do with Willie being German," I said. "I got a couple other theories."

"Like what?"

"Smuggling maybe. Willie was working in Bennett Harrington's chemical plant. Same place I'm working now, that's why I'm there. I think somebody was stealing gunpowder and stuff from the place. If Willie found out about it, that's a reason for somebody to kill him."

"Sure is."

"And here's another one: Wicket Greene is throwing games. Well, he's trying to anyway. He's making errors by the bushel. Like the way Hal Chase does, except Chase is a lot better at it. What if Willie found out about him throwing games?"

"Then Greene might kill him."

"Or whoever's behind it. Greene was marching along with us when Willie got shot. Somebody else had to pull the trigger. As a matter of fact, whatever's the real reason Willie was killed, I'm sure there was more than one person involved."

"A conspiracy?" Landfors's eyes lit up. His old muckraking instincts were aroused. "That would be wonderful."

"Why wonderful?" Besides the fact that Landfors loved

conspiracy theories as much as I liked slow hanging cur-veballs.

"When there's a conspiracy," he explained, "more than one person knows what happened. And eventually some-body will talk."

"You sure about that?"

"Absolutely. If you have an idea of who's involved, you can work one of them against another. Make them suspi-cious of each other, start them infighting. Get the weakest one to crack, and then it's all over."

Sounded simple. "I have a feeling that the Patriotic Knights of Liberty are in on it, too, somehow," I said. "Don't know exactly which ones though. If it's smuggling, that would involve different guys than if it's about throwing games." I pulled out my watch. "Oh, jeez. I better get going."

"Don't they give you a day off after you almost get your face blown off?"

"No. Anyway, I want to keep working at this. Only got a month left in the season. It ends on Labor Day, and this is August first. Not a whole lot of time to wrap things up."

Neither of us said aloud what we both knew: I couldn't wait until after the season was over, for then I'd be going to war.

Besides, I wanted to go back to the Dearborn Fuel Com-pany because it was there that I expected to find the weakest link in whatever conspiracy might exist: Curly Neeman.

•　•　•

I did a shoddy job during the first two hours of my shift. Careful to keep my face away from the front of the oven, I burned some of the peach stones and undercooked others.

I didn't worry much about it though; I knew the charcoal was sorted before going into the filter cans, so none of the sub-par material would end up in gas masks.

Curly Neeman didn't come by once during those two hours. At ten, when Agnes O'Doul and I pulled up our pails to sit down during the break, I commented to her, "Haven't seen the rat turd around tonight."

With a lick and a twist, she finished rolling a fat cigarette. "Not going to either, unless you see ghosts."

"What do you mean?"

"You really ain't heard?"

"Heard what?"

"They pulled Neeman out of the Chicago River this afternoon."

"Dead?"

"He wasn't taking a bath in it." She exhaled a cloud of smoke with a satisfied sigh. "Had a bullet in him."

Jeez. "Do they know who did it?"

"Didn't hear. But I can't imagine who would want to kill a fellow as sweet as Curly Neeman." Aggie's smile made it clear she wasn't exactly torn up about Neeman's death.

Neither was I. But I was damned annoyed. This was the one time I did want to talk to him and now I couldn't.

It must have happened in the last twenty-four hours, sometime after the Knights meeting. "What time was he killed?"

"What am I, a cop?" She rolled another, thinner, cigarette and lit it, quickly smoking it in silence, trying to finish it by the end of the break.

I tried to muster some bit of sympathy for Curly Neeman. His death didn't strike me as any great loss to humanity, but he was a human being. And from what I'd seen of him, he was more pathetic than evil. By ten past, when Aggie and I promptly resumed work, I was disappointed with myself that I could feel no sorrow for Neeman. All I felt was frustrated that somebody killed him before I could ask him if Rariden was smuggling ammunition out of the plant.

Chapter Eighteen

The Friday morning papers provided ample evidence that the Committee on Public Information—or the Illinois State Council of Defense or whatever group was in charge of censoring stories this week—was diligently at work. According to the sketchy articles published in the newspapers, Cecil "Curly" Neeman was killed in a holdup. The evidence for this conclusion: no money, watch, wallet, or other personal possessions were on him when he was found.

Neeman's body, with a gunshot wound to the chest, had been pulled from the Chicago River near the mouth of Ogden Slip. Since there was no identification on him, I wondered who identified him and how the papers knew his real name was Cecil.

More troublesome was the idea of a holdup man who bothers to dump his victim in a river. It didn't make sense. The robber shoots his prey, loots him of his belongings, and then? Instead of beating a quick getaway, he slows himself down by lugging the body to the river. I didn't buy it. Any of it.

The nonsense they were printing was so useless that I renewed my resolution to not read the newspapers anymore.

And I worried that, with Curly Neeman dead, I might have lost the weakest link in the conspiracy that led to Willie Kaiser's murder.

• • •

Buck Herzog led off the Braves' fifth inning with a bunt single to the pitcher's mound that Hippo Vaughn wasn't agile enough to field (he wasn't called "Hippo" without reason). Before taking his lead off first base, Herzog exchanged a few friendly words with Fred Merkle. The two of them had been teammates on the 1908 Giants during the first of Herzog's three stints with John McGraw. All three of us had played for McGraw for about one month in the summer of 1916. Allies one month, enemies the next.

Boston's small southpaw pitcher Art Nehf was next in the batter's box. On Vaughn's second pitch, Nehf poked a medium speed bouncer to Wicket Greene at shortstop. Easy double play for anyone but Greene, who turned every fielding chance into an adventure.

I scooted over to take the throw at second base, silently urging him, "Catch the ball! Catch the ball!" It took a true bounce, reached him belt-high, and he caught it cleanly in his mitt. Yes! Then the transfer to his throwing hand. Again clean. I straddled the bag, ready to sweep one foot across it and relay the throw to first base. Then Greene slowly double pumped before throwing me the ball. Damn! I had to remain planted on the base and wait helplessly for the ball to arrive while Buck Herzog bore down on me to break up the double play. The ball struck my mitt a split second before Herzog's spikes, with one hundred sixty pounds of Herzog behind them, impaled themselves in my left shin.

I flipped over and hit the earth hard but held onto the ball. Herzog was out; Nehf was safe at first. Herzog paused before trotting off the field to see if I was going to come up fighting. I didn't. He wasn't to blame. It was Wicket Greene who'd broken up the double play and got me spiked. For form's sake, I gave Herzog a cussing as I rose but let it go at that. Greene wasn't going to get off so easy.

The next two Braves went down on strikeouts to end the inning. Running off the field, I caught up to Greene by the third base bag. "After the game," I said. "Just you and me."

Greene bared his crooked brown teeth. "You want a piece of me?" He poked me in the chest.

"Yeah!" I shoved him in return. He tripped over the base and fell backward to the ground.

"Then get it now," he snarled. Faster than I thought he could move, Greene flung off his mitt and sprang up at me.

I dropped my glove and threw a sharp left jab at his nose. Contact! He quickly recovered, responding with a hard upper cut to my stomach. Those were more good punches than usually get thrown in a baseball fight; after that brief flurry, we settled into the traditional grappling and wrestling.

Fred Mitchell barked, "Get in here you idiots!"

Teammates pulled us apart and dragged us to the dugout. I was put at one end of the bench and Greene was placed at the other. Fred Mitchell paced the length of the dugout and launched into a managerial tongue-lashing directed at both of us. It was cut short when the umpire called for a batter and I remembered that I was leading off the inning. As I grabbed my bat, I stole a look at Greene and saw he was shoving the twisted corner of a towel up his nose to stem the flow of blood. It was a highly satisfying sight.

We played the rest of the game without exchanging blows or words. I was only vaguely aware that the Braves won the game, and I didn't know by what score.

In the locker room afterward, Fred Merkle made sure he was always in our proximity ready to break us up again if needed. Greene and I both dawdled; neither of us was going to leave before the other did—that would have seemed like running from a fight. Wally Dillard hung around, too, until he and Merkle were the only ones left besides Greene and me. "Want me to stick around?" my roomie whispered.

"No, that's okay," I said. "Thanks."

As Dillard started to leave, Fred Merkle said, "Hold up, kid. I'll go with you." Looking back at Greene and me, he said, "Go ahead and kill each other if you want. *I* don't care no more." He joined Dillard at the door, telling him, "This could be your big break, kid. If one of them ends up dead, you'll get to start tomorrow."

Don't call him "kid," I thought to myself.

Wicket Greene was the first to get off his stool. He walked slowly toward my locker and I stood to face him. His nose was red and swollen. "Why don't we just drop it," he mumbled.

"Drop it?"

"Yeah. I don't want to fight." He exposed his rotting teeth in a smile that was supposed to look friendly.

"Okay," I agreed warily. I didn't really want to touch my fist to a face that ugly again anyway.

Greene sat down on Wally Dillard's stool. "Been some crazy kind of year, ain't it?" he said.

I sat back down as well. "Yeah. Sure has." On impulse, I

decided to confront him directly. "And you been throwing games."

Greene's eyes flared. I tensed, still ready to fight. Then he sagged visibly. "No. You got it wrong."

"I checked the record books. You got more errors this year than you made in the last eight years put together. All of a sudden you forgot how to catch and throw a baseball?"

"No, no. That ain't it."

"Then what is it? What happened?"

Greene sighed. "I got old is what happened."

"Nobody ages that fast."

"It's . . ." He held out his hands, then dropped them. His head dropped, too; he shook it slowly, sadly.

"You were trying to throw games," I repeated. "And Willie Kaiser found out about it, so you killed him."

His head jerked back up. "What are you, nuts?" he squawked.

"Not yourself," I said calmly. "You were marching along with the rest of us when he got shot. Somebody else pulled the trigger for you. Maybe one of your friends in the Knights?"

"You got it all wrong."

"What's wrong about it?"

"Kaiser didn't know nothing about it! There was no reason for me to kill him."

"So you *were* throwing games, but Willie didn't know about it?"

"No—it's—what happened was—"

"For gamblers? I been seeing a lot of them in the hotel lobbies."

Greene surrendered. "For Bennett Harrington."

"Harrington?"

"Yeah. But I never threw a game. I was supposed to, but I didn't."

"Why were you supposed to? Was Harrington paying you?"

"No. He promised me I'd be starting shortstop when he took over the team."

Was Charles Weeghman right, except it was Bennett Harrington and not William Wrigley who wanted to oust him as owner of the Cubs? "You were already starting shortstop," I pointed out.

Greene grunted something like a laugh. "Not for long. I saw how Kaiser could play in spring training. He was gonna have my job in no time. Harrington said if I threw some games, he'd guarantee me a starting job."

"So you began making all those errors at the start of the season—"

"They weren't intentional," Greene insisted. "I just got so tight thinking about it that I couldn't do anything right. Harrington thought I was doing exactly what he wanted me to, but I wasn't. I wasn't trying to, anyway."

"But then Mitchell gave your job to Willie Kaiser, and to keep your deal with Harrington, you had to get Willie out of there. So you—"

"No! I had nothing to do with that. Harrington had me do other stuff when I wasn't playing."

"Like what?"

Greene hesitated. "You remember when somebody put pretzels in the concession stands?"

"That was you?"

He nodded. "Look, I didn't have nothing against Kaiser personally. I just wanted him out of there so I could keep playing a little longer. That's all."

This was too much information for me to digest. I shifted subjects. "What about the Knights? Why'd you join them?"

"Why'd you?" he shot back.

I shrugged. "Seemed the thing to do." No need to tell Greene the true reason.

"Same here."

I recalled what I'd told Landfors: that I believed the Knights were somehow involved in killing Willie. "They don't seem to do much though," I said. "Frank Timmons makes his speeches, then tries to sell everybody guns and ammo and stuff."

It was Greene's turn to shrug.

"You know anything about him?" I asked.

"Not much. I hear he was with the Klan in Georgia. Came up here a year or so ago to do some organizing for them, then he started the Knights."

"Are the Knights connected to the Klan?"

"Hell, how do I know? All these secret societies and fraternities and patriotic organizations. . . . I can't tell one from the other." After a lengthy silence, he asked, "Can we keep all this between us?"

"Who am I gonna tell?"

Greene stood and brushed off his jacket. "Well, see you tomorrow, I guess."

I remained seated and didn't answer.

He walked to the locker room door, then stopped to ask, "You wanna get a couple beers?"

"No."

• • •

Much to my surprise, on Saturday night I was at the Chapman home, the recipient of an unexpected dinner invitation. Although Edna was the one who had phoned to invite me, she'd made it clear that it was her mother who wanted me to come.

Supper turned out to be a dreary affair. There were four of us, including Hans Fohl, who appeared as uncomfortable as I felt at being there. I thought perhaps Edna's mother was trying to get back to normal, so she'd invited the same guests who had attended the last dinner she'd given before Willie's death. It was immediately clear to the rest of us at the table that with Willie gone things couldn't be the same as before.

Mrs. Chapman had even prepared the same dishes, though not as well as a month before: the whale meat was fatty and undercooked, the liberty bread grittier than usual, and the sauerkraut bland.

Edna said nothing throughout the meal. Fohl and I took turns murmuring sympathetic sounds at Mrs. Chapman's oft-repeated lament that "I'm bad luck for my men, is what I am."

Mrs. Chapman, considerably thinner than she'd been a month before, picked at her food while the rest of us finished quickly or simply gave up eating. I tried to rearrange what was on my plate to make it look like I'd consumed most of it. And I wished the dogs were under the table so I could slip it to them, though that might have gotten me in trouble with the Humane Society.

When the conversation dwindled to a long lull and we had all given up on the main course, Edna offered to serve the apple pie I'd brought for dessert. There were no takers.

"I thought maybe I'd walk off dinner," I said. "And take the dogs out."

"Go ahead," Edna said curtly. I wasn't going to have the pleasure of her company.

After getting the frisky dachshunds from their room, I asked Hans Fohl, "Feel like some air?"

"Why not," he agreed. The expression on his face reflected my own thoughts: anything to get out of this house for a while.

We left with a promise to "be back soon" and the intention to stretch out the walk as long as we could. Fohl took one of the dogs, while I tried to control three of them.

For at least five minutes we slowly progressed without exchanging a word. Then I said to Fohl, "I visited the tannery where you work a few days ago."

"I know. I saw you."

"Never saw so much leather in my life. All those hides. The supervisor, Bill Pines was his name?"

Fohl nodded.

"He told me it's almost all used for the army—belts and harnesses and such."

"That's right."

"Not much available for making shoes and purses anymore. In fact, you can't hardly find a pair of high-button shoes anywhere." I paused. "Except at your church. You remember when you were taking me around and the old man showed you those nice shoes? And he kept thanking you?"

Fohl was reddening and his droopy jowls hung a bit lower.

I was thinking of trying to blackmail him for information but chose to play it straight. "Look," I said. "If your stealing some leather from the tannery, I don't care about it. I'm not going to tell anyone. And I don't care what kind of meetings you have at the church, either. I'll bet there's more going on there than you let me see, but all I want to know is this: did any of it involve Willie?"

He shook his head no.

"Anyone angry at Willie for not joining the group?"

"Only me. And only sometimes."

"Nobody would want to kill him?"

"What? Hell, no." He paused. "You know what we do there?"

"More than give music lessons, I bet."

"Okay, yeah. Some of the guys get together and talk about what we'd like to do. But it's just talk, see? A chance to blow off steam. Can't do it anywhere else. They'll put you in jail if you do. Some of the guys talk big, but there's nothing more than that."

"You sure?"

"Yes."

I accepted his word, and we maneuvered the dogs back to Paulina Street. As we approached the Chapman house, Fohl said, "That old man you saw with the shoes, he's a cobbler. And he's been having a real tough time of it. Folks are boycotting German businesses. I'm just trying to help him put a little food on the table."

"I'd probably do the same," I said.

We stepped into the house to find a Ouija board set up on the dinner table. Oh no, I thought. There was almost a national craze for the things. Those with a son in the military used the board to find out what would happen to him; those whose son had been killed used it to communicate with his spirit. I didn't want to be talking to Willie's ghost.

Both Fohl and I had to take our turns at working the board, but it didn't do anything when we touched it. The only time the Ouija board gave a message was when Edna and her mother were using it.

I said my good-byes, probably sooner than was polite but I had to get out of the Chapman home. I left with the fervent desire that I would be invited to no more dinners and the impression that Edna Chapman shared that hope.

On the way home, I realized that tomorrow would be August fourth, the one month anniversary of Willie's death. It occurred to me that I would think of every Fourth of July from now on as the day Willie Kaiser was killed.

Chapter Nineteen

Sunday emerged warm and hazy from the muggy darkness of Saturday night. It was an off day, a break in the Cubs' baseball schedule. I made it a day of rest, determined to remain in the relative cool of my house and indulge in some badly needed idleness. And in the sultry embrace of a hot bath. My new water tank had finally been installed.

The problem was that physical rest doesn't keep the brain from traipsing about on its own pursuits.

During a leisurely breakfast of coffee and oatmeal cookies, I mulled over my conversation with Wicket Greene. If he was lying to me, he was a pretty convincing liar, and I'd seen some of the best. If he was telling the truth, then it looked like Bennett Harrington was behind the sabotage at Cubs Park.

But why would Harrington have Greene throw games if not to bet on the outcome? And if the purpose was to make money at gambling, how did the other incidents fit in? What profit could Harrington make from seats being sawed or pretzels left in the concession booths or smoke bombs tossed in the grandstand?

If these episodes were part of whatever scheme Bennett Harrington had going, could Willie's murder be part of it as well? Had Willie discovered what Harrington was up to?

And Curly Neeman getting killed—how did that fit in? If it did at all. There were also the Patriotic Knights of Liberty. To what extent were they involved?

My brain eventually wound its way to something more closely resembling my original theory: Wicket Greene, perhaps at the behest of Bennett Harrington, was throwing games; Willie found out about it; Greene got his fellow Knight Curly Neeman to kill him; then Greene killed Neeman to keep him from talking.

Breakfast finished, I called Karl Landfors at his place in Rosemont and laid it all out for him. "Neeman and Greene were both in the Knights," I said. "It could be they just met there and that's how they hooked up. But I think somebody might have been pulling their strings."

"Whom do you think it is?"

Whom. Landfors was definitely reverting to his old ways. So much for my hopes that he would become a regular guy. "Could you check on Frank Timmons?" I asked. "He's in charge of the group. I heard he used to be with the Klan in Georgia if that helps any."

"It should. You think Timmons is behind it?"

"Don't know. But he's a logical starting point. I'd bet somebody's using these guys. Curly Neeman wasn't the brightest candle on the cake, like my uncle used to say. And Wicket Greene ain't a whole lot brighter."

Landfors promised to do his best, we hung up, and I proceeded to fill the bath tub with steaming hot water. I didn't care that it wasn't the most sensible thing to do on a hot summer day. While soaking in the tub, I continued to think things over. I decided it might be worth finding out exactly what happened to Curly Neeman as well. And I was determined to do it on my own. I didn't want to be always depending on Karl Landfors for information.

After the bath and a change into some fresh light summer clothes, I plucked *The Adventures of Tom Sawyer* from the bookcase and spent the remainder of the day with Tom and Huck and the rest of the gang. It was while Tom and Becky were lost in McDougal's cave that it occurred to me: Why did Wicket Greene tell me what he had about Bennett Harrington? Why admit anything about throwing games?

• • •

My Monday morning visit to the downtown County Building, which housed the offices of the Cook County Coroner, turned out to be highly educational. For one thing, I learned that there's no great trick to obtaining information from public employees, not even from those who are supposed to keep it secret. Once you've identified the civil servant who has access to the documents you're seeking, it's more a matter of negotiation than investigation.

One of the deputy coroners, a fragile-looking, pale young man with thick spectacles, charged me ten dollars for the autopsy report and an extra five dollars to translate it for me. Landfors probably could have argued him down in price; since I didn't know what the going rates were, I paid it.

"It was routine," he explained. "Neeman, Cecil, a.k.a. 'Curly.' Killed by a single bullet to the heart—"

"What kind of bullet?"

He nodded approvingly at the question. "Don't know for

sure. The slug lodged in the spine; we dug it out, but it was badly damaged."

"Any guess as to caliber?"

"Rough guess: forty-five."

"And it was the bullet that killed him? He didn't drown?"

He laughed. "No. Neeman was one hundred percent dead before he hit the water."

"Anything else?"

He skimmed the report. "Everything is consistent with death by gunshot. And the body showed the usual signs of having been in water for . . . oh, not longer than overnight, I don't think." I could have confirmed this since I'd seen Neeman alive the evening before his body was found, but I was here to get information, not volunteer it. The deputy coroner added, "There's one thing that's unusual, but it has nothing to do with the cause of death."

"What's that?"

"Burn marks."

"Burn marks?"

"On the arm. And some bruises here and there. But like I said, that's not what killed him."

"What caused the burns?"

"That's what's interesting. They hadn't scarred over yet, so they were fairly fresh. They were small and localized, like a lit cigar would do. I've seen lots of those. A cigar's a wonderful way to torture somebody. But these looked a little different. The skin didn't pucker around the wound like it does when you touch a cigar to it. I could swear . . ." His face contorted into a series of odd expressions as he searched his memory. "Oh yes! About a year ago, I had a customer with similar marks. A bank robber. Eventually got himself shot in a holdup, which is how he became a customer. Anyway, he had a tattoo on his arm that he tried to burn off with a candle. Looked the same as what your friend Neeman had. Of course, Neeman being in the water might have affected the way the wounds looked."

"A candle. . . . Would a blowtorch make the same mark?"

"Hmm. Probably."

I sighed. "One more thing. What about the police report? Do you have that?"

"Oh no. You'd have to get that from the police." He told me who to see in the police department and added that the report was classified. That meant expensive. Which meant it would have to wait for another time. I couldn't afford to buy any more information today.

• • •

Behind the shutout pitching of Wilbur Cooper, the Pittsburgh Pirates took the opener of our series 4–0. None of their runs was due to Wicket Greene's fielding; he played a flawless shortstop. Much better than I did at second base. I booted two grounders, which led to three of the Pirates' runs. The first error was embarrassing; by the time I made the second, I knew exactly what Greene meant about tightening up.

After the game, I took a cursory shower and changed quickly into a tan poplin suit. I still had a full day ahead of me.

First stop: Charles Weeghman's office upstairs in Cubs Park. Before he got on me again to step up my investigating efforts, I thought I'd head him off by volunteering a report on my progress.

His spacious office was filled with plaques, trophies, and certificates all attesting to what an upstanding citizen, magnanimous businessman and generally fine fellow he was. Weeghman gave me little time to inspect the testimonials. The first words out of his mouth, while his cigar remained in it, were, "You got something for me?"

"Just wanted to let you know what I found out so far."

"What?" He didn't offer a seat, so I stood. That was fine with me; I didn't want to stay any longer than I had to.

"The only thing I've been able to pin down so far is the pretzels."

Weeghman yanked the cigar from his teeth. "Who did it?"

"It was an accident. One of the guys working the concession stands stocked them by mistake. After it hit the papers, he was afraid to admit it. Poor kid needs the job." It bothered me some, but not much, that I was starting to get a little too adept at lying and too willing to resort to it.

"Give me his name."

"Might be better if I didn't. If the papers find out you fired some hard-working kid for making an honest mistake, they'll really go after you."

Weeghman grunted. "You trying to protect me from myself again? Like the way I shouldn't know where you're going and who you're talking to?" A wry smile twitched at his face.

"No," I said. "To tell you the truth, I care more about the kid. He's got a family to feed." Truth? I had to remind myself that this whole yarn was a lie.

Weeghman simmered briefly, then burst into laughter. "If this ain't the goddamnedest year. I got a second baseman who tells me to my face that he cares more about some peanut vendor than he does about me, the man who can make or break him. Well, you may not be smart, but at least you're honest."

Yeah, and you're perceptive, I thought.

"Fine, keep it to yourself," he decided. "But if you find out anything about the smoke bombs or anything else, you'll tell me, right?"

"Right." That wasn't a lie—yet.

Satisfied for now, Weeghman waved his cigar at me. I was dismissed.

• • •

Next stop: the West Side, specifically Wood Street between Polk and Taylor.

On the north side of Polk Street were the manicured lawns and impressive brick buildings of Cook County Hospital. South of Polk was the Chicago Cubs' former home park, the West End Grounds. The Cubs played there for more than twenty years until Charles Weeghman moved them into his Federal League park after the 1915 season.

On Wood Street, across from the West End Grounds' left field fence, was Agnes O'Doul's apartment.

Both of our shifts at the Dearborn Fuel Company started at eight o'clock. I was in front of her three-story apartment building at quarter-to-seven. I briefly debated whether to go to her door or simply wait for her to come out. Since I hadn't had supper yet, I elected to eat at a next-door lunch counter first. While munching a grilled cheese sandwich, I kept an eye on the front window. Agnes would have to pass by on her way to work. Sandwich, ginger ale, a slice of peach pie, two cups of coffee, another piece of pie, and it was almost seven-thirty.

I'd finally decided to go to her door when she stepped outside, almost bowling me over.

"What are you doing here?" The tone was brusque but not hostile.

I stepped back and mumbled something to the effect that I'd come to talk to her. I was struck by how different Agnes looked outside of the plant, out of her coveralls and cap. She was attractively dressed in a simple, trim frock of chocolate brown with a white scarf. From her yellow summer bonnet, chestnut hair hung almost to her shoulders. She wasn't ever going to be on a burlesque stage, but there were aspects of her appearance that were most definitely feminine and appealing.

"How do you know where I live?" She sounded defensive.

"Made a couple calls."

"I'm on my way to work."

"I know. Thought I'd join you." I added, "If you don't mind."

She shrugged and started walking south at a rapid pace. "What did you want to talk about?"

I hustled to keep up with her. "Willie Kaiser and Curly Neeman." Agnes seemed a no-nonsense type, so I thought I'd be up front with her and see where it got me.

After a few steps she asked, "What about them?"

"Did Neeman tell you who killed Willie?"

She pulled up short and gave me a stony glare. I suppose I was too blunt. "Don't know what you're talking about," she said firmly.

We stood in the middle of the crowded sidewalk while pedestrians brushed past us. I said softly, "I know you and Willie were, uh, keeping company."

"He told you?"

"We were roommates." Evading isn't the same as lying.

"He wasn't supposed to tell anybody."

"I also know—you told me yourself—that Curly Neeman was always riding Willie at work."

Agnes nodded.

"And it was clear from what I saw that you and Neeman weren't exactly buddies."

"We hated each other." She resumed walking. "Don't want to be late."

As we walked, somewhat slower now, I leaned to her ear and said, "Somebody took a blowtorch to Curly Neeman before they shot him."

"What are you, a cop?"

"No. I was a friend of Willie's, and all I want is to know who killed him. If it was Curly Neeman, then I guess that's it—nothing more to do. If it wasn't, I want to find out who did it."

"It was Curly Neeman," she said simply.

"Did you—"

"I didn't kill him, no. All I did was encourage him to talk."

"With the—"

"Torch. And he admitted he shot Willie." She smiled. "The little pissant admitted it pretty quick, too."

I had to force myself not to envision what she'd done. "Did Neeman say anything else? Did he do it on his own, or were there others in on it?"

"Does it matter?"

"Yes."

"He didn't say if there were others. At the plant, Neeman was always threatening Willie with what the Knights were going to do to him. I think it was just talk though. Neeman made it sound like he had a whole army at his command. Made the little pissant feel a big man, I guess."

So that was how Willie had heard about the Knights. Maybe he learned something from Neeman that caused him to warn Hans Fohl about them. "Neeman didn't give you any other names when you talked to him?"

"No. He just kept saying it was a mistake."

"Well, there *was* somebody else involved."

"Who?"

"Whoever killed Curly Neeman to shut him up."

We said little more until our ten o'clock break at the plant, when Agnes went to her toolbox and brought me a small bundle wrapped in a dirty rag.

I tugged open the knot to find a handful of peach stones. Unlike the shells I'd been shoveling in the oven, these were whole stones. "What are these for?"

She reached over and plucked one of them from the rag. With an easy twist, she broke it open. It was filled with dark powder. "Gunpowder," she said. "Curly Neeman tried to kill you, too. I pulled these out of the bin after you got hurt that night. There were a lot in there. He filled them with gunpowder and glued them closed."

"He told you that?"

"No. But do you have any doubt?"

I thought a moment. "No." Boy, it sure was a good thing I'd started using smaller loads in the oven.

"You want to keep these?" Agnes asked.

"No, that's okay." I walked to a trash bin and dumped them. When I got back, I asked her, "Why did you think it was Curly Neeman who killed Willie? Just because of the way he was harassing him? Lots of people were doing that."

"It was more than what he said to Willie; it's what he said to me." She rubbed her nose with her palm. "After Willie was killed, Neeman liked to drop hints to me that he did it. Bragging about it, I guess."

"Jeez, what a bastard."

Agnes elaborated on that description with words that would have made John McGraw blush.

No one came to tell us when it was ten past, but we promptly went back to work as soon as the break was over.

Standing at my oven, I kept glancing over my shoulder at Aggie O'Doul. I was becoming fascinated by this woman who could put a blowtorch to a man. I had to admit that instead of being repulsed by what she had done I admired her for it.

Chapter Twenty

Lefty Rariden warmed up for the bottom of the second inning by throwing everywhere but to his catcher. He succeeded in plunking the Pirates' batboy and almost hit umpire Bill Klem. When he was younger, and capable of hurling bullets, Rariden's carefully rehearsed display of wildness planted fear in the minds of batters who'd have to face him. He could no longer throw fast enough to scare anyone but still performed his routine, either out of habit or to maintain his colorful image.

When he'd finished, Klem barked "Batter up!" and I dug in at the plate.

Rariden pulled off his dark blue cap and mussed his red hair with his glove before replacing the cap at an arrogant angle. He then made some peculiar facial expressions intended to further distract me.

C'mon, throw the damn ball already.

The next instant, without the preliminary of a wind-up, he sent the ball speeding at my head. I staggered back just in time. There was more heat on it than I expected could come from Lefty Rariden's aged right arm. Them old guys can really surprise you sometimes.

I backed out of the box and knocked the sides of my spikes with my bat. I should have known it was coming. At the Knights meeting Rariden had said that he owed me one. I stepped back in. Rariden went into a windmill wind-up this time. Just before he delivered the pitch, my memory corrected itself: he'd said that he owed me two. Sure enough, his second pitch was another knockdown, but I avoided it easily.

He'd kept his word, twice attempting to put me on my ass. I guessed correctly that the next pitch would be over the plate. It was a fat one, knee-high down the middle. I swung high, missing the ball by a foot, and sent the bat spinning out of my hands to the pitcher's mound. It spun like a propeller blade, and Rariden had to leap over it to keep from taking it on the shins. Yup, there's no end of useful things you can do with a baseball bat.

Rariden had a broad grin on his long face. It was his turn again. Another quick pitch at my head to get back at me for the thrown bat.

My turn. Once again I launched the bat at him to even things up for the latest beanball attempt.

In his finest umpire voice, Bill Klem announced loudly and calmly, "I hate to spoil your fun gentlemen, but I hope you're aware that you just worked yourselves to a full count. Now play ball!"

I dug in for the next pitch. Rariden threw a slow round-house curveball; it started for a spot a foot behind my head, then bent into an arc and kept bending. My head knew where the pitch was going, but my rear end was fooled—it was retreating to the dugout as the ball broke over the plate. I swung late and missed by a mile.

Lefty Rariden won this contest. I threw my bat on the ground, cursing Rariden in particular and elderly pitchers in general. They get so damn devious after they've started getting on in years.

He used the slow curve on me again in the fourth. It was once too often; I hung in there and drove a line single to right field. In the seventh and ninth innings, he played a little too fine with the corners of the plate and walked me both times. There were no more beanballs or thrown bats. Things were all square between us.

By the end of the ninth inning, Rariden was a very congenial fellow. He'd won the ballgame, outpitching a partially inebriated Phil Douglas. I sometimes suspected that Douglas was a pitcher primarily because it allowed him several days of uninterrupted drinking between starts. He'd cut it too close this time, but since we were as short of pitchers as we were of everything else, Fred Mitchell let him keep his turn in the rotation.

An hour after the game, I was sitting with my new buddy, the now jovial Lefty Rariden. The two of us were in an anonymous dimly lit Rush Street saloon of his choosing, swilling illegal beers, very good illegal beers, which I no longer hesitated to order. Breaking the law distressed me far less than being in Rariden's company.

Earlier in the season, a visit from the Pirates would have meant a chance to get together again with my pal Casey Stengel. But Casey had left the Pirates in June to enlist in the Navy. Lefty Rariden, whose stories and jokes were more offensive than funny, was a poor substitute for Casey as a drinking companion.

Casey got his nickname from "K. C.," Kansas City, his home town. Wally Dillard was from Oak Park. Maybe O. P. was a name for him: Opie Dillard. I'd have to see what he thought.

Rariden snorted. "Sure blew you guys away today. Hard to believe I ain't pitched a game in three years!" It wasn't the first time he'd complimented himself on his performance; through the first two rounds of beer he'd been alternating between telling dirty jokes and praising his own pitching.

"Yeah, hard to believe." It wasn't the first time I'd given him that same response, either. This time I added, "What do you think of your new team?"

"Pittsburgh ain't a bad club," he acknowledged. "Of course, if they was smart, they'd have signed me back in the spring. With me pitching for them all season, they'd be doing a lot better than third place. Be giving you guys a run for the pennant."

I ignored his conceit; few pitchers were known for modesty. "Last team you were on was the Whales wasn't it?" The Chicago Whales, Charles Weeghman's Federal League team.

The gleeful look faded from his face and Rariden called for two more beers. "Yeah, that's right," he answered. "Say, you hear the one about—"

"How'd you like playing for the Feds?" When I'd first met Rariden at the Knights meeting, he'd asked if we'd known each other from the Federal League. At the *New York Press* office, when I'd checked the *Spalding Guides* for Wicket Greene's fielding statistics, I'd also looked up Rariden's record: he'd pitched for the Chicago Feds during both years of their existence and had been out of organized baseball ever since.

Rariden downed most of the brew that the bartender

placed in front of him. "I liked it fine," he said with a belch. "Some damn fine ballplayers in that league. We drew good crowds in most cities, made decent salaries, and the Whales took the pennant in 'fifteen. Only championship team I ever been on."

"And then the league folded. Must have been tough on you."

"Damn right. Nobody wanted me anymore. The regular leagues took the younger kids back, the ones who had a future. It was us old guys who got punished for jumping to the Feds; the owners figured we only had one or two good years left, so they'd make an example out of us." He finished the rest of his beer in one long swallow and called for another. I was starting to lag behind.

"Say, Lefty, I need your advice on something."

"Sure, and what's that?" He looked relieved at the change of topic.

"At the last Knights meeting, Frank Timmons asked me about getting some, uh, material out of the chemical plant."

"Yeah?"

"Wasn't hard to put two and two together. Figured you had to be his previous supplier. So, what I want to know is, how hard is it to do?"

Rariden laughed. "It's easy if you know the right people." He made no attempt to deny it.

"And who's the right people?"

After another swallow of beer, he answered out of the side of his mouth, "Harrington."

"Bennett Harrington? He—"

"Let me take the stuff out, yeah. It was just old-fashioned black powder, anyway, not the new smokeless stuff. Talk to him. See if you can make the same deal."

"A deal goes two ways. What does he get out of it? A cut of what I'd get from Timmons?"

He laughed again. "Not even. Just do him a favor now and then."

"A favor like . . . ?"

"Oh, anything that might hurt Charles Weeghman."

I made a quick connection. "Like putting smoke bombs in the stands?" If Rariden had access to powder, smoke bombs would have been easy for him to make.

His broad wink confirmed it, though his spoken answer was, "You never heard me say that."

"And you have no fondness for Weeghman anyway," I pointed out. "When he sold out the Feds, you lost your career."

Rariden growled, "Bastard should have picked me up for the Cubs. He made a deal to cover his ass and hung the rest of us out to dry."

Lefty Rariden had a pretty sweet deal himself: he got paid by Frank Timmons for smuggling out gunpowder that he was allowed to smuggle in exchange for hurting a man he wanted revenge against. "You were doing okay," I said. "Almost sounds too bad the Pirates signed you."

He gave me a wide-eyed stare that wasn't a put-on. "Are you *nuts?* I'd rather be playing ball than doing anything else."

A trio of young bruisers in United States Navy garb swaggered into the saloon. Judging by the way they were speaking and walking, it wasn't the first one they'd been in today.

Rariden's eyes narrowed and followed the men as they took seats at the end of the bar. The presence of the boisterous sailors seemed to antagonize him; I don't think he liked for anyone to be louder or more obnoxious than himself.

While Rariden was preoccupied with glaring at his rivals, I mentally regrouped. Since Curly Neeman had hinted to Aggie O'Doul that he'd shot Willie, he might have bragged to his buddies in the Knights about it, too. Even if shooting Willie Kaiser was a mistake, as he'd claimed to Agnes, Neeman would want to get whatever glory he could for having killed a German.

"Lefty?" I said.

No response.

I couldn't capture Rariden's attention until I started a joke about a traveling salesman and a farmer's wife. At the punch line, Rariden issued a belly laugh and cried, "That's a good one! 'Do you have to use my butt for a tally board?' Hah!"

Moving quickly on, I said, "Any of the guys in the Knights ever get carried away?"

"Carried away how?"

"By putting one of those guns Timmons sells to use. I heard one of them might have killed a guy just because the guy had a German name."

"Naw. Really?" Rariden looked genuinely taken aback. "I never heard about nothing like that."

Damn. "Okay," I said. "Maybe I heard wrong."

Rariden cocked his head in the direction of the sailors. "Feel like having a little fun?"

"What kind of fun?"

"Let's take 'em on. Show 'em ballplayers are every bit as tough as navy gobs." He was itching for a barroom brawl to further enhance his colorful reputation.

"Uh, no, not for me, thanks. I got to be heading home." I ended up in enough fights without looking for new ones. Maybe I was truly a utility player at heart, for I had no desire to be colorful.

Rariden must have really been feeling his oats after the victory at Cubs Park; as I rose to leave the bar, he rolled up his sleeves and said, "Hell, there's only three of 'em. That's just about the right number for me to take on myself."

I went home with an easy conscience; whether or not Lefty Rariden survived his own foolhardiness didn't concern me.

As I passed Mrs. Tobin's house, I noticed she wasn't on her front porch. I hadn't seen her there for several days, so I paused for a moment to look at her empty rocker. Something glinted in the window behind it. It was the service flag: the blue star had been replaced by a gold one.

Damn. Harold Tobin wasn't coming back.

Chapter Twenty-One

Chicago wasn't the Windy City today. The air was stagnant and muggy, and the entire city sweltered in its sticky grip. Although noon was hours away, the thermometer had already topped ninety degrees.

The windows of Bennett Harrington's corner office were wide open, but there was no cross-breeze. All that passed through them were the combative sounds of State Street. Tempers shortened by the heat had street car conductors ringing their warning bells at automobiles, motorists honking their horns at trucks, truckers beating their horses, the animals squealing their pain, and everyone yelling at pedestrians.

Still breathless from having battled my way through the traffic snarl, I was overheated and perspiring into a lightweight worsted suit that didn't absorb moisture quite fast enough. I hoped the dark blue color would at least keep the sweat spots from showing through.

"You have ten minutes, Mr. Rawlings," Harrington drawled drowsily from behind his immaculate desk. For the first time, his loose white Dixie attire seemed entirely appropriate and sensible.

"Thanks, Mr. Harrington." I shifted carefully in my seat to keep from sticking to the leather upholstery. "I appreciate your seeing me without an appointment."

His terse secretary in the outer office hadn't appreciated it at all; it threw off "the schedule," which must have been chiseled in stone the way she referred to it.

A benevolent nod from Harrington. "You said it was urgent." He refreshed his water glass from the pitcher and took a sip. I eyed the glass thirstily, hoping he'd offer me some. He gave no sign of noticing.

Wiping a damp handkerchief over my sweating forehead, I said, "It's about Charles Weeghman." With my throat dry and my chair so far from his desk, I had to strain my voice to be heard.

"What about him?"

I had no trouble appearing convincingly nervous. "He's out to get me."

Harrington gave a small start. "Get you how?"

I shifted again. "He's been mad at me ever since I gave Willie Kaiser's mother my uniform to bury him in. Weeghman got bad publicity because of it and seemed to think I did it intentionally to hurt him. I didn't. It was just that Willie's mother asked me to and I couldn't say no." Harrington nodded impassively. "Anyway, now Weeghman says he's gonna drop me from the team and let me be drafted unless I take a pay cut." This was another lie, which I chose to think of as a "story."

Harrington chuckled. "That's a good one. I don't think even Charlie Comiskey has thought of that yet."

"It's blackmail is what it is."

"Well, some people might describe it that way. Others might call it negotiating."

"Whatever you call it, it ain't right."

He shrugged. "Why come to me about it? Mr. Weeghman runs the ballclub. I'm merely a shareholder."

"Well, like I said, the thing with the uniform wasn't intentional. But now I wouldn't mind doing something to Charles Weeghman that *was* intentional."

"I don't follow," Harrington said flatly. His sleepy left eye snapped awake, and both eyes sparkled in a way that suggested he followed just fine.

"People talk," I said. "I know you've had guys doing things—arranging accidents and such—to try and put Weeghman out of business. I want to help. I figure if somebody else—you or Mr. Wrigley maybe—takes over, I might get a fair shake." My voice wasn't much more than a whisper.

Harrington took a long slow sip of water. I'd have been grateful for a chance to lick the droplets condensed on the outside of the pitcher. "These people that talk. Who are they?"

"I don't rat."

He nodded approvingly. "And what have they been doing to hurt the Cubs?"

"Sawed the bleacher seats, put pretzels in the concession stands, those smoke bombs that cleared out the park at the end of June . . ."

"Why did they do these things?"

"Because you wanted 'em to. I figure you want to take over the team."

Harrington pulled his watch from a vest pocket, checked the time, then snapped the cover shut and tucked it back in his vest. "Actually," he said, "it's the National League that wants me to take control."

"The league?"

"Yes. The other owners and the league president."

The National League president? "John Tener knows about this?" This wasn't at all what I was expecting.

"Mr. Rawlings—you mind if I call you Mickey?"

Oh jeez, he's going to take the chummy approach. I nodded, but a warning flag went up in my head, similar to when he'd put his hat over this heart while referring to "this great game of ours."

"Well, Mickey, I'll trust you to keep this between us. Although much of it is public knowledge."

Doesn't take a whole lot of trust to confide something that's public knowledge, I thought. "I'll keep it to myself," I promised.

"You must be aware that Mr. Weeghman was one of the ringleaders of the Federal League."

"Yes. And in exchange for selling out the Feds, he was allowed to buy the Cubs and move them into his Federal League ballpark." I had as much public knowledge as any other member of the public.

"Selling out the Feds," Harrington repeated with a smile. "Appropriate choice of words."

"Uh, thank you."

"See, that's precisely the problem with Charles Weeghman. He'll sell out his own mother. The man simply is not trustworthy. It was in the interests of the National League to let him in a couple years ago. In fact, the league put up $50,000 toward the purchase price and helped him find additional investors like myself—"

"And Mr. Wrigley and Mr. Armour?"

"Yes, that's right. But now it's time for Mr. Weeghman to go. He turned on his fellow owners once before. He might do it again. These are difficult times, and we all have to be able to trust each other."

I didn't expect their motives were quite that pure. "Of course, Weeghman hurt the National League owners by starting the Federal League. Maybe revenge is another reason they want to get rid of him now?"

He chuckled and the droopy left eye appeared to be winking. "You are an astute judge of human nature, Mr.—uh, Mickey. During its existence, the Federal League did inflict a great deal of damage to organized baseball. And I expect the other owners do indeed have long memories—"

Bursting through the air came an explosion of horns, screeching brakes, an equine scream, and furious shouts. Another traffic accident. Harrington twisted in his chair and glanced at a window. "Sounds like a good one." He then turned slowly back to me; it was too hot to get up and look.

One thing didn't make sense to me, not even in this crazy year and not even for baseball magnates. "The league approved *throwing games?*" I asked.

Harrington frowned. I hadn't included that before when I'd rattled off the other mishaps at Cub's Park. "What makes you think games are being thrown?"

"It's what I heard."

"Well, it's not true. It is not sanctioned by the league anyway. Although they do not care—and do not want to know—how Mr. Weeghman is put out of business, that is not an option of which they'd approve."

"Well, I'm glad to hear that," I said. "That's one thing I won't do."

"You have some scruples."

"Yes. Not many, but some."

"In that case," he laughed, "you should have a bright future ahead of you."

Yeah, I thought, if I ever wanted to be a businessman.

The ruckus outside subsided into sporadic shouts of anger. Harrington checked his watch again. I was sure I'd exceeded my ten minutes.

"So what would you like me to do to help get Weeghman out?" I asked.

"Whatever you like. I don't want to know any details."

"But in general."

"No generalities either. Do whatever you think is appropriate."

"Same as the other owners, you don't want to know."

"Exactly."

It followed the same principle that I'd suggested to Weeghman on the train: you can't be held accountable for what you don't know. "Okay. Count me in." I stood to go. "And when Mr. Weeghman is out, my job is secure?"

"What are you batting?"

"Two-sixty-eight."

"Keep it over two-fifty, and there will be a spot for you on the roster."

"Thank you, Mr. Harrington." I turned away, then back. The same thing that bothered me about William Wrigley wanting to harm the club came to mind. "If you don't mind my asking," I said, "doesn't hurting Mr. Weeghman hurt you, too? If a business goes down, everybody with a share in that business loses, don't they?"

He smiled. "Ah, but if the share becomes larger, an investor can still do better than break even."

I didn't get it.

Harrington noticed. He tried to explain, "Let's say profits drop by a third. But your share is doubled at no cost to you. Then you come out ahead."

I still didn't get it.

Harrington's face showed that his confidence in my bright future was diminishing. "Don't worry," he concluded. "We will be adequately compensated for any fall-off in revenues. Good day."

I exited past his agitated secretary. From her scowl, she looked like she could have been Charles Weeghman's sister.

On the street, I saw the aftermath of the accident: a dead horse was being carted away and a uniformed street car conductor and a burly truck driver were grappling on the sidewalk and cursing like ballplayers. There were other scuffles among those crowded around them, as onlookers took sides and argued about who was at fault.

I watched the proceedings for several minutes. It was kind of nice to see people fighting about something I could understand for a change.

•   •   •

After the final game with Pittsburgh, before going to the Wednesday meeting of the Patriotic Knights of Liberty, I gave Karl Landfors a call.

Once the social niceties were out of the way—they were generally over in a matter of seconds when talking to Landfors—I asked if he'd gotten any dope on Frank Timmons yet.

"Some," he said. "Not a terribly interesting character, as far as I could find out. Appears to be a salesman more than a crusader. You were right about him being with the Ku Klux

Klan in Georgia, and he made a bundle of money for himself by selling them robes and hoods."

"Is that why he left Georgia—they didn't like him making money off them like that?"

"On the contrary. He was a terrific organizer. The Klan sent him to Chicago to organize here. With all the Negroes that have been moving north in the last couple of years, they thought the area would be ripe for recruiting. You know, scare the whites into thinking it's some kind of invasion and then convince them that they need the Klan for protection."

"But Timmons isn't with the Klan anymore?"

"No. He broke off with them. Like I said, he doesn't seem to have any particular cause, as long as he can make a few bucks. So he started his own group. With the war coming, he probably saw he could cash in more by scaring people about Germans. But 'Patriotic Knights of Liberty' is a broad enough name that when the war's over he can easily move on to other enemies."

"Huh. Anything else?"

"Not yet."

"Okay. Well, keep me—Oh, could you check on somebody else for me?"

"Sure. But I hope it's somebody a little more interesting than Frank Timmons."

"It's Bennett Harrington." I filled Landfors in on what I knew and what I suspected. "I'm curious about why he came to Chicago. He's from Baltimore originally and seems out of place here."

Landfors was excited about digging into Harrington's past. Going after a "robber baron," as he called almost any businessman, was one of his favorite pursuits.

• • •

Frank Timmons had completed his sermon and moved to the merchandise table to hawk his wares.

I was looking in vain for somebody to talk to. Although I didn't like anyone here, I liked being alone even less. I wanted to find somebody I knew, but the ranks of the Knights were dwindling.

Curly Neeman was gone, of course; I briefly wondered if there'd been a funeral and if he had any family to grieve for him. Lefty Rariden, who'd survived his bar fight with the sailors, was on a road trip to St. Louis with the rest of the Pittsburgh team. Wicket Greene was simply a no-show.

Their absence wasn't all that these men had in common. All of them worked for Bennett Harrington in some capacity: Neeman and Rariden in his chemical plant, Greene and Rariden as part of his scheme to oust Charles Weeghman from the Chicago Cubs organization.

Harrington certainly arranged things carefully. He needed men to undertake some clandestine activities for him, so he enlisted members of the Patriotic Knights of Liberty, a group ready-made for such trouble but with nothing to do. If any of them got caught, he could disavow them and claim they were doing it for their own political reasons. To further distance himself, Harrington had several Knights working for him, each taking a different approach so there was no visible pattern to the sabotage. According to Harrington, he didn't even know the specifics of what his minions were doing.

All the side deals had me confused, though. Wicket Greene threw games to hurt the team and maybe picked up some money on the side from gamblers. Lefty Rariden planted the smoke bombs and earned extra cash by selling gunpowder to Frank Timmons.

And Curly Neeman? All he got was killed, after he'd murdered Willie. I still didn't think shooting Willie was part of the sabotage, but it could have been the result of him stumbling on to what Greene or Rariden or somebody else was doing.

Frank Timmons surprised me from behind. "Are you *prepared,* Brother Rawlings?" he bellowed.

"Oh yes," I said. "Got a whole bunch of baseball bats at home. Any Germans come around my place, they're gonna get bopped in the head."

His round red face beamed at my enthusiastic response. He clapped a hand on my shoulder and drew me within inches of him. I smelled whiskey. In a low voice, he asked, "Have you given any thought to my proposal regarding the gunpowder?"

"Yeah," I said. "I'm trying to get transferred to that building. I think it would have helped if Curly Neeman was still around."

Timmons adopted a sorrowful expression. "Well, his death is a great loss. But I'm sure you can find somebody else to arrange the transfer."

I evaded. "You know, I think we should be getting revenge for Curly. I mean there's all this talk but no action. Oughta find the guy that killed Curly and string him up is what we oughta be doing."

Taking me by the arm, Timmons walked me out of earshot of the other Knights. "No, no, no," he said in a soothing voice. "Killing is bad for business."

"Business?"

"Yes, of course. The, uh, business of recruiting and making sure everyone is prepared. We don't want anyone doing anything rash—getting themselves in trouble, drawing attention to us, hurting the cause. You understand?"

I was starting to. Business. "I just think we should be doing something about Neeman. You know, if we showed that we take care of our own, it might draw more recruits."

Timmons considered that idea for a moment, then rejected it. "No, no. We don't want trouble. I appreciate your zeal, and I share your loss at Curly Neeman's death. No hotheaded action though, okay?"

With exaggerated reluctance, I agreed.

"Good. Now you'll see about getting that powder?"

"Sure. But couldn't that cause trouble? I mean, somebody making a bomb—"

"Don't you worry. Nobody's going to actually use it. We just want them to be prepared."

Right. Just sell the stuff. Business.

Chapter Twenty-Two

I was the second player in Cubs Park this afternoon. Wally Dillard—he'd rejected my latest nickname for him and so was not "Opie" Dillard—had beaten me as the earliest to arrive. He was carefully prowling the infield, examining the ground, occasionally giving it an exploratory kick with his spikes. It was too bad, I thought, that he hardly ever got on the field once the games began.

So far, I hadn't made it beyond the dugout. I was hunched over on the bench, the business end of my bat resting on the floor and my chin propped on the knob. I absently watched Dillard check out the field as I brooded over the situation with Bennett Harrington and Wicket Greene and the Patriotic Knights of Liberty.

Somebody was lying—either Wicket Greene or Bennett Harrington. It was difficult to determine who was the more credible. As far as I could tell, the two of them combined had less integrity than a common stickup man.

Wicket Greene. He openly antagonized Willie Kaiser and benefited from Willie's death by inheriting the starting shortstop position. He was a member of the Knights, an organization that sold weapons and ammunition. Greene admitted helping Harrington to hurt Charles Weeghman's reputation and business. Yet he claimed that he did not do the one thing Harrington wanted him to: throw baseball games. But his record was one of committing more errors than seemed humanly possible.

Wally Dillard started bouncing a ball on the infield grass to see how it would play. The grass had been cropped much too short and was starting to die. It looked like ground balls would skip across it quickly. But I knew that when the grass was cut that low, the groundskeepers tended to overwater it in the hopes of keeping it alive, and ground balls would actually be slowed down in the boggy turf. Dillard discovered the same thing from his experiment. He was doing it exactly right: you can't go by appearances; you've got to get underneath them and find the reality.

I sighed. Bennett Harrington. Talk about "appearances"—he was an actor, playing a Southern gentleman in the toughest blue-collar city in the North. He claimed a genuine love of baseball going back to the days of the old Orioles and gave ballplayers night jobs in his munitions plant so they could keep playing. Harrington also claimed that the National League owners wanted Weeghman put out of business to punish him for his involvement in the Federal League. That rang true. Magnates could keep feuds running longer than the Dodger–Giant rivalry. But Harrington said the owners did not sanction throwing games. That, too, on the face of it, I believed. Not even an owner would dare that. I hoped.

Statement by statement, Bennett Harrington's words were more believable. So why did I find myself thinking that on the whole Wicket Greene was the more trustworthy of the two? Perhaps it was because Greene admitted to so much else that I couldn't dismiss his claim that Harrington wanted him to throw games. Or perhaps I was biased: whatever else he was, and as much as I disliked him, Wicket Greene was a ballplayer. Bennett Harrington was a magnate.

I raised my bat by the handle and started whomping the thick end on the dugout floor, seeking and crushing peanut shells that were littered about.

No, there was one thing Harrington said that wasn't true. At least there was more than just Greene's word against his. What Lefty Rariden had told me about planting smoke bombs and smuggling powder supported Greene's contention that Harrington did know the specifics of what was going on, something Harrington denied to me. Of course, if Lefty Rariden and Wicket Greene were working together on a scheme of their own, they would make sure they had their stories in line.

"Hey, Mick. Wanna have a catch?"

The magic words: *Wanna have a catch?* Wally Dillard stood in front of me tossing a ball up and down in his glove. He looked like such an innocent with that babyface. Babyface Dillard? Babe, Peachfuzz, Kid . . . Kid Dillard. . . . No, he'd already told me how he felt about being called "kid."

"Wanna have a catch?" he repeated. Wanna be a boy again? Playing on a sandlot from first sunrise, with the only worry being that sunset will eventually arrive and put an end to the game. *Wanna have a catch?* A seductive incantation, a promise to make all troubles vanish for a while if you accept the invitation.

A catch. Yeah, I felt like a catch. "Sure," I said, grabbing my mitt from the bench.

We threw along the third base line, and I tried to let myself fall into the trance of the catch. But Dillard kept up a distracting chatter that broke the spell. I started to throw harder, to get him to shut up and pay attention to the ball. He threw harder to me in return, the little . . .

Dillard stopped yattering and the competition was on. Each of us snapped faster and faster tosses; each tried to catch the other's softly to avoid giving the satisfaction of a popping sound; neither would take a step backward to make the distance more comfortable. He threw a low one at my ankle; I stepped forward to catch it in the air and refused to step back again. Dillard promptly took a step closer, too. We were throwing so fast, at such close range, that it took every bit of our concentration.

I finally threw one that Dillard didn't handle cleanly. It struck the heel of his mitt, skimmed off, and nailed him on the wrist. The ball plopped to the ground as he dropped his glove and shook off the sting.

We both burst out laughing.

After he retrieved the ball, we backed up and started exchanging easy sidearm tosses.

"In a game," I told him, "don't ever shake it off. Don't give them the satisfaction."

"Hell, that didn't hurt," Dillard said with a smile. "My hand fell asleep and I was trying to wake it up is all."

I laughed again. This kid had definite potential. Then I drilled the next one at him and he barely got his glove on it in time. "Better work on those reflexes," I said.

He started chattering again, talking about how happy he was to be playing in the big leagues. I listened to him more tolerantly now that I was in a better mood.

"I'm lucky," he said. "The season could have ended any

day. I didn't think there was a chance of me getting called up to the majors."

That's it!

His next throw bounced off my chest as I neglected to put my glove up.

"Sorry!" he called. "You okay?"

"Yeah, fine," I mumbled. Then I perked up and said, "Felt like a butterfly ran into me!" Waving Dillard in, I suggested, "Come on, let's work on turning a double play."

At second base, I broke the play down into four steps: take the throw in your mitt, transfer the ball to your throwing hand, brush the bag with your foot, get out of the way to avoid the runner's spikes. I stressed that if he couldn't do all four of those, the last step was the one to omit. Getting the out is more important than getting out of the way. I also told him that it had to be done in one smooth motion. Told him, but couldn't show him. Willie Kaiser was the only player who could really achieve that ideal liquid move.

Other early arrivals made their appearance on the field. Among them was Fred Merkle, and I recruited him for our practice. Merkle hit me grounders that I fielded and flipped to Wally Dillard so he could practice his pivot moves. It would be a while before they'd blend into "move," singular.

I was feeling good, better than I had in quite a while. There's nothing like teaching somebody baseball to make you feel like you're doing something worthwhile.

And I was now confident that I knew how Willie's murder fit into things.

• • •

After considerable difficulty getting the telephone number, I was eventually connected long-distance to the Harlan and Hollingsworth Shipbuilding Company, a subsidiary of Bethlehem Steel, in Wilmington, Delaware. Pretending that I was calling from the office of Charles Comiskey, I was put through to their most famous employee.

That was the easy part. Because once I told Shoeless Joe Jackson why I was calling, he clammed up and made it clear he didn't want to answer my questions.

It was the same reaction he'd had when we were walking in Philadelphia and I'd mentioned Bennett Harrington. That was what I was asking now: Why did he have such an aversion to Harrington?

I pleaded, badgered, persuaded. Jackson didn't want to say, but he was too well mannered to hang up on me.

"It's important, Joe. Please."

Finally, I must have exhausted him. "Oh, all right." Jackson's drawl crackled softly across the phone line. "What the hell." He took a deep breath. "It was four years ago—June nineteen-fourteen. I was still with Cleveland at the time and we came in to Comiskey Park to play the White Sox. After the first game—I hit two triples off Ed Walsh, by the way—"

"I hit a homer off Walsh once," I cut in. "In Fenway. Nineteen-twelve." Right, Mickey. Like you're going to impress Joe Jackson with your hitting feats. I pulled the receiver from my ear just long enough to shake my head at myself.

Jackson chuckled. He graciously avoided pointing out that Fenway had a short left field. "Anyway," he went on, "Bennett Harrington paid me a visit at our hotel that night— the Sherman House, I think we were staying in."

He paused longer than I could take. "And . . ." I prodded.

Jackson rapidly said the words, "He wanted me to jump to the Feds."

"You're kidding!"

Having spit out the big secret, the pace of his speech slowed again. "Nope. For real. He told me he had a big share of the Federal League team in Baltimore. A 'silent partner' he called it. Said if I joined them, they could be as good as the old Orioles. He was a nut on the old Orioles."

"Talked about seeing McGraw and Keeler and all them play?"

"Sure did. Anyway, I said I ain't interested. So he offered me cash. And he had it with him, in a big envelope. A cash bonus—five thousand dollars—to sign with them. On top of what my salary would be."

"You still turned it down?"

"Damn right. I wasn't keen to jump to the Feds anyway. And there was no way I was gonna do it like this. Smelled fishy to me. You don't offer somebody cash in his hotel room if it's an honest deal."

"But why so mad at Harrington? He made you an offer, you turned it down, end of story. What's the problem?"

"The son of a bitch didn't leave it there. After I told him no dice, he said he was gonna tell people that I took the money anyway and get me in trouble."

Blackmail. Or "negotiating," as Harrington liked to think of it.

Jackson added sadly, "He told me nobody would take the word of an illiterate over his. Caused me a lot of worry. Was months before I realized it was just a bluff."

No, Harrington would have had to go public with his own Federal League involvement to accuse Jackson. "Thanks Joe. Sorry to bring all this up."

"You're not gonna tell anybody about it, right?"

"Nope. You got my word."

I had another piece of the puzzle. Or I had the first piece of a new puzzle, I wasn't sure. Harrington wasn't punishing Weeghman on behalf of the National League for having helped start the Federal League. Harrington wanted revenge on Charles Weeghman for betraying the Feds.

Chapter Twenty-Three

Karl Landfors met me outside Cubs Park after the Saturday game. "New shortstop looks quite promising," he said. I never expected to hear Landfors appraising baseball talent. And, even more surprising, he was right. Though his choice of words was poor—Dillard looked "real good," not "quite promising."

"Name's Wally Dillard," I said. "Covers a lot of ground, good hands. Hits better than I expected." Wicket Greene's fielding had improved, but he was in a batting slump, so Dillard had got his first start at shortstop. He went two-for-three with a sacrifice and a stolen base. "Once he gets some experience under his belt, he'll be real solid."

"He could use a nickname, too," said Landfors.

"I've been working on it," I said with a grin. "You got any dinner plans tonight?"

"No. But I couldn't eat anything for a while, anyway. Overdid it with the peanuts, I think." He patted his stomach for emphasis.

The weather was clear and mild, so we decided to

spend the rest of the evening at Jackson Park—go on some rides, eat some ice cream, perhaps meet a couple of young ladies . . .

On the trolley ride down Cottage Grove Avenue, Landfors said, "A baseball game is a good way to relax."

"Not if you're playing in it," I snapped at him. Not in the big leagues, anyway.

He laughed. "I don't expect to ever play in one. No, I'll just be a fan, thank you."

It was more than I ever thought he'd be, and I was happy that he'd developed such a fondness for the game. "What are you relaxing from?"

"Writing. I've been working with some fellows who used to publish *The Masses*. We're putting out some pamphlets for the Socialist Party."

I dug an elbow in his ribs and tried to shush him. There were too many passengers on the car for him to say that aloud. We immediately fell into a whispered argument about freedom of speech. My point was that there *was* no more freedom of speech.

After Landfors and I had gone back and forth about it for a while, I quietly told him, "A week before the season opened, there was a lynching." My words caught in my throat, and it was a long moment until I could squeeze them out again. "It was right here in Illinois—Collinsville. A miner named Robert Prager gave a speech on Socialism. He didn't say anything disloyal, wasn't recruiting or advocating or anything; he just gave a lecture about what it was. And a group of patriotic citizens strung him up for it."

"I heard about that," Landfors said. The eyes behind his spectacles were downcast.

I continued, my words coming loud and angry now.

"They caught the guys that hung him, which was real easy because they were so proud of it that the whole town knew who they were. And they put the lynchers on trial. Their defense was 'patriotic murder.' Can you believe that? Like it's self-defense or something. *Patriotic murder!*" It was Landfors's turn to try to hush me, without success. "And they were acquitted in twenty minutes." For me, the Prager lynching was the single event that had started me questioning all things patriotic and nationalistic.

Landfors and I agreed to not talk about politics for the rest of the day and instead concentrate on having fun. Fortunately, no one on the streetcar was inclined to do their bit to enforce the Sedition Act, so we got off the train at Sixty-Third Street without incident.

Jackson Park and the Midway Plaisance had been the site of the World's Columbian Exposition of 1893. The vast, majestic "White City" introduced to the world such delights as the Ferris wheel and the exotic dancing of Little Egypt.

Much of Jackson Park was later turned into golf courses, baseball diamonds, and tennis courts. Near the park's lagoon was the attraction Landfors and I had come to enjoy: the White City Amusement Park. In keeping with its name, all of the structures in the park were painted white. Tiers and spires dripped with every sort of architectural embellishment, causing the buildings to look like frosted wedding cakes.

If there was a place for fun, this was it—a Chicago version of Coney Island, with rides like a Shoot-the-Chutes and balloon races. There were dance halls, food vendors, bandstands, and a roller skating rink.

Landfors and I ambled about the grounds. We didn't go on any rides ourselves, nor did we meet any young ladies.

But we did consume enormous quantities of vanilla ice cream while we watched the kids who were on the rides and discreetly observed the ladies who passed us by.

After an hour or so, we sat on a bench to let the ice cream settle.

Back when the Columbian Exposition was here, there were buildings for cultural exhibits from different countries—a Persian palace, a Japanese bazaar, an Egyptian temple, and a German village. That's back when differences were considered interesting, not threatening.

"What do you think of the war?" I asked Landfors.

He exhaled slowly. Our moratorium on such conversation hadn't lasted long. "I hate it," he said. "What else can I think about it?"

"You think it was right for the U. S. to get involved?"

There was no hesitation. "Yes."

The answer surprised me. "I thought you'd have been against it."

"No. The whole thing is a monumental exercise in stupidity. But it will be over faster with us in it. And it *is* justified. Most of the atrocity stories are fabricated, but there are valid reasons for the United States to be involved. Germany has been sending arms to Mexico for years, trying to get them to go to war against us. And they have been sabotaging American plants and sinking American ships."

"I don't know," I said. "I'd enlist if it was that clear to me. But now it seems everything we're supposed to be fighting for 'over there' has been abandoned back here."

"A lot of it has," Landfors said with a sorrowful shudder. "But sometimes you can't play by the rules. Lincoln broke a lot of them during the Civil War, you know. He suspended *habeas corpus,* for one thing." In answer to my frown, he explained, "Basically, it's imprisoning people without charges and without a trial. It's blatantly unconstitutional, but quite a few politicians and newspaper editors who were pro-Confederacy were put in jail that way. If Lincoln hadn't done it, the Union might not have held together. Extreme situations sometimes require less than desirable actions. Oh, the Emancipation Proclamation was probably unconstitutional, too. Worth doing, though, don't you think?"

"Of course. Look, I'm not a stickler for playing exactly by the rule book, but I do know what's fair. And putting people in jail for disagreeing with the government, or for playing the 'wrong' kind music for chrissake, that just ain't right."

Landfors thought. "No, it isn't right. But you have to get people riled up to go to war, especially to a war that's an ocean away. So you feed them tales about horrid atrocities, you convince them that the enemy is already on these shores undermining our way of life. You tell them whatever it takes to get them to send their boys off to battle."

"Problem is," I said, "you can't rile them back down once they get going. You get groups like the Patriotic Knights of Liberty and the Anti-Yellow Dog League and the Ku Klux Klan and the rest of them. They go lynching people and burning houses. It ain't right."

"No. No it ain't."

After sitting a while longer in silence, we strolled around some more, then went to the Midway Gardens to get something more substantial than ice cream in our stomachs. Both of us picked at our dinners, thoroughly in the doldrums.

"You mentioned 'sending their boys to battle.' Mrs. Tobin, my neighbor you saw, her boy Harold just got killed."

"Damn."

"All those boys dying in France," I said, "and all I've been thinking about is Willie's death. I suppose that's kind of stupid of me, isn't it?"

"One death is all it takes," Landfors said softly. "That was enough for me."

Damn. I'd forgotten. "You, uh, you haven't told me much about her."

"That's true. I haven't. So, how are you doing with the Willie Kaiser investigation?"

Maybe it was still too soon for him to talk about his wife. "I think I'm making progress," I said, following his lead. "I've pretty much figured out why he was killed, anyway."

Landfors didn't ask me what the reason was; I don't think he much cared. He did say, "Oh, I checked some on that Bennett Harrington."

"And?"

He pulled a small notebook from his jacket pocket and flipped it open. "He is originally from Baltimore, like you said. Had a string of businesses there—trucking company, hotel, fish market; every one of them failed. Moved to Chicago about ten years ago, almost broke. His brother owned the Dearborn Fuel Company, mostly dealt in heating coal back then. Took Harrington into the business. The brother died a year after Harrington joined him." Answering my raised eyebrows, Landfors said, "No, it was tuberculosis. Nothing suspicious."

"That it?"

"So far. Bennett Harrington has done quite well for himself since then. Nothing illegal as far as I know."

"Huh. Could you do a little more digging in Baltimore?"

"I suppose."

"Check on Terrapin Park. It's where the Baltimore Federal League team played. See who owns it."

"Terrapin? Like a turtle?"

"Yeah. Stupid name, huh?"

"Not for baseball," Landfors chuckled. "Okay. I'll check it out."

When dusk came, we left the park. As we were walking out, Landfors said to me, "By the way, don't be too hard on people being taken in by propaganda. You've been, too."

"What do you mean?"

"You always refer to him as Willie."

"Well, he was my friend. Of course I call him Willie."

"You refer to everyone else by their last name. You sure it's not that you don't like saying Kaiser?"

I hadn't thought about it, but he could be right. After all, I always thought of Landfors as Landfors.

• • •

If Wicket Greene had earned any money for throwing games, he sure wasn't spending it on rent. The dilapidated wood-frame boarding house he called home was on South Halsted, in the Near West Side, not far from Jane Addams's Hull House. It didn't look like it would be there for long. The question was whether it would fall apart of its own accord before the wrecking ball got to it.

The interior showed the same signs of decay. In the shabby dark parlor where Greene and I sat Sunday morning, the wallpaper bulged from the crumbling plaster behind it. In some spots it had erupted through, leaving piles of white dust around the baseboards.

Wicket Greene sat in an overstuffed chair that no longer had any stuffing. Layers of different colored blankets draped over the seat and backrest provided the only cushions. I sat in a straight-backed pine chair that wasn't comfortable but was solid enough to hold my weight safely.

"About Bennett Harrington . . ." I began.

Greene grunted something that I took to mean "go on."

"Did he talk to you directly about . . . doing things to hurt Weeghman?" I didn't even like to say "throwing games."

"Directly?" A frown of ignorance creased Greene's immense forehead.

"Yeah, did he talk to you himself or was it through somebody else?"

"Oh!" The creases softened. "Direct."

Same as what I'd gathered from Lefty Rariden: Harrington did know exactly what was happening.

"You know of anybody else Harrington had working for him?"

He nodded. "There were some others."

"Who? What were they doing?"

Greene hesitated, then said emphatically, "No. I told you what I done, and I'll stick by it. But as far as anybody else, I don't know nothing."

"You don't want to get them in trouble? Or you don't want them causing trouble for you if it gets out that you told?"

"Right."

Right to which, you jerk? I was starting to have the sense that I was talking to an ugly male version of Edna Chapman. Okay, if Greene wasn't going to volunteer the information, the next best thing was to tell him what I suspected and see if he'd at least confirm it. "When you told me about Harrington, it was the day after Curly Neeman was killed." I paused to give Greene a chance to jump in.

He smiled nervously; at the sight of his teeth, I realized

how well he fit in with his surroundings. But he said nothing.

I went on, "Neeman getting killed put a scare into you."

"I don't scare," Greene growled.

"Sure you do. You were scared about Willie Kaiser taking your job from you. You're scared about what's going to become of you when you can't make a living playing baseball." Greene shifted in his chair in obvious discomfort, and it had nothing to do with the upholstery. "And after Neeman got killed, you were scared that you might be next. That's why you wanted to put me onto Bennett Harrington. You wanted somebody to know about him, just in case."

Greene bobbed his head slowly. After a minute, he said, "Curly Neeman was the one who sawed the bleacher seats. That's how he got his job as a guard in Harrington's plant."

"And you think Harrington killed him?"

"I don't know for sure. But that's a damn good way to shut a guy up, ain't it?"

"And you were worried he might've wanted to shut you up, too."

"Still am. Because one thing I do know is Curly Neeman told me he was going to see Harrington the night he got killed."

Chapter Twenty-Four

The problem was, with Curly Neeman dead, I'd have a tough time proving anything about Willie's murder. And I would need incontrovertible evidence to go public with what I now suspected: that Willie Kaiser was killed on orders from Bennett Harrington.

This predicament had me thoroughly discouraged until I hit upon an alternate approach: if I couldn't prove Harrington was behind Willie's death, I might at least be able to prove that he had Curly Neeman killed, and the penalty for either crime would be the same. The sentence could even be more severe for Neeman's murder since killing a "Kaiser" might qualify as "patriotic murder."

Only three weeks were left in the season, and I knew I had to step up my efforts. First thing Monday morning, I went straight to the source of the trouble.

The source granted me only five minutes this time, and no courtesy other than allowing me to sit. "What's on your mind now, Mr. Rawlings?" Bennett Harrington demanded. No more "Mickey." The chummy approach was definitely over.

Borrowing Wicket Greene's fears and passing them off as my own, I said, "I don't want to end up getting killed like Curly Neeman did."

Harrington leaned back. His right eye stared up at the ceiling, while the weak left one remained on me. I was wondering if he was going to ask, "Who's Curly Neeman?" He decided not to play coy. "And why would you be worried about that?" he asked.

"What we were talking about last time. You know, about doing things to hurt Charles Weeghman. That's what Curly Neeman was doing, and he got killed. If that's what's gonna happen to guys after they do their 'work' for you, I want out of the deal."

With a bemused smile on his lips, Harrington asked, "What have you done to keep your end of the bargain?"

"Well, nothing yet. But—"

"And you have no intention of doing anything, do you?"

"Sure I do. If—"

"Tell me something. What makes you think I had anything to do with Mr. Neeman's unfortunate demise?"

"Hey, I go to the Knights meetings. Guys talk. I think I know what's up. I just want to know what Neeman did to get you mad. I'll make sure I don't do the same thing."

"Are you armed, Mr. Rawlings?"

"Uh, no."

"Yet you come in here and essentially accuse me of killing someone. Doesn't that strike you as a foolish thing to do?"

Well, now that he mentioned it . . .

Harrington slowly sat upright. From a desk drawer he casually pulled out a colossal ivory-handled revolver and laid it on the desk, with the barrel pointed straight at me. "If the man you're accusing really is a killer, he's likely to have a weapon, don't you think? And if he does, why shouldn't he simply use it to kill you, too?" He put his hand over the weapon and cocked the hammer with his thumb. It clicked into place, sounding as loud as a gunshot.

I tried, but probably didn't succeed, to appear unconcerned. "I didn't need to bring a gun with me," I said. "You're not going to kill a Chicago Cub in your office."

He smiled. Leaving the revolver on the desk, he leaned back and folded his hands over his stomach. Sunlight sparkled off the weapon's bright silver finish. My seat was too far from his desk for me to have a chance of grabbing the gun. Harrington was toying with me and enjoying it enormously. "This is where I killed Curly Neeman," he said.

Damn! The only reason for him to admit it was that I wasn't going to live long enough myself to tell anyone.

Harrington idly smoothed the ends of his black silk string tie. I desperately tried to figure out what to do, but all I could think was that I never expected that a man who wore a white suit would do his own killing. "I don't believe you," I said. "He was found in the river. You didn't carry him all the way to the Chicago River dressed like that."

The smirk disappeared from his face. He quickly recovered. "That's true," he said. "Two very nice police officers carried him off for me."

"The police know?"

"Yes, of course. You see, I'm no murderer, Mr. Rawlings. I killed Mr. Neeman in self-defense and immediately reported it to the authorities."

"Self-defense?"

"That's what I told them."

"The police?"

Harrington was in good humor again. "And other authorities. Very high authorities. I explained to them that Curly Neeman was committing sabotage in my plant. He tried to blow you up, by the way." The smile that twitched at Harrington's lips gave me the feeling that Neeman hadn't done so on his own initiative. "In any event, it was decided that my encounter with Mr. Neeman should be kept quiet. National security, you understand. So the police were kind enough to dispose of Mr. Neeman's body."

Still trying to discourage Harrington from using the gun, I said, "Even the cops, or whatever 'authorities' you're talking about, would be suspicious at a second self-defense killing in two weeks, not to mention a second Cub getting killed. You might have clout, but so do Mr. Weeghman and Mr. Wrigley and a bunch of the other owners who wouldn't like losing their players that way."

The humor vanished from his face. The look of frustration that took its place told me he knew I was right. After letting me squirm far too long, he carefully uncocked the hammer and put the gun back in the drawer. He then pulled out his watch and announced, "Your time is up."

I was halfway to the door when he said, "Mr. Rawlings, permit me to give you some advice: don't ever get in a poker game. I knew when you first came here what you were up to. You were looking into Willie Kaiser's *accidental* death."

Harrington didn't have to shoot; his words—his message—stopped me as effectively as a bullet. I understood his meaning completely. He knew what I'd been up to all along, he was untouchable as far as the authorities were concerned, and if I continued poking around, I'd end up as dead as Curly Neeman or Willie Kaiser. And he, Bennett Harrington, was responsible for both their deaths.

"One more thing," he added. "You're fired."

• • •

Freed of my duties at the Dearborn Fuel Company, I went to a picture show Monday night. By myself.

And I went back about ten years in time, to when I was a teenager, traveling from town to town with semi-pro ball-clubs, spending my free hours in little nickelodeons. I felt less alone in my travels knowing that I could stop in any local theater and see familiar faces on the movie screen. My favorite of those faces belonged to Mabel Normand, a brunette comedienne with wide, mischievous eyes and a small, teasing smile. I'd had such a crush on her that I named my favorite bat "Mabel" in her honor.

Now Mabel Normand was appearing in a feature movie at the White Palace theater on South Kedzie Avenue. The picture was *Mickey,* with Miss Normand in the title role. It was a little disconcerting to think of a female named "Mickey," but I was also strangely flattered that they'd used my name for the title.

Mickey had been filmed two years before and was finally being released to tremendous fanfare. Because it had been shot before America had entered the war, the movie had no jingoistic political messages to deliver. It was advertised as "a wholesome romantic comedy adventure epic with thrills and heart."

Somehow the picture managed to live up to its billing. The character Mickey was an orphaned tomboy raised in the West by an old prospector. The convoluted tale involved Mickey being sent to live with a New York aunt to learn to be a lady. The wicked aunt forces her to work as a maid, but Mickey soon gains the attention of a wealthy young admirer. The story was old-fashioned hokum, with holes in the plot and a happy ending that strained credibility—Mickey wins a horse race, learns that an abandoned gold mine she's inherited had a major strike, and marries her suitor. In short, the movie was charming, a throwback to a simpler, more innocent time—pure entertainment, total escape, and a reminder of why I had once been so enchanted with Mabel Normand. I left the theater with a smile on my face and a light heart.

Back home from the picture show, I pulled three old baseball bats from the back corner of the bedroom closet. They were bats that I'd fashioned myself long before the Hillerich & Bradsby company had started manufacturing a *Mickey Rawlings* model. I hadn't used them in years, couldn't remember the last time I'd even touched them.

The one made of hickory wood was Mabel. With a dark rich luster, she stood out from all other bats as special. I'd painstakingly formed her on a lathe, turning her round and true, then carefully, lovingly, I'd sanded and honed her to a hard smooth finish.

I brought Mabel into the parlor and squeezed her handle between my fists. It seemed a childish thing to do, now, to have named a baseball bat. But I had a yearning to go back to childhood, to recapture some innocence.

Indifferent to the effect it might have on the furniture, I took a few easy swings. She felt good and right, like a natural extension of my arms. I ran my fingers along the barrel; the dry wood needed to be rubbed with sweet oil. Gripping her again, I took a closer look: there was a V-shaped chip missing from the knob. *Noooo.* Mabel wasn't perfect anymore.

I was devastated by this blemish, as if some belief I'd long cherished had turned out to be a falsehood. I ran my thumb over the notch, hard, the sharp edges of the break biting into my flesh. The bat might as well have been shattered into splinters. It wasn't the same anymore and never could be.

After some long minutes spent lamenting the damage, I realized you never get innocence back. The only way to go is forward.

Momentarily laying Mabel on the sofa, I pulled out one of the newspapers, dated July 5. I tore off the page with the story on Willie's death and crumpled it into a ball. Setting it on the headrest of my chair, I took a rip with Mabel and knocked the paper ball into the wall.

One after another, I went through every page of every paper the same way, using them for an angry batting practice.

Chapter Twenty-Five

I knew who was responsible for Willie Kaiser's death, both the man who'd pulled the trigger and the one who'd called the shot. I also knew *why* Willie had been killed. Under normal circumstances, that would have been enough information to solve the murder. Well, it did solve the crime; it just wasn't enough to resolve it.

In this topsy-turvy year, the issue wasn't who or why or how. Justice wasn't going to come that easy in these turbulent times. It wasn't even clear what justice was anymore. Not quite true—it was clear to *me* what was right. What I didn't know was how the "authorities" defined it. The legal definitions of right and wrong kept changing too fast to keep track of them.

The real question that faced me was: What the hell could I *do* about Willie's murder?

The answer that resounded back, loud and firm, taunting and haunting, was: Not a damn thing.

Could I tell the police that Curly Neeman had shot Willie from a Sheffield Avenue apartment and Harrington had been behind it? I could, but there was no reason to believe they'd do anything. The cops had already covered up Willie's murder and helped Harrington dispose of Neeman's body. They sure wouldn't be eager to investigate a crime that could reveal themselves as accomplices, not even as unwitting ones.

The other way to expose Harrington would be to break the story to the newspapers, something I'd learn from my muckraker friend Karl Landfors. Again, though, that could only be done in normal times. These days the papers were all censored, and only "approved" news was printed. Which brought it back to the authorities and the police.

I hated what Bennett Harrington had done, and his arrogance was a challenge that I found irresistible. But it would be foolish to let my hatred of him cloud the fact that in reality he was right. For all practical purposes, he was untouchable.

I tried to console myself with the fact that at least I'd accomplished what I'd promised Edna I would: I found out who killed her brother. I never guaranteed that I'd get the murderer put in jail.

All I could do now was follow through on the rest of my promise and tell her what happened.

• • •

Edna Chapman and I sat in Willie's old room, on the edge of his bed, with more distance between us than propriety required. Other than the empty space atop the dresser where the Mark Twain books used to be, the room was preserved exactly the way Willie had left it.

"Why don't you move in here?" I asked her. "I'll help move your things down if you like."

"No, I better stay upstairs with Mama," Edna said. "She wakes up in the night sometimes. Bad dreams."

"Oh, okay." I gathered my thoughts and my courage before announcing, "I found out who killed Willie."

Edna's eyes widened and sparkled. "Who was it?" Her tone was cool and controlled.

"You have to understand," I began lamely, "it didn't really have to do with Willie." What a stupid thing to say. Of course it had to do with him—somebody had put a bullet through his chest.

"What did it have to do with?"

"Business," I said sourly. I found it hard to believe that somebody could get killed for business. "And revenge."

Edna's eyebrows arched.

"Not revenge against Willie. Against Charles Weeghman."

A small frown.

"See, Charles Weeghman is president of the Cubs," I explained. "And he owns most of the team, but not all of it. There are other men, investors, who have shares in the team. Bennett Harrington is one of those. And he has it in for Weeghman."

Edna said slowly, with no indication of comprehension, "Willie was killed because Mr. Harrington is mad at Mr. Weeghman?"

"Partly. See, Weeghman was one of the leaders of the Federal League a few years back. It was supposed to be a third major league. Weeghman owned the Feds' Chicago team. And he built Weeghman Park for them to play in— 'Cubs Park' now."

Edna nodded to show she was following thus far.

"Two years ago, the Federal League folded. And Charles

Weeghman was part of the reason. In exchange for abandoning the Feds, the National League let him buy the Cubs and move them to his new ballpark. The other Federal League owners considered Weeghman a traitor for selling out."

"How does Mr. Harrington come into this?"

"He was one of the other Federal League owners. Not openly, though. He was a silent partner in the Baltimore team."

"But I don't understand. How does killing Willie get revenge against Mr. Weeghman?"

"Harrington wanted to put Weeghman out of business. Mostly for revenge, I think, but also for business. It's a baseball owner's dream come true—he gets revenge on another owner and he gets a good business deal. A double play."

Edna frowned; this wasn't the time for a baseball analogy. "Why is it a good deal?"

"Let me start at the beginning. Bennett Harrington has been having people sabotage Cubs Park all season. It did two things: it made Weeghman look bad, which he liked, and it cut down attendance, hurt business. Both these things put pressure on Weeghman to sell out his shares. And with attendance off, he'd have to sell cheap. Having somebody kill a Cub on the playing field was part of the sabotage."

"Willie," she said softly.

"Not him personally," I said. "I think any Cub would have done." I hoped it would make her feel a little better that her brother wasn't personally targeted.

It didn't. "So he was just any Cub," she said, her eyes watering.

I had even worse to tell her. "The fellow who actually shot Willie, Curly Neeman, he's dead now, too. Bennett Harrington killed him. So there's no one to testify that Harrington was behind Willie's murder. I was hoping we might get Harrington arrested for killing Neeman—the penalty's the same—but the police already know about it. And they don't care. In fact, they're the ones who dumped Neeman's body in the river. They're calling it self-defense."

Edna brought the tears under control. "So what's next?" she asked in a high, tight voice.

Now for the really hard part. "There isn't any next. There isn't any hard evidence. And the authorities won't do anything to Bennett Harrington while the war is on, anyway."

"You're giving up?"

Giving up. It was an accusation. A quitter was about the worst thing a ballplayer could be and not something any man wants to be called. "Not giving up," I insisted. "Just waiting. Maybe when the war is over, the police will look into it for real."

"You believe that?"

I shook my head, admitting that I didn't. "But there's nothing else to do."

She nodded solemnly.

"I wanted to tell you everything. I know it doesn't make things right, but at least we know who did it and why."

"Thank you."

"It may be best to let your mother continue to believe it was an accident. If there was anything else I could do . . ."

She looked at me and nodded again.

I felt like a quitter.

Chapter Twenty

Okay, maybe there was still something that could be done.

What I needed was to connect Bennett Harrington with Curly Neeman. By killing Neeman, Harrington had effectively severed the direct connection between them, but perhaps I could link them indirectly. There had to be some way of proving that Neeman had fired his rifle into Cubs Park on Harrington's orders.

I remembered what Karl Landfors said about conspiracies: people talk. If anyone was likely to shoot off his mouth, it would have been Curly Neeman. When Willie was working in the chemical plant, Neeman taunted him with threats about the Knights; after he killed Willie, he couldn't resist dropping hints to Aggie that he'd done it.

So I'd expect that if Curly Neeman shot a German, he'd want the glory of bragging about it to his comrades in the Patriotic Knights of Liberty. And if he was in league with such an illustrious figure as Bennett Harrington, he'd certainly want that to be known as well.

y one hope: that Curly Neeman talked before
Th gton silenced him.

Benn ay night I went to where Neeman was most
likel his talking: the Knights meeting in Cicero.

unately, Wicket Greene was absent again, so I
use him to introduce me to anyone. Without Greene
co th the way, I artlessly approached the Knights on my
to naking inquiries of as many of them as I could.
o wasn't subtle in my questions. I was too desperate at this
nt to have time for discretion. And I had no success. All
did was antagonize the good white men of the Patriotic
Knights of Liberty to the point where I knew this had better
be the last meeting I attended.

· · ·

The next morning, I discovered the first evidence of compatibility between Agnes O'Doul and Willie Kaiser. Her small three-room apartment was as sparsely furnished and meticulously neat as Willie's bedroom. I was sure it wasn't their tidiness that attracted them to each other, and I knew that the heart can often find a compatibility where none is visible, but I was heartened to see that they shared this trait. It helped me imagine Aggie and Willie as a couple.

I took a sip of lemonade, then put the glass back down on a thick doily, careful not to let it touch the wood of the kitchen table. "When we talked last week," I said, "you told me Curly Neeman called it a mistake to kill Willie. What did he mean by that?"

Agnes shrugged. "How should I know what he meant?"

Lemonade wasn't my morning beverage of choice, but Agnes wasn't a coffee drinker and had none to offer. I felt that I needed some badly. "Okay, let me get this straight: you're holding a blowtorch to this guy, trying to find out if and why he killed your boyfriend—" To my surprise, Agnes blushed at the word "boyfriend." "He admits shooting Willie, says it was a mistake, and you don't ask what he meant by that?" I shook my head. "I don't buy it."

The color in her face remained, but her expression changed from embarrassment to defiance. "You really want to know?" She hurled the question like a challenge. "You're not going to like it."

"Yes. I really want to know." How much worse could things be?

Agnes took a breath. "He was supposed to shoot you."

I was stunned. When I regained the capacity of speech, I could only say, *"Me?* But why?"

She warned, "You're probably going to like that even less."

I nodded for her to go ahead and tell me.

"Because Willie was too good a player."

It took a minute for that to register. Then I burst into laughter. Agnes looked at me as if I'd gone mad. I wasn't even angry at the slight to my abilities. I had to credit Bennett Harrington with one thing: he was an astute judge of talent.

When I stopped chuckling, I downed the rest of my lemonade, enjoying the coolness as it washed into my stomach. While Agnes refilled the glass from a pitcher in the ice box, I tried to gather my thoughts.

The skirt of her smart gray and white striped gingham dress swished as she sat back down across the small table from me. Morning sunlight through the kitchen window made her face seem radiant and brought out auburn tints in her neatly combed brown hair. From deep left field came the realization that I was becoming attracted to Aggie O'Doul.

I had to force myself to get back on track. "Neeman was supposed to kill me," I said. "So he was under some kind of orders. Did he say who told him to shoot me?" Please say it was Harrington.

"No. Didn't say."

"You're not holding back on me again?"

"Hell no, I'd tell you if I knew. But he wouldn't say." She smiled. "And believe me, I did my best to get it out of him. The little pissant held out though. I give him credit for that. I think he knew I didn't have it in me to kill him. He must have been more afraid of whoever he was protecting than he was of me."

With good cause. The man he was protecting did have it in him to kill Curly Neeman. Damn. I still couldn't tie Neeman to Harrington. And I never noticed before how deep and bright Aggie O'Doul's dark eyes were. The fact that she didn't have it in her to kill someone made her even more attractive.

She said, "I'm sorry I didn't tell you this before—about you being the one he was supposed to shoot. I figured you weren't in danger anymore after Neeman got killed. And I didn't think it was something you'd feel good about knowing." Her head was cocked; she was obviously still puzzled by my strange reaction to the news. Since I didn't understand it myself, I didn't try to explain it to her.

"Neeman didn't tell you anything else?"

"No. Nothing."

The conversation stalled until I remembered one of the last things Willie had said to me. "Aggie, the day Willie was shot I was trying to get him to fight back when people picked on him. He told me he was fighting back but in his own way. He never got to explain what he meant by that. Do you have any idea?"

Aggie nodded and answered slowly. "His way of fighting back was to keep doing things by the book no matter how tough it got. He worked hard at the chemical plant, he played all out for the Cubs, he would have enlisted if not for his mother being so against it. Poor kid really believed that if he did everything like he was supposed to, things would work out." She snorted. "Lot of good it did him playing by the rules."

Yeah, sometimes the rule book doesn't cover everything.

She'd given me my coat and hat, and I was about to leave, when I said, "I was wondering. How did you and Willie start, you know, seeing each other?"

"You mean how did a young, good-looking kid like him hook up with somebody like me?"

"No, I just meant . . ."

It took a minute until she decided to answer. "It started by talking, during work breaks, same as you and me. We talked and then one day we went to a movie together."

"Why didn't you want people to know you were seeing each other? You said Willie wanted to tell people, but you didn't."

"Personal reasons."

"Oh. Are you married?" I thought perhaps to a soldier overseas.

The question set her on fire with anger. "What are you, kidding me?" she said through sneering lips. "Look, my mama raised ugly girls, not stupid ones. I know what men want me for, and it's not for marrying and it's not for showing me off to their friends." Her face and voice slowly softened.

"Willie was different. He always treated me like a lady. But if it was public. . . . Well, as soon as his buddies started ribbing him about it, he'd have dropped me."

"No, he wouldn't," I said. "From what he told me, Willie was crazy about you." I almost added as evidence that he'd even stopped going to burlesque houses.

Aggie's expression was anything but angry now. "He told you that?"

"Lots of times."

If she really knew Willie Kaiser, she knew that he was unlikely to have said any such thing. But her eyes told me that she chose to believe me, anyway.

• • •

I still thought that my best bet for finding someone who could tie Curly Neeman to Bennett Harrington was the Patriotic Knights of Liberty. Neeman had taken it upon himself to shoot a German instead of the player he'd been ordered to kill—me. Why would he have done that if not to brag about it? I could almost hear him crowing to the Knights about how he'd "killed the Kaiser."

The Knight I didn't get to speak with Wednesday night, the one who hadn't been to any meetings lately, was Wicket Greene. There was something he'd said to me that didn't jibe with what I'd learned from Aggie O'Doul. I confronted him about it after the Thursday afternoon game against the Cards.

"Wick—Sammy," I said. Calling him by his real name might help, I thought. "You told me that Harrington promised if you threw games for him you'd become starting shortstop."

Greene took a quick look around. There was no one near

us in the empty tunnel outside the locker room. "Yeah. That's right."

Something didn't make sense. If I was the one who was supposed to be killed, second base would be available, not shortstop. "You remember when the Cards were here last and we got in that scuffle in the locker room?" I asked.

"I remember."

"You said you could get my job, second base, in a minute, but you wanted to play short." At the time, I'd thought it was empty talk.

"Oh that. Harrington's first offer was that I'd play second base if I helped him out. I told him it was shortstop I wanted."

"And he agreed?"

"Yeah."

Did Harrington have Neeman kill Willie instead of me just to keep his word to Greene? Not likely. "You haven't been to any of the Knights' meetings lately."

"No. Haven't wanted to."

"Ever talk to Curly Neeman?"

He hesitated. "Sometimes."

"Did you a big favor by killing Willie, didn't he?" I steeled myself for another fight.

"No," Greene whispered hoarsely. "He didn't do me any favor at all." His entire body seemed to slump.

"Tell me about it." I'd realized only recently why Wicket Greene had told me about Harrington's proposal to throw games: because compared to the bigger secret he was hiding, throwing baseball games was trivial.

Greene pointed to the locker room door. "I got to sit down." Once we were inside and seated, he said, "You got to believe me, I didn't know nothing about it. Not until afterwards. Curly Neeman bragged to me about killing Willie.

'Got me a Hun' is what he said. Then he told me who it was. And I knew he was doing work for Harrington. Like I told you, Neeman was the one who sawed the bleacher seats for him. Anyway, I felt awful. It's because of me Kaiser's dead."

"Because of you?"

"Yeah. Because I told Harrington I wanted to play short-stop. That's why he had Neeman kill him."

"That's what Neeman said?"

"No. But I figured that's what must have happened."

All this time Greene had been feeling guilty that he'd caused Willie's death. "That wasn't it," I told him. "I was the one Neeman was supposed to shoot. Harrington wasn't going to keep his promise to you. You were going to end up at second base after all."

Greene looked ill. "Damn." Then relieved. "So it wasn't 'cause of me?"

"No. It had nothing to do with you." Making Greene feel better wasn't my objective in revealing this; I thought he might more readily answer a few more questions. "Neeman tell anybody else about what happened?"

Greene promptly answered, "Frank Timmons." I should have thought of that. I remembered how eager Neeman had been for Timmons's approval. "Neeman ended up pretty disappointed, though. He thought Timmons should have considered him some kind of hero for killing Kaiser. But Timmons didn't want to hear it, and he almost made Nee-man an outcast after that."

Killing is bad for his business, Frank Timmons had said. It also explained why Timmons had asked me to smuggle out the gunpowder when he could have asked Curly Neeman to do it. He wanted to limit his involvement with Neeman.

"Anyway," Greene went on, "that all soured me on the

Knights. So I didn't want to go to any more of the meetings."

Well, at least I now had somebody who could confirm that Harrington had Neeman commit murder for him. Last question: "Would you testify about all this?"

"Not a chance in hell."

Chapter Twenty-Seven

At least two people still alive knew that Bennett Harrington was behind the murder of Willie Kaiser: Wicket Greene and Frank Timmons. However, Greene wasn't going to testify to that, and I was sure Timmons wouldn't either. There was no way for him to profit from it.

Would Harrington be so sure, though? He couldn't be entirely confident that he was immune from prosecution; he must have some fear of exposure. What if I played on that fear? Maybe I could bluff him, convince him that too many people knew what had happened for him to keep it covered up. Then again, maybe I couldn't. "Don't ever get in a poker game," he'd told me. I had a sinking feeling that his assessment of my poker skills was as sound as his choice of me instead of Willie as the more expendable ballplayer.

An entirely different approach suggested itself next: forget about the murders and nail Bennett Harrington for something else. He'd allowed Lefty Rariden to smuggle gunpowder out of his munitions plant. That should qualify as treason, and the penalty for treason was the same as that for murder. This idea withered away when I realized that Lefty Rariden wouldn't go public with what he'd done any more than Greene would. And the government would probably protect Harrington from any such charges anyway, for security reasons, of course.

I thought about it for three days. The most sensible thing for me to do would be to take the advice I'd given Edna Chapman and try to put it all behind me. But nothing else this season was sensible, so why start now?

I finally decided that my only viable option was to goad Bennett Harrington into making a move against me. There were two advantages to this scheme. One was that I knew he'd go for it. Harrington was aware that I knew too much about him, and he'd already tried to have me killed. The other, very important, consideration was that I was sure he would do it personally. Since he'd killed Curly Neeman himself, I figured he wanted to cut down the number of people involved. He wouldn't get somebody else in on it again.

This was going to be my plan. Either I'd trap Harrington when he came after me or. . . . well, I wasn't supposed to have lived beyond the Fourth of July anyway.

• • •

It was nine-twenty Monday morning when I rounded the corner from Randolph to State Street. I allowed the extra twenty minutes in case Bennett Harrington's secretary was late for work. From what I'd seen of her, I didn't think tardiness was ever a problem, but I wanted to be sure that she was there when I spoke to him. I wasn't going to repeat Curly Neeman's mistake. At this point, I only wanted to plant a seed in Harrington's mind; I didn't want him shooting me on the spot.

I took the stairs to the third floor and stepped into the outer office. The first thing I saw was that the secretary's desk was empty. What I noticed next were the two plug-uglies in the room. One, a droopy-faced bear of a man, whose crossed arms barely met across the girth of his belly, was standing outside the open door to Harrington's office. The other, a pale young man of slight build, moved up on me from the left. I looked from one to the other, then asked innocently, "Where's the secretary?"

The young fellow said, "Sent 'er home." He took a step closer to me. "You better get out of here, too," he warned in a voice too high to sound truly threatening.

I willingly moved to comply when the other man barked, "Hold him! That's Rawlings."

I was immediately grabbed by the arms. The skinny thug was stronger than he appeared; he spun me around and slammed my back against the wall. I struggled to get out of his grasp, but he got a sinewy forearm against my throat and started to push.

It suddenly came to me that both of these men were regulars at the Knights' meetings. Harrington must be employing some of them as personal bodyguards now.

I tried to twist my head to get the pressure off my windpipe. As I turned, struggling for breath, I saw the large man uncross his arms and pull open his jacket. A pistol was tucked in his belt.

Two against one. And one of them with a gun. No fair.

Before my brain could issue the order, my right knee took the initiative to throw out the rule book. It snapped up hard and fast and made full contact.

Gasping out a most amazing screech, the recipient of my well-placed kick buckled, his arm dropping away from my throat. As he doubled over, his coat gaped open to reveal that he was also armed.

Instinctively, my hand reached out and plucked the long-barreled revolver from his shoulder holster.

As my attacker fell to his hands and knees, I went down, too, taking a kneeling position behind him to use his heaving body as a barricade. The strangled, retching noises he was making told me he wasn't going to be getting up any time soon. I aimed the revolver in the direction of the man outside Harrington's door.

The fat man started to go for his gun. "Don't move!" I yelled, keeping the pistol trained on him. Actually, it didn't stay on him; it swept over him, back and forth and up and down as it wobbled in my hand. I didn't know a damn thing about using a gun. Do I have to pull the hammer back, or just pull the trigger? I cupped my left hand over the hammer so he wouldn't know if I was doing it wrong.

He could tell I didn't know what I was doing, but it worked to my advantage. Instead of pulling his weapon, he hoisted his chubby arms and tried to calm me down, repeating the words "Take it easy" over and over.

I closed my left eye and squinted with my right trying to line him up in the sights of the gun. My hand became steadier, and I ordered, "Put your gun on the floor. Slow."

He obeyed. The feeling of power invigorated me. "Slide it under the desk," I commanded next. He gently kicked the pistol until it was under the secretary's desk.

I stood up. "Move over there," I said, waving the barrel of my gun at Harrington's office door. He again did as instructed, stepping into the doorway. "Put your hands back up." They were promptly raised above his head.

After a glance down to assure myself that his partner was staying on the floor, I followed the fat man to the door.

I cautiously looked inside the office. Frank Timmons was seated behind Bennett Harrington's white desk, Harrington's glittering, ivory-handled pistol in his hand. He was aiming at me more steadily than I was aiming at him.

I jumped back half a step and slid partially behind the door jamb. It provided some protection while still allowing me to keep all three men in sight. "Where's Harrington?" I said.

Timmons answered, "Dead."

I poked my head a little farther in the door and looked around Harrington's office. All I saw was a mess of papers scattered on the floor. No body.

"It wasn't us," Timmons said, obviously appalled at the implication. "Somebody killed him last night."

Jeez. "Then what are you guys doing here?"

Timmons said promptly, "Harrington had connections to some of my men. I want to make sure there's nothing in his files that could, uh, reflect badly on the Patriotic Knights of Liberty."

Okay. Now what? The stand-off continued without incident or discussion while I considered how to resolve it.

"My suggestion," I finally said. "Is that none of us were here this morning." I allowed Timmons a moment to think it over. "Deal?"

He smiled slowly. Then he laid the revolver on the desk. "You've got yourself a deal, Mr. Rawlings."

I backed my way to the staircase, keeping the Knights in

sight. I continued to keep my eyes peeled as I went down the stairs and out to the street. I also kept the gun.

• • •

I suspended my boycott of the newspapers long enough to check the reports on Harrington's death. He was killed, shot twice, on LaSalle Street, a block from City Hall, late Sunday night by "an unknown assailant." No details on the gun.

His death got me to rethinking everything that had happened. I briefly entertained the notion that there *was* some kind of sabotage against his plant: Willie, Neeman, and Harrington all worked there. And so had I when the attempt was made on me. Then I discarded the idea, deciding that my previous theory made more sense.

Neeman killed Willie. Harrington killed Neeman, either to cut off the connection to himself or, more likely, because Neeman had disobeyed instructions when he'd shot Willie instead of me. So then who killed Bennett Harrington?

Frank Timmons? Maybe he didn't like his cause and his men being used for Harrington's purposes. But Timmons didn't have a cause, he had a business. And, like he'd told me, killing is bad for business. It's what made me certain that I'd be safe from the Knights.

Agnes O'Doul? She could have killed Curly Neeman when she had the chance but didn't. And since she knew Bennett Harrington didn't want Willie killed in the first place, she had no reason to retaliate against him.

I expanded the list of possibilities further. Finally, I thought I knew what had happened. The answer I would have least imagined seemed the most likely to be true. And I wished with all my heart that it wasn't.

Chapter Twenty-Eight

Karl Landfors promised he'd get me the information by eleven o'clock Wednesday morning. He said he'd been in town long enough to have established the necessary contacts and promised me a dinner if he failed to make it on time. I didn't want dinner. I wanted to know the kind of gun that was used to kill Bennett Harrington.

It was now a quarter past ten. I'd been up for several hours waiting anxiously for his call.

If the bullet was intact, Landfors would find out what type it was. And I was hoping with all my might that it wasn't from a Model 1892 Colt .38 revolver. At least let the slug be too badly mangled to be identified, and I'd forget about the whole thing.

The call came at ten to eleven. I grabbed the phone on the first ring and clapped the receiver to my ear. "Karl?"

"Got it!" he trumpeted.

"Was it. . . . Was it a Colt thirty-eight?"

"Close, as far as caliber. But no. A nine-millimeter Parabellum."

"A what?"

"Bennett Harrington was shot by a nine-millimeter 'Pistole ought-eight.' A Luger."

"You sure?"

"Absolutely. Two slugs were left in the body. Both of them were nice and clean, easy to identify."

"A Luger. That's German." Was Harrington killed by Germans?

"German manufacture. But they're popular souvenirs. A lot of soldiers brought them back here. Actually, Lugers aren't being used in combat much anymore. They jam in trench warfare. See, they have this toggle mechanism, and when they get muddy . . ."

Landfors was flaunting his recently acquired expertise again. I wasn't interested in the effects of mud on German side arms, so I tried to cut the conversation short.

"Wait!" he yelped as I was about to I hang up.

"What?"

"I checked on Terrapin Park in Baltimore, like you asked, which was quite confusing, I'll have you know. Terrapin Park was built across the street from Orioles Park. When the Federal League folded, the Orioles moved into Terrapin Park but renamed it Orioles Park, so now there are two Orioles Parks right across the street from each other!" Landfors sounded outraged, as if this had been done solely to make things difficult for him. "By the way," he added, "I was wondering. Are these the same Orioles that were famous twenty years ago?"

Karl Landfors had some serious gaps in his education that I felt obligated to fill. I gave him a concise history lesson: the famous "old Orioles" of the 1890s were a National League team that was jettisoned when the league cut down from twelve teams to eight after the 1899 season. The 1901 formation of the American League included a Baltimore franchise that played under the name "Orioles" until they moved to New York in 1903 and later became known as the Yankees. The current Baltimore Orioles were in the International League, a minor league.

"Oh," said Landfors, sounding like a less than avid pupil. "Anyway, Bennett Harrington owns a company that owns the land on which the new Orioles Park, formerly Terrapin Park, was built. So you're right about him. He was involved in the Federal League."

"Thanks Karl."

I didn't care about Bennett Harrington's business dealings now. I was simply relieved that it wasn't Edna Chapman who'd killed him. I was sure that if she had, she'd have used Otto Kaiser's gun, the one Willie was so proud to possess.

I was also puzzled. If it wasn't Edna, then who?

• • •

By early Friday morning, I came to the realization that I might have been only a little bit wrong—right string, wrong yo-yo.

Late Friday morning, I made a visit to the Chapman home.

Edna greeted me with polite indifference and led me into the parlor, where a battered black sewing machine on a chipped oak cabinet was positioned in the middle of the room. I hadn't seen it before. "That new?" I asked.

"New for us." She sat down at the machine. "Mind if I keep working? I promised Mrs. Schafer I'd have this dress finished for her tomorrow."

"Uh, no. No, I don't mind." Edna must have started to

take in seamstress jobs to make up for the income Willie could no longer provide. I briefly debated offering financial help, but she'd probably be insulted so I said nothing.

She started to rock the treadle with her foot; the machine squeaked and squealed as the needle flew up and down through the hem of a green serge skirt. I grabbed one of the dining chairs and sat across from her.

I watched her work for a few minutes. "Your mother upstairs?"

She nodded. "Sleeping."

I pulled my chair a little closer. In a low voice I asked, "You remember when Willie and I moved your things upstairs? When you gave the dogs your bedroom down here?"

Edna nodded while keeping her eyes on her task. With deft hands, she smoothed the cloth and guided it through the machine, producing a perfectly uniform stitch pattern.

"You have a strongbox—I remember carrying it up there—like the one Willie had in his dresser, where he kept his father's things."

The rise and fall of the needle slowed. A warm flush rose in her high cheeks. "Yes, what about it?"

"Could you bring it down and show me what's in it?"

She sat for a long minute staring at the mass of cloth. Then, without uttering a word, she went upstairs.

The box was already unlocked when Edna brought it down. She handed it to me, then took her seat at the sewing machine and methodically resumed work on the dress.

I creaked open the lid. "It's in there," Edna said softly.

The contents of the iron box were similar to those of Willie's: mostly papers and photographs. There was also a medal attached to a striped silk ribbon of blue, yellow, and green; the bronze disk was stamped "Mexican Service, 1911–

1917" and featured the image of some kind of plant—a cactus, I assumed. Lying on top of everything was a dark tarnished pistol with a skinny little barrel and a raked-back handle. A Luger.

I carefully removed the weapon and began to examine it. Karl Landfors had mentioned that Germany had supplied weapons to the Mexican army. I realized that Edna's father might have sent home a captured souvenir from Mexico the same way doughboys were now sending them back from Europe.

Attempting to check if it was loaded, I fumbled with the latch that would release the clip. Edna Chapman put a quick halt to my efforts. "There are two missing," she said. The sewing machine slowed to a stop, and Edna folded her hands in her lap. After a deep breath, she added, "I shot Mr. Harrington."

It was what I'd suspected, but as soon as I heard her utter the words, I wished she hadn't told me.

"How did you know where to find him?" I asked, placing the Luger back in the strongbox.

"Some people were watching him for me. They told me Mr. Harrington had a regular poker game at the La Salle Hotel. I met him after the game. And . . ." Her voice trailed off; she concluded with a shrug.

"Who were the people watching him?" I assumed it was some of Hans Fohl's acquaintances.

She gave me a baleful look that said I should know better than to ask her such a question.

I tried a different one. "You just walked up to him and shot him?"

"I had the gun hidden in a muff. He didn't see it until it was too late."

"And you just shot him?"

"I introduced myself first. 'I'm Willie Kaiser's sister,' I said. Then I pulled out the gun and shot him. Twice."

I didn't know what to say and didn't want to ask—didn't want to hear—anything more. I recalled her telling me once that you had to share a secret with somebody. Why the hell did she have to share this one with me?

"Are you angry?" she asked.

"No." Confused, surprised, sad. But not angry. "I think..." I picked up the weapon again. It was an ugly thing. The only pretty gun I'd ever seen was Bennett Harrington's revolver. "I think I'd like to take this with me. That okay?"

"What are you going to do with it?"

"I don't know." I really didn't know. But no matter what, she shouldn't be keeping it.

"If you like," she agreed.

I put the Luger in my jacket pocket; it made an unsightly bulge and felt heavy against my hip.

The good-byes were brief. Edna resumed her sewing, and I showed myself to the door. I felt uncertain about everything, somewhat dubious that I could even find my way home.

Stepping down from the Chapman's front porch, I met a big blond fellow coming the other way. We looked at each other for a few seconds, trying to recall where we'd seen each other before. I remembered first. "Uh, hi Gus," I said.

He stared a little longer before guessing, "Rawlings?"

"Yeah." This was the man from Hans Fohl's church, the one who'd said I didn't belong there. We exchanged awkward nods and moved on.

When I reached the sidewalk, I looked back, suddenly aware of what he'd been carrying: red roses wrapped in white paper. I was sure they weren't for Edna's mother.

Chapter Twenty-Nine

I'd been up all night, sitting alone at my kitchen table, staring dull-eyed at the darkness outside the window next to it. The latest cup of coffee had been in front of me for about two hours. Now and then I took a sip of the cold, bitter brew, but I didn't need it to stay awake. Thoughts of Edna Chapman mingled with memories of Willie Kaiser and Curly Neeman and Bennett Harrington, were all that were necessary to prevent me from sleeping.

In my heart I felt that Edna was justified in killing Bennett Harrington, and in a way I admired her for it. The admiration was mingled with frustration; Edna's action had relegated me to a minor role in the matter. After all this time worrying about not doing anything for her, it turned out she didn't need me at all.

And because she admitted to me what she'd done, I was now in the position of having to make a choice: keep her secret and do nothing more or turn the Luger over to the police and tell them who killed Bennett Harrington. Some choice.

I wanted there to be laws and rules, but I wanted them to be fair and reasonable. I wanted them to be effective, to take care of people like Bennett Harrington so that an eighteen-year-old girl didn't have to commit—. According to the law, what Edna Chapman had done was murder. The dilemma for me was whether I was willing to be what I think they called an "accessory after the fact"—whether I was going to align myself with the law or with a more pragmatic justice.

I looked out the kitchen window through a porthole of clean glass that I'd produced by rubbing hard on the dingy pane. The moonless night sky was as black as my coffee, with only a few stars twinkling dimly. I estimated that there was still an hour, maybe two, until Sunday dawn. Fall was approaching; the days were getting shorter and sunrise was coming later.

A light went on in Mrs. Tobin's house. Its glow lit up the narrow space between our homes and cast a yellow sheen on my window. She probably hadn't been able to sleep much after getting the news about Harold. I remembered what Mrs. Chapman had looked like after Willie's death and could imagine what Mrs. Tobin was going through.

I couldn't fathom why I should feel any concern about Bennett Harrington's death. Harold Tobin was somebody to mourn. So was Willie Kaiser. But Harrington? No.

Not that I really grieved for Bennett Harrington. His death didn't strike me as any more of a loss than Curly Neeman's. So what was it exactly that had me so troubled? Perhaps it was disillusionment that the rules I wanted to believe in had proved useless. And if I went along with what Edna had done, I'd be giving up on the way things were supposed to work.

I wasn't going to bother trying to fall asleep in what was

left of the night, so I put on another pot of coffee and pretended that I had just gotten up extra early in the morning.

Sipping on a hot cup of the fresh brew, I sat back down. Perhaps it wouldn't mean giving up on the system to let Edna Chapman get away with it. Maybe the Harrington case qualified as one of those "extreme situations" that Landfors talked about, like the Civil War when Lincoln suspended *habeas corpus* or whatever it was.

Mrs. Tobin's light shut off. My train of thought jumped rails from the Civil War to the present war in Europe and all the lousy things that were being done to promote it. I didn't like the propaganda, but if I let it keep me from going to fight for the things I did believe in, I was letting it control me the same as it was influencing people like Curly Neeman and the Patriotic Knights of Liberty. I told myself that in all things I needed to focus on the ideals, keep them in view, not be distracted or dissuaded by the imperfect means sometimes used in struggling for them.

Maybe what was really bothering me was the knowledge that after this season I would never again be able to ignore what happened outside the ballpark. There was more to life than baseball, and many new things, most of them complicated and some of them troublesome, would be part of my life.

The sky grew brighter as I pondered, but answers became no clearer.

A loud clanking noise and a rumble of muffled curses echoed from the alley. The sounds shook me loose from my tangled musing. I sprang up from my chair and went to the back door, drawing aside the curtain far enough to peek out.

Two scruffy boys of about fourteen or fifteen were hauling a hot water tank out of a neighbor's cellar. They must have dropped it and were moving quickly to take it away. Leaving the cellar door open, the boys staggered with their unwieldy load to another house four doors away down the alley. A man's arm opened the back door for them and they slipped inside with the tank.

I mentally marked the location of the house, then grabbed my coat.

Minutes later, I was knocking on that same door. There was a flurry of movement within the house, then a young voice called, "Who's there?"

"Me," I grunted. What the hell, I thought, that's the answer most people give.

Footsteps approached the door. The curtain started to move, and I leaned away to avoid being seen. An unintelligible exchange of words took place inside, then the door cracked open a cautious inch. I immediately gave it a hard shove, forcing my way in.

I was met by no physical resistance, but my nose was struck by a smell nearly as vile as that of the Union Stockyards. It was the sickly sweet odor of something fermenting.

The boy at the door stared at me with his mouth agape. Equally surprised were his two accomplices: the somewhat younger boy who'd helped carry the tank and a gnarled, gray old man. They stood at the far end of the kitchen, next to the stolen water tank. No one spoke for a minute, giving me time to survey the filthy residence. A wall had been crudely torn down between the kitchen and parlor to make one large room. It was an uninhabitable room, cluttered with plumbing fixtures, metal pipes, and several other hot water tanks, one of which, I was sure, was mine. Tin washtubs along one wall were filled with the brown liquid responsible for the noxious fumes.

Slamming the door shut, the boy behind me said in a tone that he tried hard to sound threatening, "What should we do with this guy?" I turned my head and gave him a look that warned he better not try doing anything to me.

The old man wiped his hands on his stained undershirt and growled, "Depends on who he is."

"Mickey Rawlings," I piped up. "Believe you have something of mine." I nodded at one of the tanks and noticed the spiral of copper tubing attached to the top. I'd seen something like it once in Texas. Scattered about the place were boxes of yeast and bags of sugar and cornmeal; many were broken open, with their contents spilled over the dirty floor. They were moonshiners!

It was obviously a bush league operation. The scene looked like the aftermath of a pie-throwing episode in one of Mack Sennett's slapstick comedies.

The boy next to the old man said, "We better do somethin' about this guy. Make sure he don't talk."

I recalled that amateurs often did very stupid things and momentarily wished that I'd thought to bring the gun I'd acquired in Bennett Harrington's office. It was hidden next to Edna's Luger behind my Mark Twain books.

The old guy relieved my worry somewhat when he boxed the kid's ears. "Goddamn idiots. Shouldn't have let him follow you."

Ignoring the boys, I directed myself to the man, hoping that he'd acquired enough wisdom in his years to be a little less stupid than the boys. "Look," I said. "I don't care if you want to set up a still and brew a little corn whisky. But don't go stealing stuff from my house to do it."

"Well, I didn't like having to," he grumbled. "We ain't thieves." He smacked the boy in the head again. "If we was,

these damn kids would be a helluva lot better at it." He
turned to me. "We'd buy what we needed if we could, but it's
hard to get plumbing supplies these days. There's a war on,
you know."

Why did people always tell me this as if it was news?
"Then buy bootleg booze," I said. "What do you have to
make your own for? This is Chicago, for chrissake. A drink
ain't exactly hard to find."

He ran a hand over the tank and gave me a sly wink. "It
will be," he said. "When Prohibition passes. And we're
gonna be set up to make a killing selling our home brew!"

I couldn't keep from laughing. They sure weren't going to
be good businessmen. "Then you're really stupid to be stealing from your neighbors," I said.

The grin vanished and his brow furrowed. "Watcha
mean?"

"You're going to need these people as customers. You go
stealing from them, word gets around, and you're out of
business."

"Hmm." He rubbed his unshaven chin and said thoughtfully, "Man has a point boys." With a shake of his head, he
added, "But ain't no other way to get the equipment."

"Got a pencil and paper?"

He punched the kid in the shoulder, and the boy went to
another room. He returned a minute later with the writing
materials.

I scribbled down a name and phone number. "This is my
landlord," I said. "He's got vacant buildings and he'll sell you
the tanks and plumbing from them. It'll cost you, but you'll
be better off doing it that way." I held out the slip of paper,
and the old man walked over and took it from my hand.

"You'll also pay him thirty dollars for the one you stole from me. Tell him to apply it to my rent."

He shrugged and agreed. "Fair 'nough."

"And you'll return the other ones you took," I added, pointing to the one they'd stolen that morning.

He nodded, and I went to the door, pushing the older boy aside. I said to him, "You're lucky it was me who saw you and not Mike the Cop."

All three of the aspiring bootleggers laughed. The old man snorted, "Hell, we woulda got off easier with him. He wouldn't'a done nothing!"

I stepped into the alley thinking he was probably right.

. . .

By mid-morning, the lack of sleep caught up with me. It seemed slothful to go to bed at this time of day, so I stretched out on the parlor sofa. A Sunday nap was entirely permissible.

I'd enjoyed just enough sleep to be wanting more of it when shouts from the street put an end to my dozing. Half awake, I listened. It was otherwise quiet, another Gasless Sunday with no automobiles to disturb the morning peace.

"Go on! Beat it!" yelled Mike the Cop. In his efforts to keep the neighborhood quiet, Mike generally made more noise than the children he was trying to silence.

I turned on my side so at least one ear wouldn't have to hear him. Then I twisted and sat upright. I had it! A way out of my quandary. Those inept moonshiners were right about one thing: Mike wouldn't do anything.

Quickly slipping on my clothes, I ran outside in time to catch him. Mike was standing at the curb, his arms akimbo, observing the children as they disappeared around the corner. I drew up next to him. He gave me a glance, then resumed watching his tormentors. "Damn kids," he puffed.

Confident that Mike wouldn't want to hear anything about Harrington even if I offered to tell him, I put on my most innocent face. "Don't suppose you'd want to hear my theory about who killed Bennett Harrington," I said.

He turned and directed his eyes fully at me.

No, no. Ignore me. Tell me to get lost. Worry about the kids.

Eagerly, he answered, "Sure I would."

Damn. Mike has to pick today to get conscientious in his duty.

I wasn't going to get off the hook easy; I had to make a decision. Nothing was coming easy for me this year. After a deep breath, I said, "I think it was Charlie Comiskey. See, I figure he was mad about the Cubs doing so much better than the Sox this year and—"

Mike cracked a smile that had no amusement in it. He tapped me on the shoulder, hard, with his billy club. "You better lay off the hooch, boy. It's illegal you know."

With that warning, he walked away, trying to whistle. He sounded like a straw sucking at an empty ice cream soda.

I stood and watched him and slowly began to smile, then grin.

An exhilarating sense of relief washed through me. It felt so good, so reassuring, that I knew I'd made the right decision not to tell him about Edna.

Maybe it wasn't in the rule book to let her get away with what she'd done, but it was fair.

Chapter Thirty

From his perch atop the pitcher's mound, Burleigh Grimes tried to stare me down. I ignored his glare; my eyes were fixed on the blue *B* insignia sewn on the front of his jersey, "B" for Brooklyn. Although I was no longer a Giant, the sight of a Dodger uniform could still raise my body temperature several degrees.

I scraped my spikes in the batter's box like a bull pawing the ground, eager to charge. It was bottom of the first, one out, nobody on base. In my grip was Mabel, brought out of retirement for this one game. I gave her hickory shaft a twisting squeeze, knowing she would understand it as a caress.

C'mon, give me the high hard one, I silently challenged Grimes.

He loaded the ball with saliva, wound up, and let it fly. The pitch came high and hard and straight.

I unleashed Mabel and was wishing the ball a pleasant journey before she even made contact. When she did meet the horsehide—oh, what a feeling. A powerful sensation surged through my arms, the magic tingle that only comes when the sweet spot of the bat contacts the ball dead on.

Grimes's futile spitter was on a rising path to straight-ahead centerfield, the deepest part of Cubs Park, as I reluctantly dropped Mabel and began my race around the bases. The ball headed to the wall, not quite high enough to go over it. As I rounded second, I saw it carom off the scoreboard and bounce into the tricky corner near the right field bleachers. Heading to third, Fred Mitchell waved me on, screaming, "Go! Go!" Seconds later, I slid safely into home with an inside-the-park home run that put us up 1–0. Before the Cubs batboy could pick up Mabel, I retrieved her myself and carried her into the dugout.

I faced Grimes again in the third. Two effective spitballs put me behind oh-and-two in the count, then he tried to jam me with a fastball. I swung. Mabel took the pitch on the handle but was strong enough to drop a loop single over the third baseman's head.

By the time I came to bat in the sixth inning, Burleigh Grimes was out of the game on the losing end of a 5–1 score. Rube Marquard, my one-time teammate with New York who had to suffer the indignity of going from the Giants to the Dodgers, replaced him on the mound. I greeted him with a hard grounder up the middle that went through for another single.

My final at bat was in the eighth. Marquard threw a couple of fastballs for called balls, then hung a slow curve knee-high on the outside corner. I couldn't have asked for a nicer going-away present. Mabel got all of it, driving a solid shot up the right field foul line, and I pulled into second base with a stand-up double.

Four-for-four on the day. Perfect. The first time I'd ever gotten four hits in a major-league game.

After our 8–2 win, still in uniform and carrying Mabel and my mitt, I stopped in Fred Mitchell's small office adjacent to the locker room.

"Good game," the manager said with a grin.

"Thanks. It's my last one."

"Huh?"

"I went to a recruiting office this morning. I enlisted."

"Damn." Mitchell seemed uncertain how to react to the news. "But the World Series. All you have to do is stick around a few more weeks and you'll be playing in the Series."

I was well aware of that. We'd already clinched the pennant, and the Cubs' management had already arranged to play the Chicago home games in Comiskey Park because of its larger seating capacity. "I know, Fred. But I don't want to wait."

"Well, if it's what you want to do, I won't try to talk you out of it. Sure gonna miss you, though."

"Thanks. You know, Wicket Greene would probably do okay at second. I'd leave Rube Dillard at shortstop."

"Rube?"

I nodded. It turned out the kid liked my most recent suggestion. A dachshund, a teammate. . . . If I had a daughter, I'd probably end up naming her Rube.

"They'll make a decent double play combination," I said. Dillard and I had turned a couple of them in today's game. It wasn't the same as with Willie Kaiser, but they'd clicked well enough.

Mitchell accepted my advice with good humor and

wished me luck in my new vocation; he also said he hoped I'd be returning to baseball soon.

I showered and changed before making my next stop: Charles Weeghman's office upstairs.

Weeghman was in a visibly chipper mood. It was disconcerting to see him smiling and content.

He became less happy when I informed him, "I haven't been able to find out who's trying to put you out of business, and I'm gonna have to drop it." As the scowl that I'd come to know so well crawled over Weeghman's face, I explained that I was going into the Army.

Weeghman sat motionless for a minute. Then he did something totally unexpected: he opened the cedar cigar box on his desk and asked, "Have one?"

"Thanks," I accepted. I took one of the long slim cigars and put it in my breast pocket. "I'll smoke it later." I had no intention of smoking it later, but it seemed impolite to refuse.

Weeghman took one for himself and bit off the end. "It doesn't matter anymore, anyway," he said.

"What do you mean?"

"Well, it looks like when you get back you'll be playing in Wrigley Park after all." He struck a match and rolled the end of the cigar in the flame. "This ain't public yet, so don't tell anybody, but I'm selling out to William Wrigley at the end of the season."

I wasn't sure if I should congratulate him or express regret. So I said, "Oh."

After enjoying a few puffs of the aromatic cigar, Weeghman asked, "Why don't you stick around for the World Series? Hell, we got the pennant sewed up. Why leave now?"

That was a question I'd thought about long and hard. Part of the answer was that I didn't intend to let my desire to play in a World Series determine the decisions I made in life. "I can't explain it," I answered. "It's just something I got to do now."

Besides, not even playing in the World Series could salvage this season.

• • •

Edna Chapman and I took the dachshunds on one last walk through Ravenswood. As soon as we left her home, she became the next person of the day to receive the news of my enlistment. Edna quietly suggested that I "be careful," and we completed the rest of the journey without exchanging another word.

On our return to the house, we remained outside, sitting on the top step of the front porch, three of the dogs curled up at our feet. Rube sat down next to me, his brown eyes squinting in the evening sun. I scratched him under his chin; he hopped up and flicked his tongue out, licking the tip of my nose.

"There's something else I have to tell you," I said to Edna.

She reached down and stroked the head of the dog nearest her. "Yes?"

"That, uh, family heirloom you lent me. . . . I'm afraid I lost it."

Her head spun to face me. "Lost it?"

"Yes. It's gone." I'd disposed of the Luger in the same place that Curly Neeman's body had been dumped. Unlike Neeman, though, the gun was never going to float to the surface. I added emphatically, "Nobody's ever going to find it."

She blushed and smiled with understanding. "Oh."

"Hope you're not angry."

Smiling more fully, Edna shook her head no. In a whisper, she added, "Thank you."

•   •   •

I took a break from my packing when Karl Landfors came over later that night. I didn't really know what to pack anyway. I'd never been on a road trip all the way to France before.

After we sat down in the parlor with a couple of cold soda pops, I gave him the news that I'd enlisted. Landfors became the first person to express pride in my decision. "You're doing the right thing," he said approvingly.

He then became the third person to point out, "But if you go now, you'll miss playing in the World Series." People were telling me that I'd be missing the Series the same way they kept informing me that "there's a war on, you know."

I laughed it off. "Well, they say this is the war to end all wars. That means it's my only chance to get in one. I'll have plenty more chances to get in a World Series. They have them every year."

Landfors smiled weakly. He seemed to catch on that I didn't want to go into the reason for my enlistment. It wasn't something I completely understood myself; I knew only that it felt right and that it had something to do with keeping ideals foremost in mind.

He switched to a subject I was equally reluctant to discuss. "Inconvenient about Bennett Harrington getting killed," Landfors said.

That was a curious way to describe it. "Inconvenient? How so?"

"It makes it difficult for you to determine who was ultimately responsible for your friend Kaiser getting killed. Harrington was clearly involved to some extent, but there had to be others, right?" His eyebrows rose above the rims of his spectacles. "You said it didn't make sense for one of the Cubs' owners to be behind whatever was going on. Doesn't that mean somebody other than Harrington had to be orchestrating things? And who killed Harrington? You don't believe it was a holdup, do you?"

I decided to satisfy his curiosity on everything except the circumstances of Harrington's death. "You're right," I said. "I guess it is kind of inconvenient that he's dead. Probably means there's some things we're never going to know for sure. One thing I am sure of, though: Bennett Harrington was the one behind the sabotage at Cubs Park, including Willie's murder."

"Why? What could he gain by it?"

"That's the question I had the toughest time with. Why would one of the team owners do anything to frighten away fans and decrease revenues? He might be able to buy the club cheaper that way, if he wanted to, but it wouldn't be worth much once he got it." I paused for emphasis, then added, "Not if the team was staying in Chicago, that is."

"I don't follow," said Landfors.

I explained, "I'd bet that Bennett Harrington's plan was to buy the Chicago Cubs and move the team to Baltimore. You told me he still owns Terrapin Park, Orioles Park now."

Landfors nodded. "I see. And the sabotage was to drive down the buying price?"

"Well, he's a businessman, so I expect that was part of it. I don't think it was the main factor though. Harrington's munitions factories are doing great, so he probably had plenty of money. No, the most important reasons were to put pressure on Weeghman to sell and to drive down attendance.

"See, once Harrington became owner, he'd have to get permission from the league to move the franchise to Baltimore. The best way for him to do that was to prove that fans weren't coming to Cubs Park, that Chicago wouldn't support two major league teams anymore."

"No National League team in Chicago? You think the other owners would have gone along with him?"

"Until this year, I would have said not a chance. But this season's been so strange, the owners have been making so many crazy decisions, I really don't know. Harrington might have been able to make a case for it. Attendance has been way down in every city in the league. Harrington could have pointed out that the Feds' Baltimore franchise always drew great crowds. And, of course, Charlie Comiskey would love for his White Sox to be the only show in town, so you can be sure he'd have done whatever he could behind the scenes to help Harrington move the Cubs to another city.

"If Harrington pulled it off," I went on, "he would have been a hometown hero for bringing major league baseball back to Baltimore."

Landfors protested, "But he did own part of the Federal League team in Baltimore, and he kept that a secret."

"That's different. The Feds were an outlaw league, not part of Organized Baseball. If they didn't succeed, anyone mixed up with them could end up in Dutch with the established leagues. So Harrington kept his role with them secret, and when the Feds folded there was no taint on him. Of course, if the new league had succeeded, I'm sure he would have eventually gone public with his involvement."

I concluded, "Moving the Cubs to Baltimore would have been a real coup for Harrington. They're a National League team, same as the old Orioles."

From Landfors's expression, he was having a tough time understanding the business side of baseball. "But why kill Willie Kaiser?" he asked next.

"Same reason: to scare away fans and pressure Weeghman into selling the team. That took a while for me to figure out, too. Most of the sabotage wasn't violent—annoying, frightening, but not really dangerous. I didn't think killing Willie was part of the scheme because it was so different from the rest of the pattern."

"So how did it fit in?"

"Wally Dillard gave me the clue when we were playing catch. He said he was eager to get to the Cubs before Secretary of War Baker shut down major league baseball. It looked like he might do it any day, remember? Harrington must have had the same worry. If the season was canceled, it could have taken the pressure off Charles Weeghman. By next year, people would have forgotten about the sabotage and Weeghman might have had time to regroup financially. So Harrington tried to finish him with one blow, something he thought would totally kill attendance. He had a Cubs player murdered in the ballpark in full view of a packed crowd."

"What do you think—"

"That's all I know," I cut him off. All that I intended to tell him, anyway. "It's over. Let's leave it at that."

Landfors started to open his mouth, then nodded in agreement and took a gulp of ginger ale.

"One other thing," I said. "I've paid a few months ahead on my rent. You want to stay here until . . ."

"Until you get back?"

"Right. Till I get back." I fully intended to be coming back.

"Sure," he agreed. "Thanks."

"Good. You can keep an eye on the hot water tank for me," I said with a smile.

Landfors chuckled, but he soon turned serious again. "You know," he said, "Newton Baker may not think so, but what you've been doing here, playing baseball, is important, too. I didn't know until I was over there how much baseball means to Americans. It's what the doughboys play when they get a break from the battles. And they follow the pennant races to take their minds off the war." His voice rose. "Don't underestimate how important the national pastime is for morale. Baseball is—"

"Karl," I said, interrupting before he got around to using the phrase "this great game of ours."

He pushed up his slipping eyeglasses. "Yes?"

I leaned forward. As if revealing a great secret, I whispered, "Karl, baseball is a game that you play if the weather's nice."

Not long ago, I'd have slugged Landfors if he'd said such a thing.

Chapter Thirty-One

Eight and a half pounds of black walnut and blue steel, carefully assembled into a balanced instrument forty-three inches long. Standard issue of the U. S. Army's Ordnance Department: a Springfield .30-06.

"Tennn . . . *hut!*"

A rifle. Bolt-action, .30-caliber, fed by a five-round box magazine, with a bayonet attachment on the barrel. An instrument complicated in design, yet simple in purpose: to kill.

"Presennnt . . . *ahms!*"

In the hands of a trained soldier it could do so in many ways. And during the last two weeks, I'd learned most of them. I could disembowel a straw-filled dummy with the bayonet, use the rifle stock as a cudgel in hand-to-hand combat, and fire a bullet into a target seventy-five yards away. Not often in the bull's-eye but usually somewhere in the target.

"Shoorrr . . . *ahms!*"

With a brisk move I slammed the rifle to my shoulder. As

always, the heft of the thing felt wrong; it was unwieldy, tricky to handle, and no amount of practice could make it feel comfortable in my hands. I was intimately familiar with every component of the weapon, having assembled it, broken it down, and cleaned it a hundred times. Yet it remained alien to me, and a little repellent.

Our entire company stood in formation on the rain-soaked parade ground of Fort Benning, Georgia. I was no more comfortable with my gear and uniform than I was with my rifle. Everything the Army put on my body seemed intended to restrict movement. Heavy boots anchored my feet in the mud, the puttees wrapped from boots to breeches bit into my calves, and the stiff brown wool uniform was like a scratchy strait jacket. Strapped to my back was sixty pounds of additional equipment. I had to lean slightly forward to keep my balance.

"Fowarrr . . . *march!*"

I promptly plucked my left foot from the grip of the mud and stepped forward, as did every other recruit.

As we plodded through the soupy red clay, the drill sergeant, whose personality combined the worst elements of Ty Cobb's and John McGraw's, barked, "Left . . . left . . . left, right, left." In unison, our boots responded: Squish, *plup,* squish, *plup* . . .

This outfit had been drilled to perfection. When we passed the reviewing stand, the order came "Eyes *right!*" and I could almost hear the eyeballs click into place as they turned to face the officers.

My mind wasn't nearly as disciplined as my body. I knew that at the same time I was marching in Fort Benning, the Chicago Cubs were taking the field in Fenway Park for what could be the final game of the 1918 World Series.

While I was learning the rudiments of war, baseball had gone on without me. The regular season ended on Labor Day, a month earlier than usual. To save a month's payroll, the owners promptly gave unconditional releases to all the players, after agreeing among themselves that they wouldn't steal any ballplayers "freed" by another club.

The World Series opened on September 5, with Boston's big left-hander Babe Ruth outpitching Hippo Vaughn for a 1–0 win. A few days later, Ruth won his second game of the Series, beating Shufflin' Phil Douglas. If the Red Sox took today's game, they would be world champions for the third time in four years. And with Babe Ruth pitching for them, the Sox would probably keep winning World Series for years to come.

Someday, though, I'd be playing in one of them.

The scene on the parade ground began to dissolve before my eyes and transform itself into a brighter vision: the felt campaign hats became baseball caps; the suffocating uniforms were now baggy, pinstriped flannels; and instead of marching in formation, we were stepping onto the green living turf of a baseball field for the opening game of the World Series. I imagined the cheers of the fans and the feel of the breeze blowing the flags and pennants. I hadn't missed my chance to get into the Series, it had merely been deferred.

I now felt more confident that I'd be coming home alive from this war. No way was I going to die without getting into a World Series.

Yes, somehow or other, I would manage to survive. I'd even use my rifle if I had to. But I wouldn't feel truly alive again until I had a Louisville Slugger in my grip.

After selling a controlling interest of the Chicago Cubs to William Wrigley, Charles Weeghman resigned as president in December 1918.

The baseball park Weeghman built, variously known as Weeghman Park, Whales Park, and Cubs Park, was officially renamed Wrigley Field in 1926.

Wrigley Field is the only remaining Federal League ballpark.